THE OMPHALOS

BOOK 5 OF THE MAQLÛ

JC HOLMBERG

Library of Congress Control Number: 2024906479

This is a work of fiction and is a product of the author's imagination. Any references to historical events, real people, or real places are used fictitiously.

Learn more about the history and background of this book at:
www.JC Holmberg.com

Front cover image by Rebecacovers
PCIP provided by Five Rainbows Cataloging Services
Names: Holmberg, John C., 1956- author.
Title: The Omphalos / J. C. Holmberg.
Description: Pine Knot, KY : Tist Fiction, 2024. | Series: Maqlû, bk. 5. | Summary: Alex Scire and his friend Chrysophylax are whisked away to Greece and into the clutches of Atlantians. | Audience: Grades 5 & up.
Identifiers: LCCN 2024906479 (print) | ISBN 978-1-956342-22-2 (hardcover) | ISBN 978-1-956342-21-5 (paperback) | ISBN 978-1-956342-24-6 (large print) | ISBN 978-1-956342-20-8 (ebook) | ISBN 978-1-956342-23-9 (audiobook)
Subjects: LCSH: Adventure stories. | CYAC: Wizards--Fiction. | Magic--Fiction. | Fantasy. | Young adult fiction. | Historical fiction. | BISAC: YOUNG ADULT FICTION / Fantasy / Historical. | YOUNG ADULT FICTION / Fantasy / Wizards & Witches. | YOUNG ADULT FICTION / Action & Adventure / General.
Classification: LCC PZ7.1.H65 O47 2024(print) | LCC PZ7.1.H65 (ebook) | [Fic]--dc23.

To Steph,

Who changes lives with a mix of chalk and challenges.

CONTENTS

"If you are going through hell, keep going."

Winston Churchill

CHAPTER 1

TO DARE AND ENDURE

Alex Scire took one look at the glowering faces of the Druid women piling out – and jumped. His knees buckled when he hit the ground – sending him crashing down the steep hillside above Loch Ness, stopping only when he crashed into a fir tree. Despite the pain in his ribs, he struggled to his feet and headed for the lake far below.

He slowed when the sounds of pursuit grew fainter, then slumped to the forest floor when he couldn't hear them anymore. Exhausted from all he'd been through it took him some time until he'd caught his breath and was ready to continue his descent. But just as he was about to stand, he heard a twig snap nearby. Holding his breath, Alex lowered himself back to the forest floor, hoping whoever was nearby wouldn't spot him.

Seconds later, a woman's whisper cut through the stillness. "How are we ever supposed to find that demon in all this wilderness?"

Another voice, even closer than the first speaker, replied, "I fear this is a wild goose chase because the boy magically appears and disappears. In fact, I heard he escaped from Stormhold by flying out the window as if he had invisible wings."

"I don't believe half the stories about him, the first woman replied. He's just – different."

Before the second woman could reply, her walkie-talkie sprang to life with orders to shift their search.

Alex's heart rate was just returning to normal a few minutes later when Sibyl's now-familiar disembodied voice said, *"You must get out of here before they come back."*

"What are you doing here?" Alex hissed. "You're never around when I need you and only show up when all the dirty work is done."

"Lower your voice, or one of the Bandruí will hear you and come back. I have castigated myself far more than you could ever do for my inactions to date – which is why I'm here tonight. I've decided that I want to help you complete your quest. I didn't help earlier because …, well, because I was confused about everything that was happening. But you're accomplishing something I didn't think was possible – destroying the Maqlû. Which is why I've come to tell you that your friend awaits you down at the lake. Now hurry. Before the witches spot you."

"Who are you talking about?" Alex asked. He waited for the enigmatic ghost to say more, but when all he got was silence, he assumed she'd disappeared again. Heaving a deep sigh, he continued down the hillside, hoping to find whoever Sibyl meant before the quickly fading daylight was gone. He just hoped that whoever was there could provide food and shelter, as he'd left all his gear on the other side of the lake when he'd hopped a ride on Nessie the day before.

Soon, a heavy fog started rolling up off the lake, making it near-impossible to see more than an arm's length away in the gloaming. Alex's hopes rose with the worsening weather conditions as he figured his pursuers would give up their hunt. But they were quickly dashed when he saw lights appear above him, stretching out in a long line across the hillside.

Seeing the Druids were hemming him in and knowing there was no way he could cross Loch Ness, he began looking for a hiding spot. He'd just about given up his search when a familiar voice inside his head said, *"Stop making so much noise, Little One. I'll get you out of here."*

"But, how do I ...."

"Be quiet, your pursuers might hear you. If you feel like you must speak to me, remember, I can hear your thoughts. When my mother adopted you into our weyr, not only did she share our lineage with you, but she also passed several of our abilities on to you, including telepathy. So, just follow my thoughts down to the lake."

"But, how do I find you?"

"Be quiet, your pursuers might hear you. Remember, when my mother adopted you into our weyr, she passed several of our abilities on to you, including telepathy. So, just follow my thoughts down to the lake."

A beam of light hitting his face, followed by shouts of, "I've found him," caused Alex to throw caution to the wind and race down the hillside. Crashing through the woods, he didn't worry about the noise he was making, as all he could focus on was reaching Chrysophylax and hoping he would save him.

When he finally reached the opalescent-colored dragon standing on the shoreline, he stopped and asked, *"How are we getting out of here? I can't swim across the lake because it's too cold, and I'd freeze to death."*

"I don't see how Apalāla can stand living here because I have no great affinity for these waters either. But don't worry; we're going to fly out. Now hurry and jump on. We don't have much time before your pursuers arrive."

Alex scrambled on and settled down between Chrys's wings but asked, *"How will I hold on?"*

"Lay low and hold on tight. I'll try not to make any sudden moves and will fly as level as possible. But hurry. They're almost here."

Nearby voices drove Alex to scramble on. No sooner had he'd settled himself than Chrysophylax took a few quick steps and launched into the air. Soon, they were flying high enough that Alex could see the lights of Inverness glowing in the sky to the northeast. For a moment, he thought the dragon was taking him toward the city, but then Chrysophylax banked left and made a slow 180-degree turn. Surprised at the change in directions, Alex asked, "Where are we going? It looks like there's nothing ahead of us."

"To my world – Berellus. We can hide there until things die down here."

"But how are we going to get there? Do you have a spaceship or something?"

"We'll go through the nearest wormhole portal, located inside Fingal's Cave – a little over a hundred of your Earth miles southeast of here."

"What's this portal you're talking about and how does it work?" Alex asked.

"They're gateways that connect different parts of the galaxy. We're not sure who built them or how many there are, but we've used them safely for millennia."

"How do they work?" Alex asked.

"Do you remember how you traveled to that castle in Romania, when you rescued my mother? Kind of like that."

"But how do you know where we'll come out?"

"I don't understand exactly how they work, but I know that if I use certain portals, I end up where I want to go."

"You're sure you won't get lost and wind up on some remote world?" Alex asked.

"I'm sure, Little One. Now just relax, because it'll be okay."

Alex was quiet for a few minutes, trying to wrap his mind around space travel through wormholes. At last, he said, "Why do you think we should go to your planet?"

"My Uncle Nabu has been working for ages to bring the Maqlû back to Berellus. But when you took your dad's ankh, you threw his plans to control them into total disarray," Chrysophylax replied. *"At first, he was upset. But he's been rethinking his plan since you've destroyed three of the objects. Which is why I think it would be good for you two to work together. Maybe you'll find an easier way to eliminate all the Maqlû and thus end a threat to both our species."*

Alex wasn't sure what to think of Chrys' suggestion, especially the terrifying idea of traveling through space on the back of a dragon. Yet, even though the idea nearly petrified him, he couldn't help but be excited about traveling to another planet. With his thoughts in turmoil and the mist changing into a steady rain, he lapsed into silence as they flew towards the portal.

All too soon, they were over the Hebrides Sea, and Chrysophylax had started his descent. *"We're almost there,"* the dragon warned him. *"But you should be aware that it may take some time, because I have to fill up its magic reservoir before it has enough power to open. Don't worry, though. Between a hiding spot inside the cave and my glamour spells, no one should be able to find us. If all else fails, I'll just look into any intruder's eyes and put them into a trance – like what I did to your friends in Lamanai."*

Chrysophylax dropped his wings to slow his speed as they entered Fingal's Cave. Before he could get a glimpse of any of the thousands of perfectly shaped hexagonal columns in the sea cave, Alex felt something yanking him forward – much like what he'd felt when he'd entered the wormhole in Romania.

An instant later, the wormhole sucked them in.

Tiny pinpricks of light zoomed past them as they slipped through the invisible space tunnel, turning first one way and then another as they crossed two of the outer arms of the galaxy. Before Alex could get his bearings, they'd popped out on a steep, rocky mountainside.

"Sorry about that," Chrysophylax said. *"I've never seen a portal open so suddenly and wasn't prepared for that instant acceleration."*

"That's okay," Alex replied. "At least we survived. But I thought your planet would look a lot different. This looks like some of the European mountains I've seen in pictures."

There was a long pause before Chrysophylax hesitantly replied, *"That's because they are. We've just exited the portal on Mt. Olympus in Greece."*

CHAPTER 2
TO LIVE FOR SOMETHING

Diana Bennet saw Alex leap down the hill and was about to chase after him when Jane Roland grabbed her arm and whispered in her slight Scottish accent, "Let him go. We won't help by chasing after him. I think it's better to stay here and try limiting the pursuit. Besides, I have a feeling he'll escape them.

Diana looked up at her friend and cupped a hand behind her ear. "You'll have to speak up. You know I can't hear very well, especially with all this noise. After Jane repeated her observation, Diana asked in her thick accent, "Do you really think so?"

Jane didn't get a chance to reply as a van pulled up, and another half dozen Druid women jumped out. Diana's mother, Sophie, quickly instructed the reinforcements to fan out and head down the hillside after Alex before turning to her daughter and saying, "I'm disappointed in you, Diana. I thought you had more respect for our order than running away with that boy."

Ignoring her mother's caustic comment, she asked, "How in the world did you find us? We didn't know where we were going until only a couple of hours ago."

"It wasn't hard to figure out. You might not know it, but we have a valuable object hidden nearby."

Knowing Alex had just destroyed the Chintamani, one of two Maqlû the order guarded, Diana looked to Jane for guidance on what to say.

"Does Lady Yvaine know what ye're doing?" Jane asked. "She's been very clear in the past that no one is to harm him."

"So, we're expected to do nothing while he rampages around, destroying centuries' worth of our work?" Sophie retorted. "She's the only one on the High Council who defends the boy. Even his grandmother thinks he's a threat and wants to eliminate him. But, I won't stand around here and argue with you two about him.

Sophie motioned for a woman standing by one of the cars parked nearby and said, "Take them back to Stormhold. And don't let them out of sight until you're inside the compound. Got that?" She turned back to her daughter and added, "I'll let Lady Yvaine deal with your constant rule-breaking."

The woman nodded and motioned for Jane and Diana to get into her car.

The girls made the trip to Stirling in silence, waiting until they reached Jane's room before Diana asked, "What do we do now? We can't leave Alex to the mercy of my mother and that mob of hers. And shouldn't we tell Lady Yvaine we've returned?"

In her usual calm manner, Jane replied, "There's not much we can do right now. It's late. I'll bring Lady Yvaine up to speed tomorrow. But for now, we'll have to hope Alex's luck holds out and yer mother won't do anything drastic. If she does, the consequences will be grave as I believe Lady Yvaine will kick her out of the order."

Diana's stomach took that moment to complain about its neglected state. Looking sheepishly at her friend, she said, "I'm starving. Let's go raid the kitchen and bring our dinners back here to figure out our next steps."

It wasn't until Diana had finished scarfing down her dinner that she spoke again. "By the way. I've been wondering how you could hear Nessie's thoughts, and I couldn't."

Jane held up the golden dragon-shaped necklace with a flaming pearl set in the middle that Alex had given her in Hispaniola and said, "I believe this little thing is what allowed me to hear Apalāla's thoughts."

Diana scrunched her face in disbelief. "That's not fair. The ring he gave me does nothing but sit on my finger and look bizarre."

Jane's eyebrow arched upwards. "I wouldn't be so sure about that. I've been thinking about the ankh Alex wears and believe he has stumbled upon some advanced alien technology that directed him to our jewelry pieces when he was rummaging around those treasure chests. I'm guessing your ring has powers, too. Ye just haven't discovered what they are."

"But what if you're not right? What if something else is causing all this? Then what do we do?" Diana asked.

"I don't know. No matter what, the first thing I'm going to do tomorrow morning is bend Lady Yvaine's ear and get her to call off that rabid pack of dogs going after Alex. If he manages to survive his current predicament, then we'll worry about figuring out what to do next. But I'll tell ye one thing: I'll do everything I can to help him because I'm guessing his other enemies want him dead before he can destroy any more of the Maqlû."

"Agreed," Diana replied.

Both girls lapsed into silence until Diana sighed and said, "I know it's not important in the big scheme of things, but I have to tell you – I'm not looking forward to telling my mom that I lost another cell phone."

"Is that regret, I hear in yer voice? Didn't ye have a blast flying across Scotland with ghosts and riding on the world-famous Loch Ness monster?"

Diana began absent-mindedly tracing the loops of the triquetra tattoo on her arm. "Of course, I don't regret it.

Sometimes I just wish it weren't always so uncomfortable trying to help him. Plus, I want to be able to tell someone about what we're doing. It's frustrating having to keep all the cool things we've seen and done a secret." Seeing Jane was about to protest, Diana held up a hand and said, "I know he's sworn us to secrecy. Besides, I also know it would be wasted breath because no one would believe us."

There was a long silence until Diana said, "I keep thinking that there's got to be something bigger going on than we can see."

"What's bigger than finding the Maqlû?"

"I don't know," Diana replied. "I mean, I keep getting surprised at who's involved and wonder what they all want. We know our order, ghosts, dragons, assassins, and some mysterious woman named Pythia are chasing him. But what are they all trying to achieve?"

"That is the question, isn't it," Jane replied.

CHAPTER 3

KNOW NOT WHAT WE MAY BE

"Greece! I thought we were going to your home planet Berellus, to get advice from your uncle," Alex said. "What do we do now?"

Chrysophylax didn't immediately respond. Instead, he banked left and headed west, away from the coastline and over the rugged landscape flanking Mt. Olympus. *"I'm surprised at your reaction, as I didn't think you were that enthusiastic about my plan."*

"I've thought about it and have decided that it's probably a good idea to get someone else's thoughts on what's happening," Alex replied.

"Are you sure you're not subconsciously opposed to going? Because, maybe, deep down, you wanted to remain here on Earth. It's the only thing I can think of on how we ended up here. You must have overcome the portal's controls and somehow willed us here."

"That's absurd. How could I do that? I had to ask you what a portal was."

"It's not as crazy of an idea as you think," Chrysophylax replied. *"My uncle told me that the ankh you wear is an extremely powerful alien device. You must have unlocked its powers – something Nabu has never been able to do. I suggest I drop you off near a city where you can get food, shelter, and transportation to wherever you want to go while I go to Berellus and try to get answers. I'll return when I know how to help you."*

"But I know nothing about Greece," Alex replied. "Where would I go? The only thing I know for sure is that

I probably need to catch a train or bus to Athens to go home."

"I'm not very familiar with Greece, but I believe there's a city not too far away with some rock formations that could shield our arrival, allowing me to land without being seen." Chrysophylax craned his neck to look at the sun's position and added, *"It looks like it's pretty late in the day, but I'm going to find a hiding spot nearby where we can stay out of sight until the sun goes down."* They flew only a few more minutes before he said, *"Hold on, I'm heading down."*

They landed in a small alpine meadow and quickly ducked into the surrounding tree line. Only after Chrysophylax was satisfied they were deep enough in the forest did he kneel, letting Alex slide off the dragon's back.

"Why do we have to hide? I thought you said you used a glamour spell to hide yourself when flying around," Alex said.

"I do. But I don't want to take any chances as I'm not very good at it yet, and I don't want anyone to catch a glimpse of us. Now, why don't you get some sleep because we won't be taking off until after it's dark."

Even though he'd gotten little sleep the previous two nights, Alex was too hungry to sleep. Having left most of his gear at Loch Ness, all he had left was what was in his dad's Army rucksack. He quickly gobbled down his last protein bar and drank the last of his water but was still hungry and thirsty when he'd finished them. Reminding himself he'd been in worse predicaments, he gathered some needles and leaves for a makeshift bed and lay down, hoping sleep would take his mind off his discomforts.

He was so tired that he fell asleep as soon as his head hit the ground. The next thing he knew, Chrysophylax was nudging him to wake up. *"Come, Little One. It's time to go."*

As soon as they were in the air, Chrysophylax turned southeast and landed an hour later amongst a jumble of towering rock formations.

"Where are we?" Alex asked, his head still spinning from everything that had happened that day.

"I believe they call this area Meteora. I know it looks isolated, but don't worry, there's a town down below."

Seeing Chrys was ready to leap off the tall rock column, Alex asked, "Do you have to leave?"

"I need to get my uncle's advice on what to do next," Chrys replied. *"And I need to leave now before anyone sees me. But don't worry. I'll be back soon."*

"Do you really think we need to get him involved? From my perspective, he hasn't helped much yet. And since he can't travel between worlds, he seems to be mostly an armchair quarterback. Why don't you stay with me, and we'll figure this out together," Alex pleaded.

Chrys shook his head and said, *"That's not true. Yes, he's been wrong on a few things, but he was the one who sent you the ankh and he's been working on this problem longer than anyone else. I'm sure he'll be able to help us."*

"All right. Do what you think is right. I'll muddle along until you return." An overwhelming fear of loneliness drove him to add, "You are returning here, though? Aren't you?"

"I plan to, but my home planet is in turmoil. The High Council arrested me the last time I returned, and it took me months before I found a safe way back here which means it will be difficult for me to return soon. Now, I

really must go. I need to be gone by daylight, and I can't count on the portal opening as readily as it did with you."

Without another word, Chrysophylax leaped over the edge and disappeared into the night.

For a minute, Alex felt desolated. But seeing the lights of a city far below cheered him out of his funk as it meant he was near civilization. He thought about setting out immediately, but being unsure of his surroundings, he decided to stay put for the night.

Despite it being early summer, the temperature was uncomfortably cool, driving Alex to look around for a place where he could get out of the wind. He found a snug spot and tried getting some sleep, but hunger, thirst, and cold made his night a long and miserable one.

His relief with the coming of dawn was short-lived, though, when he saw where Chrysophylax had deposited him. Instead of being on some low-lying hill, he discovered he was on top of one of the towering rock formations surrounding Meteora. He looked for an easy way down, but couldn't find one – except for jumping over the edge.

Frustrated that he was stuck on top of a thousand-foot-tall rock with no apparent way down, he threw his head back and screamed to the heavens in frustration. When he'd calmed down, he forced himself to walk the edges of the rocky column, hoping to find some unseen way down.

He'd gone about halfway around when he spotted a dark crease and hurried to the slit. His relief was palpable when he got there and spotted a narrow, well-worn walking path cutting down through the rock.

Anxious to return to civilization, he started down. But before he'd taken two steps, he felt the hairs on his neck stand up. Feeling like someone was watching him, he whirled around – but saw nothing. Figuring he was just tired and imagining things, he resumed his descent.

He worked his way down for the next hour, often having to sit and scoot down the path because it was so steep. His spirits soared when the trail finally leveled out. But he quickly discovered that the challenges he faced just changed in nature – because instead of making his way down a steep path, he found himself having to fight his way through thick undergrowth.

He growled in frustration when the path abruptly ended in an impenetrable brush wall. Alex looked for a way around but didn't see a way out. As he swung his pack off to get to his knife, he accidentally hit a well-worn stick jutting out of the natural barrier. There was a soft click, then, like a door, the brush swung outward. Not wanting to chance being trapped, he ran out.

When he saw a parking lot nearby filled with cars, buses, and people a few minutes later, he closed his eyes and gave a silent prayer of thanks to the Great Spirit.

CHAPTER 4
THE FLASH OF A FIREFLY

Lady Yvaine heard the door to her study slide open and whirled around to see who had overcome her magical barriers and entered. It took a moment before she recognized the ancient-looking woman standing inside her doorway, as her guest looked like she'd aged a hundred years since she'd last seen her. "Hellwain? Is that you? What's happened?"

"I could almost say the same thing about you, as I see grey streaks in your hair for the first time," Hellwain replied. She shuffled across the room using a cane to steady her and sat down in one of the overstuffed leather chairs across from Yvaine.

"I'm sorry about my greeting, but you came at a bad time. I'm a little distracted because Alex Scire, Jane Roland, and Diana Bennet have disappeared again. Sophie is out searching for them as we speak."

"I know."

"But how could you," Yvaine asked. "They disappeared only last night."

Hellwain smiled and said, "That's an interesting question without a good answer."

Yvaine's eyes narrowed. "Why are you here instead of guarding the Chintamani?"

"Given all we've talked about recently, I'm surprised you even bother to ask," Hellwain replied.

Yvaine sat down in a chair opposite Hellwain and dropped her head into her hand. "It can't be. How could he find it? I thought nobody could do that."

"Does it matter?" the crone asked. "I believe this definitively answers our question of whether he's found any of the other Maqlû."

"But how did he get in? Did he blast the doors open? Did he magically appear? What?"

"None of the above."

"But how'd he do it if he didn't use magic?" Yvaine asked.

"I didn't say he didn't use magic. I said he didn't magically appear. Do you remember the back door – the exit we thought was the most secure as you had to dive over 100 meters into the dark, frigid waters of Loch Ness to get into the outer caverns before having to open two magical doors?"

"Of course, but how does that have to do with how he got in?"

"That's the way he came in. Obviously, he used some sort of powerful magic to get through the doors, but what is most intriguing was how he told us he got to the cave entrance in the first place." Hellwain waited for Yvaine to ask the obvious question. When the head of the order remained silent, she said, "He told us Apalāla helped him."

"Who's that?" Yvaine asked.

"It took me a while to figure out the answer to that question, too. I'm sure you'll recognize her more common name – Nessie."

"What! How could he tame a beast that's a myth?"

"The circumstances lead me to believe she's a dragon. Which seems impossible because I thought her kind had all left Earth."

Yvaine sat in stunned silence until Hellwain said, "You might also be interested to know he brought Jane and the other girl with him."

"Are they safe?"

"They were the last I saw them. They also entered through the back door but arrived sometime after the boy." Hellwain grew silent and sat with furrowed brows, staring at the floor. "I believe I got one answer to some of the boy's strange behaviors, though. He can speak to spirits."

"Why do you say that?"

"Well, while trying to figure out what he was doing, I asked him why he was in the area. His response was quite unexpected."

Yvaine sat forward in her seat. "And?"

"He said he was helping William Wallace," Hellwain replied.

"That's impossible."

"I thought so too, but then he started talking to someone I couldn't see or hear. And whoever he was talking to was waving a sword around in the air."

Yvaine shook her head again and said, "What does all this have to do with you being here? Is the Chintamani okay?"

Hellwain shook her head. Seeing Yvaine was about to protest, she held up her hand and said, "Hear me out. My sisters and I were distraught when the boy first entered our chamber. We wanted to kill him for trespassing but decided to give him the option of choosing the cauldron with the stone."

"That's not giving him a choice, as all the options lead to death."

"Precisely. And yet he seemed ready to accept his fate, for he believes the Maqlû are too tempting for humans, and we should destroy them. Which is what he did to the Chintamani."

"How could he even pull the stone out of whichever cauldron it was in?" Yvaine asked.

"Again, I can't answer your question. I know he was in great pain, but somehow, he pulled the stone out unscathed. It reminded me of the Gom Jabbar test in *Dune*. That's when I believe the spirits entered. But rather than give the stone to whoever was there, he tossed it into my cauldron. Then he got me to throw our *Sibylline Book* in as well. They're both gone now," Hellwain said.

"You seem to be relieved at the whole incident."

"I am, as are my sisters. I never realized what a burden protecting that thing was until it was gone. All three of us feel like we've regained our freedom. But, as you can see, it also no longer feeds our life forces. We're dying. And by the grey streaks in your hair, I can see this has impacted you, too."

"We've been friends for such a long time… it's hard to accept this might be the end," Yvaine said quietly.

"Yet, you need to prepare yourself for what lies ahead. He'll come for all of them if he continues pursuing his current course. And, since the rumors about him are already spreading, you need to think about what you'll say to the order about all this."

The two women sat in companionable silence until Hellwain asked, "What will you do about the Omphalos? I think you should assume he'll go after that, too. Will you increase security or allow him the opportunity to find and destroy it?"

"I'll have to increase security, or else I'll have an insurrection on my hands," Yvaine replied. "It's funny, though."

"What?" Hellwain asked.

"I'm surprised I'm suddenly reluctant to do so. Anyway, it won't matter. There's no way he'll find it.

And even on the remote chance he does, there's no way he'll get to it. It's too well guarded."

"That's what we thought," Hellwain said. "Even though he was 150 miles away when I last saw him, with no obvious means of transportation, I wouldn't put it past him to find his way back here quickly."

"I don't think he'll come here," Yvaine replied. "Remember, he was here for months and made no move to take anything."

Hellwain scoffed. "He didn't have much choice as he was in a coma almost the entire time. And remember – as soon as he got out of here, he went straight after the Chintamani."

"You know there were extenuating circumstances with his running away."

"Perhaps, but I believe we've been missing the big picture. What if we've gotten our order's mission all wrong? What if we shouldn't have focused on finding and protecting the Maqlû and, instead, should have focused on destroying them – like the boy is? This whole incident makes me feel like a failure."

"You're not a failure." But no sooner had she said it than doubt began creeping into Yvaine's thoughts. "Do you really think we've been wrong all this time?" she asked.

"Possibly. I wish you'd have been there to see what happened. As I said, I don't believe he was interested in the Chintamani when he entered the room, but he destroyed it anyway because he thought it was the right thing to do."

Hellwain grimaced as she shifted in her chair to get more comfortable and added, "I don't know what's worse – suddenly getting old or growing older gradually. At least with normal people, you have time to adjust to all the discomforts of growing old." She waved her hand across her body and said, "But that's beside the point. If we're to understand what's going on, we need to figure out what resources he is able to marshal because he couldn't have penetrated our protection spells without help. It appears he's already using ghosts, magic, and dragons, but given what you've told me of his personality, I wonder if he sought them out or if they sought him?"

Lady Yvaine got up and went to the windows to stare down at the lake below the manor house. "Does it matter? As fascinating as I find how he entered your hideaway, I'm more interested that he survived your no-win scenario."

She was so preoccupied that she didn't notice her scrying dish come to life. Nor did she hear someone calling her name until Hellwain brought Yvaine's thoughts back to the present, saying, "Someone's calling you."

Yvaine looked down at the waters in her scrying dish, which were starting to calm, and said, "Apkallu. I'm surprised to hear from you. Is everything all right?"

"No, your Ladyship. I just spotted the boy."

Yvaine grabbed the table the dish sat on for support and said, "How can that be? He was in Scotland hours ago."

"I can't answer that. All I can tell you is that he was standing a few feet away from our entrance in Meteora an hour ago."

"What did he do?"

"Nothing. He must have appeared here sometime during the night because I saw him wandering around the hilltop as the sun was rising. Surprisingly, though, he didn't seem to be looking for us, as he left as soon as he found the trail leading down. I followed him until he got to one of the nearby monasteries and got in a taxi. What should we do?"

"I'll have to think more about this and get back to you, but do nothing for now except keep an eye on him. Report back to me immediately should he approach your location again. And thank you, Apkallu. You did well to notify me."

Yvaine waved her hand over the dish, severing the connection, then turned to her guest with a questioning look.

"So, we have an answer to another question," Hellwain said. "He's not coming here. He must be going after the Omphalos, as I thought."

"Perhaps, but right now, I'm more concerned about you and the others. What can I do to help?"

Hellwain smiled and said, "Don't worry about me, Puckle, or Hecate, as we haven't been this carefree in a long, long time. I just hope we can live long enough to see what this is all about. Now go, do what you must. At the very least, you must ensure our members don't get out of control. They already want his head for everything else he's done. I can only imagine what they'll do when they hear he destroyed one of the few Maqlû we possess."

Yvaine pressed her longtime friend's hand and smiled weakly. "I don't know how long I'll be gone, but you're right. I have to intercept him and escort him home to keep him safe. Maybe he'll open up and help me understand what's happening. Farewell, my friend." And with that, Yvaine rushed out of the room to pack her bags.

CHAPTER 5

WAKAN TANKA

"Thank you for agreeing to meet me here in Denver," Lady Yvaine said as she thrust her hand towards Alex's grandfather, Ignacio. "I hope it wasn't too long of a drive for you."

"Don't worry about us, Ma'am. We had a much easier time getting here than you did." He turned to the sixteen-year-old girl beside him and said, "This is my granddaughter Chipeta, Alex's cousin."

Motioning to the tall, gangly girl beside her, Yvaine said, "Of course, you've both met my assistant, Jane Roland. Where can we talk privately?" she asked.

"I've booked rooms for you at the airport hotel and have a van waiting outside," Ignacio replied.

Seeing how tired Lady Yvaine was, Ignacio said nothing on the short trip to the hotel, letting her unwind. But as soon as they were ensconced in a room, Yvaine said, "As I told you on the phone, we're here because I need to learn more about your grandson. He's … done things I don't understand. You told me long ago that he has no magical ability, but the evidence suggests otherwise. I don't know what it is, but I have a feeling you do. Will you share what you know?"

Ignacio looked down and shuffled his feet.

"It's okay, sir," Jane exclaimed. "I've known about the ankh for some time. And recently, yer grandson felt comfortable enough to tell our friend Diana Bennet about it too."

When Ignacio didn't respond, Jane turned to Lady Yvaine and said, "I don't know much about the background of it, but right before his family died, Alex accidentally took a necklace from his dad that had a rather unusual ankh on it. I believe it's the ankh that gives him his unusual powers. I don't know everything it does, or how it works, but I know it protects and guides him. I also know it enables him to see spirits."

Ignacio, relieved at finally being able to talk about the family secret, nodded and said, "It's been handed down through our family for generations and has been nothing but a curse to us. In fact, it's often driven its owner mad. I wore it for a while but couldn't handle it. The same was true for my mother and son, Alex's father. None of the bearers were ever comfortable with it. Maybe the Shakespearean line that says, 'Uneasy lies the head that wears a crown,' is apropos."

"Why do you think your grandson can handle it?" Yvaine asked. "For that matter, why did you keep it?"

"Concerning your second question, all I can say is that our family has been leaders in our tribe for as long as anyone can remember – because of the ankh. As for why it doesn't seem to affect my grandson the same way as all the rest of us, I have no explanation," Ignacio replied.

"I have a theory on that," Jane said. "I believe the ankh has a mind of its own – like a tiny supercomputer with immense powers. When I first met Alex, he was always doing strange things with no rhyme or reason. But, as he's gained experience with it, the randomness of his actions has smoothed out. His relationship with the ankh seems to be gradually changing to more of a give-and-take. The ankh still protects him, of course, and it still wants him to go certain places, but he appears to be making more of his own decisions now. And when he does, the ankh seems to support him."

"How can that be?" Chipeta asked. "He's always been pretty laid back."

"Ye're right, but he's been through some difficult times that have changed him," Jane replied. "But I can tell ye that I wouldn't wish those experiences upon anyone."

"Then why do you keep putting up with the danger and hardships to be with him?" Yvaine asked.

"Because he's determined to do the right thing, whatever the consequences, and I admire that. Also, ye told me to look after him, so I couldn't, in good conscience, let him go off on his own."

"You know I never meant for you to put yourself in harm's way," Yvaine said. "And why haven't you told me any of this before? Why keep it a secret?"

"First of all, Alex asked me to keep the ankh's existence and powers a secret. But, since we're here with his grandfather, and he's started opening up about it, it seemed time to share what I know. Secondly, I haven't been entirely sure how ye felt about him. The rest of the order is out for his blood, and I was unwilling to put him at further risk."

"You trust me now?" Yvaine asked.

"Not entirely, because I know ye're still undecided about him."

"Ouch," Yvaine replied. "I don't think I've had that harsh of criticism in cent…, I mean ages."

Seeing the high priestess of the Bandruí about to protest, Jane hastily added, "But the situation is spiraling out of control, and we need to work together."

"Pardon me," Ignacio said. "This has been an interesting discussion, but what's caused you to come here now?"

"Your grandson has found and destroyed a precious magical object of our order that … well, I don't see how he did it. I hoped you could explain his behaviors to help us prepare for similar future events." Yvaine turned to

Jane and said, "Since you have been so forthcoming, why don't you shed light on how it happened."

It was Jane's turn to wince from the censure in her preceptress's words. She took a deep breath and said, "Well, he never meant to go after the Chintamani, but he happened to come across the spirit of William Wallace and promised to help him move on."

"Excuse me," Chipeta said. "Are you talking about *The* William Wallace? The hero of Scotland? The one who was in *Braveheart*?"

Jane nodded. "I don't know what led him to Wallace in the first place. I wasn't there with him, but our friend Diana was. It could've been by chance … or not. But, whatever it was, he wound up agreeing to help Wallace move on." She abruptly stopped talking and shifted in her chair until she faced Yvaine. "This isn't right. Since we're being open here, ye need to hear the whole story. Well, at least as far as I know it. This quest of his started because he wanted to help his sister move on."

"Wait. How's Deborah mixed up in all this?" Yvaine asked. "She's been dead for years."

"Apparently, Alex's parents moved on after the accident, but his sister didn't," Jane said. "After he found the first *Sibylline Book*, Deborah begged him to find one of the Maqlû, thinking it was her destiny, and doing so would help her move on in the afterlife. To make a long story short, he found the Palantir but chose to destroy it so it wouldn't end up in the wrong hands again. Distraught over the belief he'd ruined his sister's chances of moving on, he went after the Fountain of Youth. And, like the Palantir, in the end, he felt he had to destroy the Pair Dadeni to keep others from abusing it. In my opinion, though, the most intriguing part of his story was the nine months when he disappeared, which he still insists was only a couple of weeks to him. Because he's bound to secrecy, he won't tell me what happened, but I believe he found the Holy Grail and spent most of that unaccounted-for time restoring it to its rightful place."

Seeing everyone stunned into silence, Jane thought it best to continue. "As I was saying, I'm not sure how Alex found Wallace, but he did and agreed to help the spirit find his remains so he could move on. Since it's a matter of public record where King Edward displayed Wallace's body parts, he didn't have much trouble finding Wallace with the aid of the ankh and Wallace's friends, who hadn't moved on either. The only problem he encountered was when a group of spirits attacked him outside of Falkirk – which was what caused the coma. Ye're probably wondering what's the link between helping Wallace and finding the Chintamani's hiding place – but I have no idea what it is. Right up to the end, Alex insisted he wasn't interested in finding that object, which leads me to believe the ankh was pushing him towards it."

"You keep mentioning the Chintamani. What is it?" Chipeta asked.

"It's a very powerful magical object that our order has been guarding for a long time," Yvaine replied. "The reason Alex's actions are a big deal is because only four people knew where the object was hidden, and we thought it was impossible to break through all our barriers protecting it." She turned to Jane and asked, "Do you think the ankh led him to our hiding place?"

"Probably, but I believe that luck also played a role. Think of everything that happened to lead him to the object's hiding place. First, Alex decided to help Wallace. Then Diana mapped out how to get to the general locations of Wallace's body parts. I have no idea, though, whether it was luck, the ankh, the spirits, or Alex's instincts that led him to the exact spots where Wallace's body parts were buried. The only leg of the quest that was clear about who selected where to go was Loch Ness, which William Wallace's friends chose. And that was when we got the most unexpected help."

"I was surprised, nay – stunned, to hear Hellwain tell me about that," Yvaine said.

"Who are you talking about now?" Chipeta said. "You can't leave us in the dark about who this mysterious helper was."

"Her name was Apalāla," Jane replied.

"And who's that," Chipeta asked.

Yvaine smiled at Jane and said, "Go ahead and tell her. I know you're dying to."

"Well, it was pretty cool. And very unexpected," Jane said. "Nessie took us to the Chintamani's hiding place."

It took Chipeta a moment to internalize what she'd heard. When it sunk in, Chipeta nearly exploded. "What! How come he gets to do all the cool things? It's not fair."

"It's not all fun and games when we're with him," Jane said. "Admittedly, I wouldn't mind meeting Nessie again, but I never want to go through what happened with her as it was nip and tuck whether we'd die of hypothermia, drown, or survive."

Ignacio laid a hand on Jane's arm and said, "I never got to thank you for taking care of my grandson when he was in a coma, so thank you. But why were you so secretive about his illness?"

"We were concerned about how upset you'd be if you knew how close he was to dying, Yvaine replied. "Plus, we couldn't let you, or any other outsiders, see him, as most of the order views him as an enemy. But I can assure you that he wouldn't have made it without Jane's incredible healing skills and her round-the-clock attention for months."

Jane ducked her head to hide her deep blush, letting her long ginger-colored hair hide her face.

"I don't doubt anything you've said, but perhaps you're all missing one of the most obvious reasons for all this happening." Ignacio paused, then said, "Every person has different beliefs about religion than the next person. I'm sure you've heard that many American Indians worship the Great Spirit, as I do. Many think of the Great Spirit as an entity, like the Christians' belief in God, your Gaia, Buddha, etc. But, I believe the divine is much more than a single entity. I believe it's the unifying life force of everything around us – including the mountains, the stars, the sun, and the moon. It's the animals all around us, the plants, the air, even the rocks underneath us. It's like thinking of your Gaia as Mother Earth, but encompassing the totality of life and the universe. We call this concept – Wakan Tanka, or the Great Mystery. After hearing everything you've said, I have come to believe that what's happened is that the ankh has opened part of this mystery to him, including the spirits that now define much of his life."

Jane was nodding in agreement as she said, "Interesting. I hadn't thought of it like that. But none of what we've discussed explains why spirits seek him out, wanting his help."

"What makes him different than his father, myself, and others in my family is that he accepts the world around him as it is, unlike his predecessors," Ignacio said. "I believe his motivations come not from the world we know, but the universe around us. And that is truly magical."

The four sat silently for some time, each trying to internalize all they'd discussed. At last, Yvaine slapped her hands on her legs and said, "Thank you, Ignacio and Chipeta, for your time and your perspectives. But I think it's time we go to the source."

As Ignacio drove Yvaine and Jane back to the airport, he asked, "Have you found out how he got from the wilds of Scotland to the wilds of Greece so fast?"

Yvaine smiled. "If I knew that, I'd be closer to solving the puzzle that is him."

CHAPTER 6

ASK QUESTIONS FROM YOUR HEART

After two days of nearly non-stop traveling, Yvaine felt her vast age catching up as she exited the plane in Kalabaka, Greece. She rubbed her eyes as she sank into the waiting limo and wearily asked Jane, "Why do you think he's here?"

"I've got a hunch," Jane replied. "Who knows what he was thinking when he came here, but he seems to have a nose for the Maqlû, and this area isn't a bad starting point for finding the next one."

"But it's been two days since our people last saw him. Based on his history, I'd think he'd be long gone by now."

"Possibly. But I'm counting on human frailty to slow him down. Remember, it hasn't been that long since he recovered from his coma, and he's been going non-stop since then. I'm thinking he'll take a break and figure out what he's going to do next. And even though I don't know how he got here, he couldn't have gone that far if he'd been on foot in Meteora two days ago," Jane replied.

"I can understand his not contacting you or Diana, but why hasn't he contacted his grandfather?"

"He knows Ignacio supports what he's doing, and he knows that our whole order is out to get him. If I were him, I'd also assume that we're tapping their phones. Besides, if he's out and about, someone could spot him. It's happened to him before, which is why I'm guessing he's laying low and recuperating."

"But why here of all places? It can't be coincidence."

"Maybe. But I doubt he planned it this way. It makes me wonder, though, if his grandfather was right and some greater entity is interceding."

"That's not important right now," Yvaine said. "What I want to know – is how you plan to find him, as I don't have the same confidence you do about him being here. For all we know, he could be anywhere in the world."

"I know ye're having a hard time believing we can find him, but it's like what happened with Diana and Elizabeth in Romania," Jane replied. "Diana had no idea where he was, so she tried to think illogically – like Alex often does. And, as you know, she eventually crossed paths with Alex and I. Or, think about how I found him when he ditched me in Scotland and wound up in Seville." Seeing Yvaine was still unconvinced, Jane changed tacks. "Okay, think of it this way. Do ye believe in Murphy's Law?"

"What's that got to do with anything?" Yvaine snapped.

"I believe there's a good chance he'll be wherever it makes us most uncomfortable. And right now, that's here. Ye'll just have to trust me and hope for the best."

Yvaine studied her protégé briefly before saying, "Can you read other people's minds? Is that how you know he's here and plan to find him?"

Jane blushed and tried clearing her throat before she stammered, "I…I can't read his mind. I've learned a lot about how he thinks and can sometimes read his body language, but that's it. The only times I've been able to predict his actions are when I step back and look at the big picture. Then, I can take educated guesses on what he might do."

"Hmph. I'll let you go on that answer, but don't think I didn't notice you answered only part of my question. So, what do we do now?"

"You're about to drop, so I suggest we go to our hotel room and get a good night's rest," Jane replied.

"I won't argue with you, but why don't you look tired?"

"Remember, I'm a lot younger than ye are."

"That might be, but you never seem to tire, no matter how active you've been."

Jane looked away and didn't answer.

By the next morning, Yvaine felt refreshed and was ready to resume their search. "What do you recommend we do today?" she asked.

"As I've told ye before, if ye want to understand Alex, ye have to think like him – but don't overthink it. So, I thought we'd wander around Meteora for a bit, then return to Kalabaka and wander around. If he's here, there's a decent chance we'll find him."

"Why not start here in Kalabaka? It's a much bigger city, with more resources, and easier to hide."

"He was on foot and exhausted when he reached our sanctuary, which means he had to hike miles to get to Meteora."

"But, how do you expect to find him if he's holed up?" Yvaine asked.

Jane smiled, flipped her long ginger-colored hair back, and said, "I'm easy to spot as I stand out wherever I go with my hair color and bright-colored dresses. If he's here, we'll run into him."

They wandered around the tiny downtown of Meteora, then headed up the road to the nearest monastery. As they passed a small outdoor café, Yvaine heard a chair scrape across the stone pavers, turned to look, and was surprised to see Alex running after them.

"What are you doing here?" he called out.

Jane turned and ran towards him, engulfing him in a hug. When she finally let him go, she said, "Looking for ye, of course."

"But, how did you know I was here? I barely know where this is," Alex said.

"Someone recognized ye and called us. Figuring ye were in a bind, we came to help," Jane replied. "Why don't we go back to the café and chat while ye finish yer breakfast?"

Alex looked skeptically at Lady Yvaine but turned and headed back to the cafe. Having already eaten breakfast, Jane and Yvaine only ordered drinks. Before they could get comfortable, Alex asked, "What's the real reason you're here? Is it because of the Chintamani? Because I'm not sorry I destroyed it. I couldn't let it fall into the wrong hands."

"I'm not here to reproach you," Yvaine said. "And to put your mind at ease, I'm not here to take you back to Scotland either. What I want to know is – what are your goals?"

"It's okay, Alex. Ye can talk freely here," Jane said as she wrapped her hands around the steaming cup of hot chocolate she'd ordered. "She knows about the ankh as we've jest returned from talking to yer grandfather about it."

"What were you doing talking to him?" Alex asked.

"I want to understand you better," Yvaine replied.

"You ask me to trust you, but not two days ago, a bunch of your group were trying to kill me. Why in the world would I tell you anything? You'll just use it against me."

Hurt by the blunt critique, Yvaine sat for some time in silence. At last, she said, "I understand how you might feel that way, but your grandfather thinks it'd be good for you to share your burden."

Alex didn't hear her comments as he got distracted by the strange ring on Lady Yvaine's hand. It had six stones of various colors in a round setting with what looked like a tiny sliver of a dragon's scale in the middle. "I've never seen you with that ring on," he said. "Where did you get it? It's interesting."

Yvaine's gasp was inaudible as Jane asked, "Are ye feeling okay, Alex? Lady Yvaine never wears jewelry."

Realizing he'd seen something he wasn't supposed to, Alex looked away and mumbled, "I guess I'm tired and seeing things."

An uncomfortable silence descended over the table and wasn't broken until Yvaine said, "You're right. We haven't given you much reason to trust us, but Hellwain, one of the women you met in Scotland, suggested I share some of our order's secrets if I wanted information from you. My dilemma is that most of the women in our order fear you're a warlock and, therefore, a threat to us, as our history is fraught with problems caused by men with lesser powers than yours."

Alex shook his head. "We've been over this countless times. I've seen the things Diana can do, like conjuring fires, moving earth, and growing plants, and I can't do any of that. Heck, I struggle to start a fire in the woods when I have matches and dry wood."

"Maybe ye can't do any magic, but yer ankh can," Jane said.

"Heh. That is supposed to be a secret. Who have you been blabbing to?"

"Your grandfather trusted us with your secret and told us about your family's history with the ankh," Yvaine replied.

"Where is all this going?" Alex asked. "What do you really want?"

Yvaine took a deep breath and blurted out, "I want you to stop destroying the Maqlû."

"So, you're saying I should stand around and do nothing as people misuse the blasted things," Alex retorted.

"I'm asking you not to go looking for them. Let sleeping dogs lie," Yvaine replied.

"I think this meeting was a mistake," Alex said. Before Yvaine could say anything, a picture of a steaming mug of hot chocolate flashed in his mind. Images of the sweet brew combined with feelings of bliss and ecstasy filled Alex's brain. A second later, a furry, odd-looking, cat-like creature jumped onto the table and attacked Jane's hot chocolate, greedily lapping the rich drink up.

Startled, Jane shrieked and jumped out of her chair.

The creature's emotions gripped Alex so powerfully that he couldn't move or think until his little dragon friend had finished lapping up the last drop in Jane's cup. Only then was he able to react. Not wanting Yvaine to figure out what had attacked Jane's chocolate, Alex scooped up Sadie, grabbed his pack, and said, "I'm sorry about her. Excuse me." Then he headed to the back of the café.

Jane stared at his retreating form and shook her head in wonderment about his odd actions. She barely heard Yvaine saying, "Well, this has been a disaster. I don't know what I was thinking we'd accomplish."

The two stared out at the street until Yvaine asked, "Does he usually take his pack to the bathroom?"

"He tends to keep it nearby at all times, just in case something happens," Jane replied. Suddenly, her eyes grew wide, and she pushed back her chair. "Oh my god. That wasn't some random cat. That was Sadie."

"Who's Sadie," Yvaine asked. "And how would both of you know a cat in this town?"

"That's not important right now. What's important is that he's escaping." Without another word, she ran after Alex.

CHAPTER 7

THE COMMITMENT TO BEGIN

Chrysophylax hurtled out of the portal and pulled up, flapping his wings hard in a desperate attempt to climb above the great sandstorms that regularly swept across the Great Sareer Desert. He'd thought about coming through one of the more commonly used portals on Berellus but had decided it was safer to risk the deadly storms over the desert island rather than returning through one of the heavily guarded portals.

He kept climbing until his lungs felt like bursting, and every muscle screamed in protest. Knowing he couldn't last much longer at that rate, he scanned the horizon for signs of one of the destructive sandstorms that left the island the only uninhabited part of the planet. Not seeing one, he decided he could afford a more leisurely climb and eased back on his ascent. When he finally reached an altitude where he was safe from the storms, he leveled off to conserve energy for the flight to the mainland and the long journey to his home weyr.

Several hours later, he crossed the coastline and headed out over the Laccadive Sea, and away from the deadly island. Seeking a tailwind, Chrysophylax slowly descended until he caught one a few miles above sea level. He rode it steadily eastward for the rest of the day until he finally spotted land and glided down, nearly collapsing from exhaustion when his feet hit the ground. Chrysophylax folded his wings and promptly fell asleep. When he awoke late the next morning, he went hunting to satisfy his grumbling stomach, then continued his journey home.

He arrived home several days later, bugled a greeting, and landed on the rock ledge outside his uncle's laboratory. Before he could enter, Nabu whispered, *"Hurry up and get in, but don't say anything until I tell you it's safe."*

Curious, Chrysophylax waited until his uncle had set up a magical shroud around the lab before asking, *"Why all the secrecy? Have things gotten even worse since I left?"*

"I fear Thoth is gathering power and means to take control of the High Council, though I don't understand what he hopes to achieve, as our society has worked together harmoniously for millennia."

"What does he crave?" Chrysophylax asked.

Nabu stared at his nephew as if he were some alien creature. *"What has that to do with anything?"*

"You forget," Chrysophylax replied. *"I've been around humans quite a bit over the last few years, and they seem to want only three things – more power, more wealth, and love. Which one is it for him?"*

"I never thought about it that way," Nabu replied. *"But it makes sense. Thoth has always been interested in human behavior, and I know he's not interested in wealth or love. If your theory is right, that would indicate he's after more power."*

"For what purpose?" Chrysophylax asked. *"He has to have a reason that's driving him to act so out of character for our species."*

Nabu stared at the large blank monitor in the center of his lab before replying, *"Possibly revenge. He's lost several family members to the humans and has one of the greatest reasons to hate them. But I'm not sure. You seem to know a lot about these emotions. What would you suggest we do?"*

"I'm torn. Before I went to Earth to discover what happened with the ankh, I'd have said we should wait and see what Thoth is planning to do. But now... I'm not so sure. Maybe we should take a cue from the boy and stop Thoth and his minions."

"What are you getting at?"

"Well, the boy has witnessed the temptation to abuse the power of the objects and is doing something about it. He's seen what too much power does to people and is eliminating the Maqlû one by one."

"No! You've got to go back and stop him," Nabu roared. *"You've got to return to Earth, find and bring the remaining Maqlû here so we can protect them. Those objects are too precious and might be needed to stop whatever Thoth is up to."*

"I don't know if I can do that," Chrysophylax replied.

"Why not?"

"Well, there are several problems. First, I don't know how to find the objects because the boy seems to be the only one who can. Second, how do I even get off this planet? If what you say is true, then they'll be guarding the portals even tighter than before. I was lucky this time – I flew over the Sareer desert to avoid being. Since it often takes several hours for them to open, it would be suicide to wait for the portal in that hellhole. And lastly, I know we think of humans as lesser beings, but I've come to respect the boy's choices. Look at how he helped my mother. Heck, even Apalāla and Kraken have been willing to help the boy, and you know what they think of humans. Then there's that little Ryūjin dragon who's following him around everywhere. It all adds up to – I

think he's doing the right thing to destroy the objects. Which means we've got to find another way to defeat Thoth."

Nabu sighed. *"Maybe you're right, but let's not make any decisions now. You need to rest after your journey and I need to think about what you've said. We'll talk about this more over the coming days."*

CHAPTER 8

ATHENS

Alex splashed water on his face, trying to clear his mind of his discussion with Lady Yvaine and the uncomfortable feeling he'd had as his ankh pulled him towards the mysterious ring she'd worn. Before he could process what he'd seen, something bumped into his leg. An image of a ruined ancient Greek temple sitting high atop a hill popped into his mind. Looking down, he saw Sadie weaving between his legs. An instant later, the little dragon ran out the door, flashing more images of the Greek ruins.

Despite knowing he'd seen the structure before, he struggled to place it. As he left the bathroom, he looked to where Lady Yvaine and Jane were still sitting and, for a moment, thought about returning to them. But Sadie's insistent messaging drove him out the back of the cafe.

Although he wasn't too worried about the two Druids pursuing him, he ducked into a nearby alley and headed away from the town's center. After ten minutes of winding his way downhill, he popped out onto the main street of Kalabaka, directly across from the bus station.

Looking down at Sadie, he said, "I wish I knew what you were trying to tell me so I wouldn't go off half-cocked again." But the only reply the little Ryujin dragon gave him was to nudge him towards the bus station before running away. Knowing he was on his own again, he sighed and crossed the street.

Once inside the station, he sat on a bench and wracked his brains to remember where he'd seen the ruins Sadie had shared. And even though he felt he was wrong, all that came to mind was the Acropolis – high atop a hill overlooking Athens. Figuring the capital of Greece was so full of ancient buildings that he couldn't be far off, he went to the counter and bought a one-way ticket to Athens.

Learning he had an hour before the bus left, he went back outside and looked for a grocery store where he could buy food and water for the trip. After filling his pack, he stopped at an ATM to get more Euros, then returned to wait for the bus.

When he was finally on the road, he settled back and pondered what new mess he was getting into. His thoughts soon drifted to wondering what Diana would say when he told her he'd visited a UNESCO site without her. But he soon forgot about his friend and drifted off to sleep. A few hours later, he was in the middle of Athens.

Despite the city's history, he felt disappointed at first glimpse as it looked like every other big city he'd been in – modern, crowded, and noisy. More importantly, though, he didn't see any sign of the Acropolis. After half an hour of wandering around, he still hadn't spotted the ancient site and decided to head away from the central part of the city.

He felt like a dunce when he walked a couple of blocks off the main strip and got his first glimpse of the rocky outcrop that dominated Athen's skyline. But his heart sank when he saw it wasn't the ruins Sadie had pictured and realized he was in the wrong city.

He found an empty table at one of the many street cafés, ordered lunch, and tried figuring out where to go next. After half an hour of fruitless analysis, he decided to see the famous site anyway, hoping to find some clue on where Sadie had meant for him to go.

With a clear view of the ancient citadel, he worked his way towards the base of the hill and spotted a crowd of people milling about a set of gates. A woman passing by paused and said, "If you're trying to see the Acropolis, I'd suggest you do it first thing in the morning when there aren't nearly as many tourists. Because right now, it'd take you an hour just to get in. Then you'd wait in a long line to get to the top, where you'll be in a crowd so dense that you won't be able to see much. If I were you, I'd go see the Agora now and come back tomorrow."

Alex thanked the woman and started in the direction she'd pointed but had only gone a short distance when a wave of cold air washed over him. He stopped when he saw a short, stocky spirit standing before him, dressed in a white chiton, staring intently at him. Not feeling the ankh thumping against his chest, Alex figured he wasn't in danger.

"So, it's true," the ghost said. "You can see us. I was skeptical, but I had to come see for myself."

"You have the advantage of me," Alex replied. "Who are you?"

"I am a citizen of the world." The old man paused, waiting for acknowledgement of his status. When Alex shrugged, the spirit rolled his eyes and said, "I was hoping you had some education and had read my works. I'm Socrates."

"Ah, I've heard of you. But I'm not sure what you did."

"It's not important. I was hoping you were wise."

"Well, if there's one thing I know, it's that I don't know much," Alex replied. "For instance, right now, I don't know why I'm here, nor why you're talking to me. But I'm assuming there's a reason for both."

"That gives me hope for you," Socrates said. "Since that's the case, I'd suggest you stroll through the Agora here."

"Why? It doesn't look like much."

Socrates pointed to the Acropolis towering above Athens. "Most people want to visit that place. It does have great views and an interesting history, but down here was where the heartbeat of the city was when I lived. It's where the greatest philosophers of my day came to seek wisdom. If you stroll through there, I believe you'll find some of the answers to your questions. I'd remind you that nature has given you two ears, two eyes, but only one tongue, so you should hear and see more than you speak." Before Alex could reply, the spirit disappeared. With the sun beating fiercely down on him, Alex pulled his Tilley hat down and headed in the direction Socrates had pointed, hoping the trip wouldn't be for nothing.

He'd gone only a few steps when cold air once more enveloped him. A second later, his sister, Deborah, apparated and said, "Thank Gaia, I found you at last. How did you get here? I wasn't in the Netherworld that long."

Alex jumped and nearly fell at her unexpected arrival. When he'd recovered his balance, he said, "I wish there were a way of telling me when you're going to arrive. I swear I'm losing years of my life with all the ghosts appearing out of nowhere and wanting something from me."

Deborah huffed and said, "I doubt if surprise is what will kill you. It's more likely you'll die on one of your crazy adventures. But you outdid yourself in Scotland. I've never seen the order in such an uproar – everyone wants your head. The only ones on your side are Jane, Diana, the three Crones, and Yvaine."

Hoping his twin would relieve some of the guilt he was feeling for his actions, he said in a plaintive tone, "But I did the right thing by destroying the Chintamani and not letting Edward have it. Didn't I?"

"Of course you did. It's just that I worry about you. Your adventures are getting more dangerous by the day. By the way, what did the ghost I saw you talking to a minute ago want?"

"I don't know," Alex replied. "But Socrates hinted that there's something important nearby."

"That's who that was! I would've thought he'd moved on a couple of millennia ago. I wish I'd interrupted you two so I could've met him."

With sweat dripping down his face from the bright Aegean sun, Alex walked closer than usual to his sister, using the cold emanating from her to offset the Greek heat. As they neared the remains of a temple near the entrance to the Roman Agora, Alex noticed a familiar-looking rotund priest wearing brown robes and a tonsure haircut. Figuring this must have been why he'd come to the Agora, Alex broke into a jog to catch up. When he got close, he called out, "Brother Stafford."

The man turned to see who was calling and said something in Italian. Disappointed, it was an unknown middle-aged man with glasses, Alex held up his hands and said, "I only speak English."

The priest smiled and said, "Ah, you're an American."

Alex nodded and said, "I'm sorry. I thought you were somebody else for a minute."

"That's okay because we have a Brother Stafford in our group. Is he expecting you?"

"No, but I've met him a couple of times and thought you were him since you look the same from behind."

"My name is Brother Henry Phillips," he said, sticking out his hand. "Come on, let's try finding him. He's around here somewhere."

"I'd appreciate that. I'm Alex Scire by the way."

The man froze. "What did you say your name was?"

"Alex Scire. Why? Did I say something wrong?"

Deborah nudged her brother. "Watch what you say. I'll leave you alone for now, but I'll be close by in case you need help."

Alex nodded and listened as the man said, "No, it's that Brother Stafford has told us about you, and I was hoping I'd meet you one day."

"Why would he talk about me? I barely know him. In fact, I haven't seen him in over a year."

Brother Phillips shook his head while continuing to stare at Alex. "I'll have to apologize for doubting some of his stories about you. This is the first time our order has gotten together in the last couple of years, and he was worried that you'd crash our party. And now – here you are, just like he feared, I mean predicted."

"I'm sorry. I don't want to intrude," Alex said, "so I'll be on my way."

"Nonsense. Brother Stafford will be more upset if I don't take you to him. Now, come on."

As they strolled through the Ancient Agora, Brother Phillips introduced Alex to several other men, all dressed in the same monkish robes and all startled to meet him. After the sixth such occurrence, Alex said, "I don't get it. Why is everyone looking at me so funny? It's like I'm some alien from outer space."

Brother Phillips smiled. "As I've said, Brother Stafford has told us quite a bit about you."

"Why would he do that? I've only met him a few times and am not that interesting."

"If you're trying to be discrete, I'll accept your answer. If you're trying to be modest, I'd urge you to be more genuine with those who know your story."

"Can I ask you a question?"

"You can always ask," Brother Phillips replied.

"Now you're even sounding like Brother Stafford," Alex said.

Brother Phillips laughed. "I apologize, but we've found it's better to be discrete, as people usually misunderstand our work."

"Well, that's my question. Who are you guys? What do you do? You know something about me, but I know nothing about you. And it seems like I only run into Brother Stafford right before something weird happens to me. It can't be coincidence."

"He'd probably say the same thing about you," Brother Phillips replied. "Perhaps it's God's will bringing you two together."

They stopped when they reached the Stoa of Attalos – a long, two-story building with dozens of fluted columns. "If you wanted to see Brother Stafford, then you had exceptional timing because we'll be going our separate ways in a few hours. And who knows when we'll get together like this again." Brother Phillips spotted Brother Stafford in the distance and nudged Alex. "I see our quarry up ahead. Let's surprise him because I can't wait to see the look on his face."

Alex grinned, nodding his acceptance. They walked up quietly to Brother Stafford, who was gazing up at the Acropolis. Phillips tapped Stafford on the shoulder and said, "I've got someone here who would like to meet you."

Brother Stafford frowned, turned around, and stumbled backwards when he saw Alex standing a few feet away. It took Stafford several seconds before he managed to stammer, "What, what are you doing here?"

Alex hesitated, trying to figure out how to reply to Stafford's surprised reaction, and decided to lie, saying,

"I was doing some sightseeing and happened to see Brother Phillips and thought he was you."

Seeing the two staring at each other made Brother Phillips uncomfortable. He waved his hand between them and said, "I'm going to leave you two alone and return to the others."

Alex watched Phillips for a bit before turning back to Brother Stafford. "I didn't mean to bother you. It's just that things have been crazy the last few…" His words trailed off as Deborah reappeared beside him.

"Did you expect to see him here?" she asked.

Alex shook his head to get his sister to leave him alone, but Stafford noticed the gesture and asked, "Is everything all right?"

"I'm fine. I was just thinking how odd it is to run into you here."

"I was thinking the same thing," Stafford said seeming to drift off to another thought before returning to the present. "Today is the last day of my group's meeting, and I was debating whether to go home or visit an old acquaintance in Delphi. I think I'm going to do the latter. Would you like to come and meet her? I think you'll find her a most fascinating person."

"Who are you talking about," Alex asked.

"Her name is Pythia."

Alex jerked and stepped back at the mention of a person he'd heard was pursuing him. "Why would I want to meet her?" he asked.

"You're probably thinking of 'The Pythia' from ancient Greece – the High Priestess and Oracle of Delphi. I'm talking about a live person who has been most anxious to meet you."

"No, that's…."

Do it," Deborah whispered in his ear. "You're here for some reason, and I can't believe this meeting isn't fortuitous. Especially not when we're talking about going to Delphi – one of the most intriguing spiritual spots in the whole world."

"I'll go if you think it's the right thing to do," he replied to his sister.

Thinking Alex was talking to him, Stafford replied, "Good. I can pick you up at your hotel tomorrow morning at, say, eight." "Uh, I don't have a place yet, as I just got into town."

"Okay, what about giving me your phone number? I'll call you tonight to coordinate pickup tomorrow."

"Uh, I don't have a phone either."

"What! Everybody has a cell phone nowadays," Stafford said.

"Not everybody. A friend thinks I'm a Luddite because I'm not into technology."

Stafford shook his head as he mumbled, "And I thought some of the members of my order were living in the dark ages." In a louder voice, he said, "Okay, how about meeting me outside the train station at eight tomorrow? It's a little north of here and easy to find."

"Sounds good to me," Alex said, shaking hands. He watched Stafford return to his group before turning to his sister and saying, "He probably thinks I'm crazy."

Deborah smiled and said, "You are. That's why I like hanging around you. But that's beside the point. Do you think meeting Pythia was why you came here?"

"I don't know, but we'll find out tomorrow. Now, where am I going to stay tonight?"

CHAPTER 9

DELPHI

Alex had difficulty finding Brother Stafford outside the train station the next morning, causing them to get a later start than planned. Once underway, the peculiar duo drove in silence, as both were uncomfortable with the other's presence. But the views were so stunning once they left the outskirts of Athens that Alex soon forgot his worries about going with the strange monk and stared out the car window for the rest of the trip.

There were already so many tourists at Delphi by the time they finally arrived that they had to park nearly a quarter mile from the museum complex. After buying their entry tickets, they headed up a sloping paved stone walkway to the right.

Alex kept looking around for signs of the ancient archeological ruins but didn't see anything until they made a sharp left turn and came upon a gravel path that cut across the steep mountainside, with ancient building blocks and columns strewn around. Above them were more ruins, but at first glance, Alex thought it was an underwhelming UNESCO site. He began changing his opinion, though, as they wound their way up the mountain, and he saw more substantial ruins, like the Treasury building, enabling Alex to imagine better what the site once looked like.

The views were equally stunning. A steep rocky mountainside provided an impressive backdrop to the ancient religious site, while a line of forested mountains rose across a deep valley, giving the place a spectacular setting.

Stafford paused at the ruins of the Temple of Apollo and told Alex to wait there while he went to find Pythia.

No sooner had he gone out of sight than Sadie appeared, bumped his leg, and ran towards the backside of the temple.

Unsure what she was telling him, he followed the little dragon past the Temple of Apollo and headed up the hill, pausing a short time later to get another view of the surrounding scenery. When he turned around and looked down on the Temple of Apollo, he gasped – as it was the image Sadie had shared in Meteora.

Deborah apparated just then and asked, "What are you expecting to find here?"

Alex looked around to see if anybody could hear him. When he saw they were clear, he replied, "I'm not sure, but this is where Sadie sent me."

"Who's Sadie?" Deborah asked.

"You haven't met her yet because she tends to disappear when others are around. She looks like a cat but is actually a Ryujin dragonet who saved my life at the Fountain of Youth and has literally and figuratively nudged me along the path I've been taking ever since. I don't understand everything she tries to tell me because she communicates only by flashing images into my head. But I've learned that I should pay attention every time she tries to warn me or push me in a certain direction. For instance, I'm here in Delphi because she sent me images of ruins atop a hill. I went to Athens first because I thought she meant the Parthenon since those were the only Greek ruins I knew about. But now that I'm here, I realize this is where she wanted me to come."

"What have you learned so far?" his sister asked.

"That monk I told you about wants to introduce me to Pythia."

"Why would you want to talk to that witch?" Deborah asked. "You were the one who said you thought she was trying to kill you. It seems like you're purposely looking for trouble."

"I know it sounds crazy, but fate pushed me here, so I figured I might as well embrace it," Alex replied. "And I'm hoping this place will give me clues to the next object." He looked around for Sadie but didn't immediately spot her. Knowing she was a chameleon and could blend in with any surroundings, he looked closer and spotted her on a grassy trail ahead. He pointed to the little dragon and said, "If you'll excuse me, I see Sadie's growing impatient for me to follow her."

He headed after Sadie, who scampered up the curving grass trail beyond the temple. Alex followed but had taken only a few steps when he heard a whistle, followed by shouting. He stopped and looked up the hill to his right, where he saw a small guard booth. "How am I going to get past that without them seeing me?" he asked. "I'm sure I'm going someplace I shouldn't."

"The guards are trying to keep tourists from damaging the site." Deborah grinned and said, "But don't worry. I'll take care of them."

"You're not going to hurt them, are you?"

"Of course not. I'm just going to give them a little scare. Now, go. Follow your dragon friend."

Alex walked to the end of the Sacred Way gravel path, then waited for Deborah's diversion. A few seconds later, a scream, followed by shouting and whistles, told him she'd done the job.

He ran after Sadie up the well-worn trail curving around the backside of the archeological site. A few minutes later, he entered a thick grove of trees completely hidden from the Delphi complex and slowed to a walk as he headed up the steep slope of Mount Parnassus.

It was such a steep climb that Alex needed a break after only ten minutes. As he caught his breath, he noticed the ankh beating excitedly against his chest.

He didn't get to rest long, for a series of head bumps from Sadie and images of a rock face forced him to reluctantly resume his ascent.

Soon, they were past the last of the ruins, but they didn't stop until they'd reached the end of the trees and a tall cliff blocked their way. Sadie turned and scrambled along the cliff face until she stopped in front of a crease in the rocks he hadn't noticed before.

Alex felt the ankh thumping even harder against his chest and, for an instant, wondered if he'd found another one of the Maqlû. He looked around nervously, but there were no sounds except for the wind rustling through the trees. Eager to discover why Sadie had led him here, he slipped through the narrow crevice.

The sudden change from bright sunshine to gloom forced him to pause and let his eyes adjust. When he could see again, he discovered he was in a wide stone tunnel. Taking a deep breath to still his nerves, he stepped forward. A pair of wall torches came to life, reminding him of the Crones' hideout near Loch Ness. Hesitantly, he pushed deeper into the tunnel. A new pair of torches lit up every few feet while the ones behind him sputtered out.

A short distance in, he bumped into a metal wall that blended into the rocks so well it was invisible in the gloomy light. He felt along the surface, looking for a door handle, but before he could find one, the door slid silently open, revealing a small chamber with several dark openings in the back wall and a tall tri-legged stool and table standing in the center of the room.

He walked over to the unusual-looking pieces of furniture and noticed a glistening ring on the table. Alex reached out to swipe at the liquid to see if someone had been there recently and froze when he saw it was similar to the silvery liquid in his grandmother's scrying dish.

A nudge from Sadie, followed by an image of one of the openings he'd seen at the back of the room when he'd entered, drove him to leave the table and head to the back left side of the chamber.

More torches sprang to life as soon as he stepped in, highlighting a bedroom suite with all the modern amenities. Feeling he had unwittingly invaded someone's privacy, he hurriedly stepped to the next opening, which turned out to be a well-appointed but small kitchen and dinette. The third entrance held a comfortable-looking lounge with a television and sound equipment.

Thinking the last room would be as mundane as the first three, Alex was shocked when he stepped inside and saw a chamber filled with racks of swords and staffs and shelves of jewelry and other items.

Although none of the objects looked dangerous, Alex could feel a power emanating from the room that disturbed him. Worried he'd stumbled into a trap, he turned to leave the cave and crashed into a nearby rack, causing a gnarled old stick to fall on the floor.

His sister's voice echoing in the rock chamber startled him. "What's all this?" she asked.

"I don't know, Sis, but this is where Sadie brought me."

"You should get out of here now before whoever owns this place returns," Deborah said.

In total accord with his sister's suggestion, Alex hastily turned and headed out, but he wasn't watching where he was going and tripped on the staff he'd knocked over. Wanting to hide all traces that he'd been in the unusual home, he picked it up to put it away, but as soon as his fingers wrapped around the stick, an energy surge shot up his arm. Startled, he jumped back, accidentally striking the staff on the stone floor.

A flash of light blinded Alex, so it was some time before he could see the stick had turned into a hammer with a large rectangular head. Lifting it, he was surprised at how light it felt and tentatively swung it around, trying to imitate Thor. But, instead of whirling around at a controlled speed, the hammer spun Alex so fast that he became dizzy and stumbled into a rack of staffs, causing an explosion that knocked him out of the room, across the central chamber, and into the tunnel. Rocks began tumbling down, forcing Alex to scramble to his feet and run. He didn't stop until he was outside. An instant later, a cloud of dust rolled out of the opening.

Aghast at what he'd done, Alex froze and gazed into the now-demolished cave.

"Don't just stand there," Deborah said. "Run!"

CHAPTER 10

THAT PIECE CANNOT BE MOVED

Still shaken from Alex's unexpected appearance, Brother Stafford headed back to the museum, where he spotted Pythia standing in a cream-colored toga in the shade near the entrance. He paused to admire the woman he'd long thought was the most beautiful woman he'd ever seen, with her emerald green eyes, bronze skin, and copper-colored hair.

Pythia shattered his reverie by striding towards him and saying, "This is a mistake. Why did you insist on bringing the boy here?"

"I thought you'd want to meet him. He's waiting for us at the Temple of Apollo," Stafford said.

"I wanted to observe him, but not here on my home turf. Did you bring Solomon's Seal, at least?"

Stafford shook his head. "I lock it up in Assisi when I travel. I don't want him, or anyone else, anywhere near it."

"Oh. So it's okay for you to keep your valuables hidden, but not me? How thoughtful of you," Pythia said sarcastically.

"I'm glad I left it behind. This is the fourth time he's popped up out of nowhere and surprised me. It's like he's got a tracker on me. And, although I share your concerns about the location and timing of all this, I didn't have much choice. I couldn't let him disappear again near both our homes. Left alone, who knows what havoc he could wreck. No. I have him in my grasp, and I'm unwilling to let him go. Besides, I thought you would've used your Cup of Jamshid to learn more about him and divine his intent."

"As I've told you, ever since he came into the picture, my cup has only worked sporadically, which is one of the many reasons why we should've met somewhere else," Pythia said. "He's dangerous. I've sent half a dozen ghosts equipped with multiple magical objects after him, but none have returned. You should know because you've failed just as spectacularly as I have at getting rid of him. I'm curious, though. How did you convince him to come with you? He's got to be suspicious of us."

"It was surprisingly simple," Stafford replied. "I told him I wanted him to meet you, and he agreed. He doesn't appear to think he's in danger because he wasn't too nervous on the way up here."

"That should have made you more nervous," Pythia growled.

"Maybe he trusts me. To his knowledge, I've never done anything to harm him. Or, maybe he's comfortable coming here because somebody is protecting him. Someone like Gilgamesh. It would explain a lot."

"It can't be him. Gilgamesh has been gone for centuries now," Pythia said.

"I hope you're right. Although I initially agreed with him, his increasingly brutal methods to achieve our goals became repugnant to me," Stafford said.

"Enough about the ancient past," Pythia said. "What do we do with the boy now that he's here? I don't feel comfortable letting him just wander around. Who knows what trouble he might cause."

"Relax. Everything will work out. I told him I'd introduce him to you and really think you should meet him. That way, you can get an up-close opportunity to study him. You're a lot more perceptive than I am, so I'm hoping you can figure out what makes him tick so we can stop him once and for all. Or, we can always take the direct approach and lure him to your home, where you can kill him with one of those magical objects you have. It's hidden and would be easy to dispose of his body."

"I don't know," Pythia replied.

"Why? What's wrong?" Stafford asked.

"I don't know, but I'm suddenly having qualms about killing him. I'm not sure I can do it. I mean, what has he ever done to us? I can't help but wonder, if he's doing us a favor by cleaning up the mess we created."

"You can't let him get to you," Stafford interjected. "If we don't stop him now, I fear he'll eventually come after us. Are you willing to die for your newfound conscience?"

"I don't know what to think," Pythia said in exasperation. "Let's let the Druids handle him. They're not going to let him destroy all their work."

"They had him for months and didn't get rid of him. Besides, my information tells me he's got several allies within the order, including Lady Yvaine and the Crones. No, if we're going to take care of him, you and I will have to do it ourselves or pray for some accident to befall him."

"Maybe I'm getting too old for all this subterfuge. Or maybe, all our failures to get rid of him are Gaia's way of telling us to let him go about his business. It's a dangerous game we're playing, and I don't have the energy to risk it all for some long-ago goal," Pythia said.

"I never thought I'd see the day when you no longer had the stomach for this fight. Maybe we should part ways," Stafford said, "as I still believe in our cause and will not let that boy interfere with our plans. Yes, we've made mistakes in the past. We should have stopped Gilgamesh from having free rein to do what he thought was best, but that doesn't mean we're wrong for wanting to use the Maqlû to help humanity dig out from its self-made morass.”

A muffled explosion from far above them interrupted their discussion. Stafford looked around for the cause but couldn’t see anything.

Pythia grabbed two handfuls of her hair and shouted, “No, no, no, no, no.” She glared at Stafford and screamed, “I knew bringing him here was a bad idea,” before she took off running.

Stafford hurried after her but couldn’t keep up and had to take several breaks on the way up. When he finally caught up with her inside what used to be her home, he was panting so hard that it took him a couple of minutes before he could ask, “What happened?”

“You!” Pythia shouted. “You brought that monster here, and look what he’s done. He’s destroyed everything, including all my magical armaments.”

“Is there nothing left?” Stafford asked.

“No. Nothing! You can see it’s all gone.” Pythia looked around her ruined home in a daze until her unseeing eyes fell on a spot on the far wall. She smacked her forehead and said, “I was so distraught that I didn’t check.” She hurried over to one wall, chanted an incantation, and sighed when a hidden panel slid open, revealing The Cup of Jamshid.

“This makes no sense. Why would he come all this way and not destroy one of the Maqlû? That cup is worth more than all the other magical objects you had put together,” Stafford said.

Pythia glared at the doorway and said, “I don’t know what his plan was, but this means war.”

CHAPTER 11

DO NOT PRAY FOR AN EASY LIFE

Alex scrambled down the mountainside and broke into a run as soon as he reached the trail behind the ruins. Seeing a familiar-looking woman with a glowering face running up the Sacred Way, he ducked behind a tree. He wasn't able to recognize her as the woman he'd seen in his grandmother's scrying dish years earlier, until Brother Stafford came huffing by.

He stayed hidden until both Atlantians were out of sight, then raced the rest of the way down the hillside. Alex didn't stop running until he got to the parking lot, where he slowed to a walk to catch his breath and figure out what to do next. Spotting a line of buses, he headed over and began asking the drivers if he could buy a ticket for Athens. It took him six attempts before he found someone who would take him. After paying his fare, he got on, found a seat, and anxiously waited until the other passengers returned and he could escape.

He was just starting to relax when he saw Stafford and Pythia appear and start searching the parking lot. His heart skipped a few beats when Stafford boarded the bus he was on and looked around. Luckily, the other passengers were getting back on board, forcing Stafford to get off. But Alex didn't feel safe until the bus finally pulled away and headed back to Athens.

As his worries about being caught gradually faded, guilt for his unwitting destruction of Pythia's home threatened to overwhelm him. He was almost at the point of confessing to the police what he'd done as soon as he got to Athens when Deborah apparated in the seat next to him.

"Good job, brother."

Alex reflexively looked around to see if anyone had noticed, then lowered his voice to a whisper. "How can you say that? Look at the mess I've caused. I destroyed someone's home and almost caused the mountain to crash down on a world-famous site. What do I do?"

"Do what you're doing – get as far away from here as possible. I followed Stafford and listened in on his conversation with Pythia, which was entirely about killing you. So, I wouldn't feel bad about destroying her home. She'd have done the same to you if she had the chance."

"You shouldn't have risked going near Pythia because she can see ghosts," Alex said.

Deborah shook her head and said, "Na, she can't. I learned that she can only see ghosts when she uses some magical object, which, regrettably, survived the explosion."

Alex stared out the window for a minute before turning back to his sister and whispering, "Did you find out what was that stuff I found in her home? It gave me the heebie-jeebies being around all of it."

"Yeah. You destroyed her arsenal of magical objects – things like that staff Stoughton tried to kill you with in Lamanai."

"How many magical objects were there?" Alex asked.

"I don't know, but it's more than I could have imagined," Deborah replied. "What I do know is that none of the Druids knew there were that many magical objects lying around, which leads to the questions of: how many more are there, who has them, and how much of a threat do they represent?"

Alex lifted the gnarled stick he'd picked up in the cave. "Do you know what this is? It's giving off some weird vibe and is what caused the explosion back there."

Deborah grabbed the staff and tried pulling it towards her – but it wouldn't budge. "What's wrong with this thing? It weighs a ton."

"I have no idea, as it just feels like a stick to me."

Deborah rolled her eyes at her brother's nonchalant attitude towards the strange object and scooted closer to him to examine it.

After several minutes of close scrutiny, Deborah gave up her study and said, "I have no idea what this is, but I think you need to treat it like the ankh and keep it safe at all times. Switching subjects, have you decided what you're going to do next?"

"Why would you ask that question? You know I don't have a plan. As usual, I'm making this stuff up as I go."

Their talk soon turned to lighter topics until they got to Athens. Alex had been so intent on escaping Delphi that he hadn't asked where the bus was headed. Instead of winding up at the city bus terminal, as he'd intended, he discovered he'd arrived at the ferry terminal and that the bus's passengers were heading back to their cruise ship. "This is great," Alex said, throwing his arms up in frustration. "Now, what do I do?"

"I heard your stomach gurgling on the bus," Deborah replied. "Why don't you get something to eat and take time to figure out your next steps?"

"Sounds good, but can you scout around and tell me where there's a nearby café?"

Without replying, Deborah disappeared but was back in less than a minute. "Come on. There's one that looks good a little ways from here."

He followed her to a waterside café, ordered a gyro, and was about to sit down when he heard a familiar Haitian accent say, "Alex? Is that you?"

Turning around, he saw Jean Paul standing over him. Alex jumped up and hugged him. "I'm glad to see you. You're my favorite person to bump into. Where's Francis?"

Jean Paul flashed his toothy smile and said, "He's on *La Amistad*, getting everything ready so we can go out with the tide. I was about to order dinner. What are you doing here?" He didn't wait for Alex to reply before he said, "Wait a minute. Don't tell me. You've gotten separated from your party again?"

Alex smiled wanly and replied, "Not exactly. I was heading home but accidentally wound up here."

"Uh, huh. What trouble have you gotten into this time?" Jean Paul asked.

Alex kept his eyes fixed firmly on his feet. "What makes you say that?"

"The first time we encountered you was on a deserted island, where we found you practically dead. The next time was just after you'd come ashore in the middle of no-place England. And now, here."

"Hey, at least this time, I'm in a city where I can easily get food, lodging, and transportation."

"That's true," Jean Paul said, looking skeptically at Alex. "Does anybody know you're here?"

"Pretty much everybody by now. I met with Lady Yvaine yesterday and Brother Stafford today. But you should be aware that just about everybody wants my blood because I've happened to break a few things."

Jean Paul gasped and closed his eyes as if in pain. "You didn't. Which one?"

"Which one what?" Alex asked.

"Let's stop pretending we don't know what's going on," Jean Paul replied. "Francis and I grew up with the Maqlû. In fact, a long time ago, our job was to guard them. But when a group of witches and warlocks stole them, we shifted our focus to helping people as best we could."

"So, it wasn't chance that I ran into you?"

Jean Paul shook his head. "Not entirely. Do you remember the object Francis wears?"

"Yeah, but I can't remember its name."

"It's called Sharur. It's not one of the Maqlû, but it's a magical object that, among other things, helps Francis find certain things – like you. One other trait of the object is that it's invisible to all but the wearer, myself, and now you. And the reason Francis and I can see it is because we made it. As for how you can, well…."

"What do you want from me?" Alex asked.

"Nothing. But Francis believes we should help you when we can."

Alex's eyes narrowed as he looked at Jean Paul skeptically. "How do I know you're not lying or trying to get me, like everybody else?"

"Have we ever given you any reason not to trust us?"

"No, but that hasn't stopped others from turning on me." He pointed at Jean Paul's head and asked, "What's with the sudden silver streaks in your hair? Did you stop dying it or something?"

"That's an odd question. I've been wondering about it myself because both Francis and I are suddenly turning grey. Why do you ask?"

Alex hemmed and hawed for a few seconds until he finally said, "Well, I recently learned that my destroying the Maqlû has affected those who've lived around them for a long time. The same thing is happening to Lady Yvaine."

"Interesting." Waving a hand across his face, he said, "Well, that's not important right now. Have you talked to your grandfather recently?"

"As you know, I don't carry a phone, and I haven't been to any place where I could call."

Jean Paul pulled out his cell phone, dialed the prefix to the U.S., and handed it to Alex. "Call home. I'll get Francis and bring him back here. He'll want to see you." With a wave of his hand, he left.

Alex had just finished updating his grandfather and cousin on his recent actions when Francis came up from behind, lifted him from his chair, and engulfed him in a bear hug.

When Francis finally set Alex down, the three sat down, ordered food and drinks, and spent the next hour catching up on events over the last year, with Alex being very selective about what he shared. Jean Paul remained unusually silent throughout, not prying into the gaps in his story until Alex mentioned he'd seen Pythia and Stafford earlier that day. Jean Paul looked knowingly at Francis and asked, "And how were they when you left them?"

"Do you work for either one?" Alex asked warily.

Jean Paul shook his head. "Not anymore. We've never worked for Pythia and only sporadically with Brother Stafford, but lately, we've chosen to go our separate ways. But you still haven't answered my question."

Alex couldn't look either of his Haitian friends in the face as he quietly said, "They seemed a little upset."

"Damn!" Jean Paul reached into his pocket, pulled out a wad of Euros, counted out a handful of bills, and handed them to Francis.

"What's wrong?" Alex asked.

"Nothing. It's that Francis and I had a bet on when we'd see you next and what type of trouble you'd be in. My friend here seems to see the bigger picture better than I do."

"What does that mean?"

"Nothing, except that we should leave before either of those two finds you here," Jean Paul replied. He paused and said, "We're on our way to Crete. Would you like to come and help us?"

"What are you working on?" Alex asked.

"Most of our work is helping educate women and girls in Third World countries. We believe women's education is one of the best ways to help a nation rise from poverty. It's also very personal for us since Francis and I both grew up in single-parent households with illiterate mothers. If it weren't for Brother Stafford coming to our village and taking us and our mothers to where we could get a good education, we would have died a long time ago. It made such a difference in our lives that we've dedicated most of our time and resources to the cause. In fact, besides buying a better ship to get us around faster, we've used most of the proceeds from selling that gold bar you gave us on our mission. Would you like to come with us? It would help you become scarce, and we could take you to some interesting sights."

Alex's eyes lit up. "That would be fabulous, but are you really okay with me tagging along? This would solve a dilemma for me since I wasn't sure what I was going to do next."

"We're sure. So, let's get going," Jean Paul said. "The sea won't wait for us."

A couple of hours later, they were heading into the Aegean Sea on their way to Crete.

CHAPTER 12

ERRA

Pythia finally gave up searching for Alex and climbed to the cliffs above Delphi to look out over the Gulf of Itea and try to calm her nerves. It was several hours before she got over the shock of losing almost every magical object she'd collected over the centuries and realize she had more immediate concerns – like where to stay for the night.

As she lay in her bed that night, she found she couldn't sleep, as she kept second-guessing her actions towards Alex. So, it was long past midnight before she finally gave up trying to sleep and started pacing the small hotel room, wracking her brain for new ideas on dealing with him since all her previous efforts to kill him using ghosts and magical objects had failed.

The sun was just starting to kiss the eastern horizon when her thoughts drifted to her early days on Earth – working with people like Ishtar and Enkidu, now known under the pseudonyms Yvaine and Stafford, developing the Cradle of Civilization. Pythia began mentally reviewing the men and women she'd known back then and paused when her thoughts turned to a man renowned for his short-fused temper and propensity for violence – the being the ancient Mesopotamians believed was the God of Mayhem.

Of all her former compatriots, the half-demon Erra was by far the largest, standing a head taller than the next tallest person. Behind his thick, bushy beard and long dark hair, all a person could see of his face was a thin slice of forehead and a pair of coal-black eyes – making him appear as if he were the devil himself. And everywhere he went, death followed. Surely, she thought, Erra would be able to eliminate the boy.

But just as quickly as hope had risen in her breast, doubts arose, as she hadn't seen him since the great schism and didn't know if he was still alive. She hurried back to her ruined home, set up her table and stool, then pulled the Cup of Jamshid from its hiding place. Stirring the silvery liquid in the cup, she chanted,

> *"By the powers of Water, Earth, Fire, and Air*
> *I ask of thee to help me now*
> *Send my voice across the sky*
> *So Erra can hear my words.*
> *Oh, brother mine, I need thee now*
> *So come with haste to me."*

Having done what she could, Pythia ran her hand over the cup, stilling the waters inside, then secured it in her safe and headed down to the nearby town of Delphi.

She spent the next two days cleaning up her home and sorting through the debris in her magical objects' room, seeing if she could salvage anything. The sun was starting to dip below the mountains when Erra magically appeared.

If it weren't for his size, she wouldn't have known who he was as he'd cut his hair and trimmed his beard, making him appear much more approachable than he'd ever looked before. His clothing, unlike hers, reflected modern casual styles – a t-shirt, jeans, and cowboy boots. Goosebumps popped up all over her arms when she heard him say, in a low and soft voice, "You called?"

It took her a minute to recover from the shock of his sudden appearance and changed looks. Her first instinct was to run over and hug him, but she remembered he'd never been a touchy-feely type of person. "Thank you for coming," she said at last. "I wasn't sure if you would or not. How has life been treating you?"

"Cut the chit-chat," Erra replied curtly. "You didn't ask me to come here to talk. You could have done that any time in the last few millennia, yet you stayed away from me as everyone else did."

"Can you blame us?" Pythia asked. "You were always so angry that it was dangerous to get close to you. Plus, you seemed to want to be by yourself."

"Maybe. But I've changed. I like my life now – it's peaceful. And I can't help but wonder why, after all this time, did you call for me?" Erra looked around the destroyed home and asked, "What happened?"

Pythia studied the new, calmer Erra, trying to figure out what button to push to get him to do what she wanted. After a long pause, she said, "A boy is destroying everything we worked for all those years ago."

"Why should I care? You, Gilgamesh, and Enkidu were always the ones with the grandiose plans, expecting the rest of us to do your bidding as if we were lackeys. I don't care if your plans fail. I told you; I like my life now."

At one time, long ago before they'd gone their separate ways, Pythia had thought Erra had a crush on her. Figuring her only remaining option was to play the knight-rescuer card, she said, "The other day, this boy I'm concerned about broke into my house and destroyed almost everything. I can only imagine what he would have done to me if I had been home at the time. I'm scared of him."

Erra set aside his lion-headed mace and stepped forward, his fists balled. "Has he hurt you?"

"Not this time, but I was lucky, as I'd gone for a walk when he came. The thing is, I fear he's going to keep coming after me if someone doesn't stop him. He's threatened Enkidu, too. We've both sent men to kill him, but none have returned. I don't know where he is, but I'm sure he'll keep coming after me until I'm dead. Which is why I can't sleep easy until he's gone - for good."

"If you don't know where he is, how will I find him?"

"I don't think it'll be as hard as you think, as he's trying to find and destroy the Maqlû. He's a dark-skinned teenage boy who always has his hair in two long braids. You should know that he's also terrorized the witches, including destroying one of their hideouts in Scotland. I don't think it's a coincidence that he's here in Greece, since I live here, and the witches have strongholds in Meteora and Crete. All you have to do is follow his trail of mayhem. He'll be at the end of it."

Erra took Pythia's hand and gently kissed it. "Have faith, my lady. I'll protect you."

She watched him fade into the quickly darkening night and thought, "I pray to Apollo you will."

CHAPTER 13

FEAR DOES NOT PREVENT DEATH

"How could you? Have you lost all sense of morality?" Sidney Carton yelled. His older brother, Robert Stafford, had returned to their order's villa overlooking Assisi less than an hour earlier. "I thought you weren't going to have anything more to do with her. What would possess you to keep asking that woman for help? You can't trust her – ever!"

Like a little boy in trouble, Stafford looked up at his taller, trimmer, more elegantly garbed brother and glared back defiantly. "You weren't there. You don't understand how upsetting and shocking it was when I turned around and discovered that kid had found me again – in Athens, of all places. Our meeting was secret. Nobody should have known we were there. We stayed hidden our entire time there except for our excursion to the Parthenon." He paused, then looked sharply at his brother. "You didn't tell him we were there, did you?"

"Do you hear yourself?" Carton asked. "You're making it sound like there's some conspiracy, and everybody, especially the boy, is against you. Of course, I didn't help him."

"I can't help myself. The boy has rattled me. I'm telling you, he scares me far more than Pythia does."

"Why did you go to Delphi in the first place? You said you were going to come straight back after your meetings."

Stafford didn't immediately reply. Instead, he poured a glass of wine and took it to the balcony. When Carton had joined him outside, Stafford said, "I was hoping if she met him, she'd figure out how to defeat him. But it was a colossal mistake."

"Why would you think she'd be successful? She's already tried killing the boy countless times, only to fail every time – just like you. Besides, if you're so intent on getting rid of him, why didn't you get rid of the boy when he was with you? It would've been the simplest way."

"First of all, I don't want to be implicated in his murder," Stafford replied. "And secondly, we don't know what he's capable of. If we attacked him directly, he could use his powers on us. Then everything we've worked for all these years would be for naught."

Carton stared at the lights of Assisi far below and said, "I still say you should let him be. Don't worry about what he's doing. It's time you give up on our original dream of reshaping humanity using the Maqlû. I know I have no interest in it anymore. Besides, given human nature, I'm not sure if it was ever a feasible idea in the first place. Instead, let's focus on our goal of educating women. It's a good project. We've only been at it for 150 years, and look at our progress, especially in the Western World." He leaned forward and said, "Plus, our former comrades Utnapishtim and Urshanabi would support us, and we'd eliminate two threats to us."

Stafford shook his head. "I'm not giving up on our original goals. World peace, elimination of poverty, and better living conditions are too important."

"Those are all great, but I've come to believe that the goals are too big. They're not actionable, as human nature will prevent us from ever getting there. As a species, they're too greedy, narrow-minded, and short-sighted. Too…human."

"I can't accept that. While the rest of the Maqlû are out there, waiting for us to find and use them, there is hope,"

Stafford said, more to himself than his brother. Speaking in a louder voice, he added, "Which is why we must redouble our efforts to find them, even if it means working with the witches. If we don't, that boy will destroy all of them."

"You shouldn't get worked up over things you don't have control over. And besides, no one has ever gotten them to operate to their full potential."

"I'm sure we'll figure it out when we have them," Stafford replied. There was a long pause before he added, "I haven't told you the worst of it." Seeing the questioning look in his brother's eyes, he said, "I thought I was bringing him up to Delphi to bring about his downfall. But the boy used me. I left him alone for a few minutes to find Pythia. But while I was talking to her, he found her lair, broke in, and destroyed everything, including her entire chamber of magical artifacts."

"How could he find her home?" Carton asked. "We've searched the entire Delphi area countless times and never found it."

"I have no idea, which is what scares me. As Pythia and I were talking, there was an explosion up on the mountain. She instantly knew what had happened because she ran straight for her place and I followed. I'm sure her enchantments were as strong as mine, if not stronger, yet all that remained of her entrance was a pile of rubble, which took us a while to clear, even with our magic. She was so upset that she ran in and didn't bother trying to hide anything from me."

"Does she at least still have the Cup of Jamshid?"

"Yes, it's safe. But everything else in her house was destroyed – except for maybe one item, which she couldn't find any traces of in all the debris."

"Which one?" Carton asked with a sense of foreboding.

Stafford grimaced as he said, "The object Donar made. The object Pythia coveted so much that she killed him to get it. Of course, it was a wasted effort because she could never lift it from the spot where Donar died."

"Mjölnir?" Carton asked in an awed voice.

Stafford nodded. "It was gone. She was able to identify the remnants of all the other magical objects – except for that one. Pythia believes the boy stole it." Stafford slammed his fist on the table hard enough that it rattled the wine glasses. "I'm telling you, we've got to stop the boy, for he's destroying all hope for ever achieving our goals."

Carton began pacing the deck, trying to internalize everything his brother had told him. At last, he said, "Go back to the beginning. How exactly did he find you?"

Stafford threw his hands into the air. "How does he ever find me? This time, his excuse was that he'd been talking with Lady Yvaine in Meteora and had come to Athens to catch a plane home. He said he was wandering around the Agora when he spotted Brother Phillips and mistook him for me. As you know, I've told our members about him but haven't told them to fear him. Brother Phillips thought he was doing me a favor by bringing him to me."

"Do you believe the boy's story?" Carton asked. "It sounds improbable."

Stafford's eyes got a faraway look in them. "Surprisingly, I do. I wouldn't have believed him if it wasn't for the Lady Yvaine part. I mean, what is she doing seeing him when the rest of the Druids are out for his blood? Is she the one who's guiding his actions? It scares me to think so. As for his saying he was heading home and was just happening to visit the Agora when our group was there – no. He had to be lying."

"But that would mean you think he was using you to find Pythia. If so, then where is he headed now?" Both remained silent until Carton abruptly sat down and said, "You don't think he's going to Crete, do you?"

Stafford's eyes grew wide in horror. He slammed his fist on the side table, this time knocking his wine glass over. "Of course. That's got to be where he's headed. I need to warn the witches."

"How are you going to do that? They don't know that we know what they have there."

"I won't have to mention Crete at all. I'll call his grandmother and tell her he made a surprise visit here, then disappeared. She'll put two and two together and alert the right people."

"I'm surprised Lady Yvaine is helping him," Carton said. "But it would explain how he's avoided your and the witches' attacks all this time."

"It doesn't matter," Stafford said grimly. "Once the rest of the Druid order learns he's coming, they're bound to react violently. Since they know the boy better than Pythia and I, they should be able to take care of the problem once and for all."

CHAPTER 14

SAMARIA GORGE

"They were well out to sea before Alex confessed he had no idea where Crete was, much less anything else about the island they were going to.

Jean Paul pulled out a map, laid it on a table, and pointed to a large island south of Greece in the eastern portion of the Mediterranean Sea. "The bigger cities generally have more educational resources, so we focus on the rural areas on the southern coast and northern Africa where we can make a bigger difference, as they tend to be a little lower on Maslow's Hierarchy of Needs."

"Huh? What's this Maslow stuff?" Alex asked.

"It's a psychology theory that suggests people will focus on meeting their basic needs first – things like food, water, and shelter, before trying to meet 'higher' needs like relationships, education, and fulfillment. Since money tends to follow opportunities, most rural areas are poorer and don't have as many opportunities to advance."

"But I thought European countries have pretty good education systems."

"In general, they do," Jean Paul replied. "But not where we're going. We'll head along the south coast and drop off school supplies to some associates we've been working with. They use what we give them to help educate girls in their areas and take the rest to remote villages of North Africa."

"Why don't you work directly with people in Africa?" Alex asked.

"We found it too difficult to sustain an operational base in North Africa because it's pretty unstable there, with the constant fighting and climate extremes causing food shortages, and general lack of opportunities. So, we decided to work with some of the locals on Crete who can more easily get to North Africa. Besides, we live too far away and work in other areas – like the Caribbean. It might not seem like we're doing much, but it's only the two of us. We plant the seeds of better education in places we can get to relatively easily, then come back every year and nurture them. It takes time, but we've had some success, encouraging others to get involved and help."

"I think it's a great idea," Alex said. "What can I do to help?"

"You can help carry the supplies ashore and distribute them. But I'd suggest you spend most of your time talking with the people to learn about their experiences. Maybe it'll encourage you to get involved in similar efforts one day."

***

The next few days flew by. Every night, they arrived at their next destination then unloaded their supplies the next morning. They bypassed the densely crowded shoreline areas except when they needed to restock their ship stores or properly dispose of their waste. Sometimes, their destination was a small village; sometimes, it was an isolated hotel on the beach where only one child was living. Seeing how excited and grateful the kids and parents were, Alex felt guilty about the relative abundance of his life growing up.

Near the end of the week, they arrived at an area where the mountains that dominated the island's interior reached all the way to the coast. At their base was a small town with a handful of multi-story white buildings clustered along the beachfront. As there wasn't much there, Alex didn't give the town another thought and continued getting everything ready to go ashore. But he felt a tremor just after he'd finished loading the last of the book boxes in their skiff. He looked up to see what could have caused the shaking but didn't see anything out of place. Not even the waves gently lapping on the shore seemed disturbed. Hoping it was his imagination, he asked Francis, "Did you feel that?"

The stocky Haitian shook his head and continued with his work.

Uncomfortable that his friend hadn't felt the tremors, Alex looked around again and noticed a narrow gap in the mountains behind the town that he hadn't seen before. It wasn't the area's natural features that arrested his attention, though. Instead, it was the ghost of his childhood yellow lab sitting at the entrance to the opening. Alex turned to Jean Paul, who had come up from below and, with more than a little trepidation, asked, "Where are we?"

"Agia Roumeli, the endpoint of the Samaria Gorge."

Feeling like his dog was inviting him in, and curious about the tremors he'd felt he pointed to the gorge opening and asked, "What is that?"

"It's a spectacular national park that climbs about ten miles into the mountains. But it's rugged and steep and almost everyone who hikes through it starts at the top and comes down. Then, they take a ferry from here and return to the other side of the island. Why?"

"Is it safe to go for a walk in there?" Alex asked.

"Yes, but hikers have to be careful. It's very rocky and easy to trip and fall. It can also get scorching hot, so hikers need to carry lots of water and take it easy, ensuring they get in the shade and cool off if they get too hot. But it's hard to get lost as there's only one way in or out. But again, why do you ask?" Seeing Alex hesitate, Jean Paul added, "Why do I get the feeling I won't like your answer?"

Instead of answering the question, Alex smiled and asked, "Would you mind if I do a little exploring today instead of helping?"

Jean Paul eyed Alex, for what seemed like eternity, before replying in a cautious tone, "We're not planning to leave until tonight, so you have plenty of time to go a couple of miles in and return before dark. And since it's the height of the tourist season, there'll be plenty of people inside the park to help you, if you have any problems." He sighed, as if he wouldn't see him again, and said, "Now, go below and have Francis pack you some water and food for your hike."

Half an hour later, Alex waved goodbye to his friends and headed up the beach towards the dry river bed. As he neared his ghost dog, Sport got up and trotted inland, with Alex following him past a collection of houses to the mouth of the gorge.

The first part of the hike was relatively easy, as there was a well-groomed trail that gently rose in elevation. Less than a half-mile in, the mountain slopes started closing in until he reached the famous Iron Gates, where the gorge's walls were barely ten feet apart and soared almost a thousand feet up. After that, the trail became much rockier and crisscrossed the stream that had carved the gorge for millennia.

Even though Jean Paul had told him most people started at the top of the gorge and hiked down, Alex began growing uncomfortable an hour in when he still hadn't met anyone. As the path became ever more challenging, Alex began thinking of turning around and heading back, but every time he turned, Sport would stop and wait for Alex to resume his climb.

When the sun's rays finally broke the crest of the ravine's steep walls, it turned the gorge into a natural oven, causing Alex to take frequent breaks and be grateful Francis had packed so much water for him. Not having a watch, he kept wondering if he'd gone too far and was relieved when he heard Deborah's voice echoing through the narrow canyon, saying, "Alex, up here."

Seeing her high above him, his first instinct was to ignore his sister and save himself the trouble of climbing up the steep path. But the tremors he'd felt on board his friends' ship had gotten steadily stronger as he'd made his way up the gorge, and he knew it wasn't chance that Deborah had taken that moment to appear. Hoping he wouldn't regret his choice, he looked around and found a narrow path cutting up the left wall, then heaved a sigh and started climbing.

It was such a difficult climb that when he finally reached her, all he could think about was sitting on the narrow ledge she was hovering over to rest. When he'd finally caught his breath, he asked, "Can you feel it too, Sis?"

"Feel what?" Deborah replied.

"The tremors. I've been feeling them all morning."

"I have no clue what you're talking about. Ever since you fled Delphi, all I've been doing is keeping an eye out for any pursuit of you."

"And?"

"Luckily, I've seen nothing. Although, that doesn't mean much, as I've focused my energies on ensuring you're safe rather than finding out what Pythia plans to do now that you've wrecked her place. But I have to ask, what the heck are you doing here?"

After taking another swig of water, Alex said, "I'm not sure. I felt those tremors I was telling you about, then saw my ghost dog at the mouth of this canyon and followed him in. Whatever is going on, it's up here."

He looked around for Sport and, noticing he was gone, asked, "Have you seen my dog?" When she shook her head, he groaned and said, "Once again, he got me to follow him and then disappears after having led me straight into, what I'm sure will be, trouble. You'd think I'd know better by now. Maybe I should give up and head back."

"Why ask me where your dog is?" Deborah retorted. "You know you're the only person who can see him. Besides, I think his appearance is a good sign since he keeps helping you find your way towards the next object. And you shouldn't be blaming him for you always getting embroiled in trouble. Last time I checked, you chose to follow him each time. He's never forced you to go on. But none of that matters right now. You're the one who needs to decide to keep going, or turn back."

Alex pulled his ankh out for the first time that day and studied it, hoping it would give him some indication of what was going on. But when he felt it tugging him further up the canyon wall, he wasn't sure whether he should be relieved he hadn't been imagining things or worried. Alex pointed above them and said, "It wants me to keep going up that way."

Deborah waved her arm in the direction he'd pointed and said, "Since you have the ankh, lead on. I'll be right behind you."

Alex slipped his arms through the straps on his pack and shrugged into it. Then he slapped his Tilley back on his head and used his new-found staff to push himself to a standing position.

Alex had only gone a short ways up a winding beaten track when he heard voices echoing from the trail below.

After hours of seeing no one but ghosts, the sound of living people's voices had a therapeutic effect on him, making him feel that he wasn't far from help if he needed any. With a little more vigor in his step, he continued his ascent.

But he quickly forgot about the tourists when he came upon a slit in the mountain. Alex looked from the black hole to his sister and said, "Remember those tremors I told you I'd felt? They're even stronger here, which tells me we're close. But I'm worried about going in."

"Then don't," Deborah replied. "No one is forcing you. These adventures of yours have long since ceased to be about helping me. They're all about whatever your destiny is." Her eyes and tone grew softer as she said, "Only you can decide whether you want to continue, but I've seen some of the good you've done when you've followed your instincts."

Placing his hand over his chest, Alex said, "The ankh is going crazy on me, which means there's something important, and undoubtedly dangerous, in there." He shook his head in disbelief. "Which means I'm going to regret it if I go in, but I'll kick myself even more for chickening out." Before he could talk himself out of it, Alex took a deep breath and entered.

CHAPTER 15

THE LABYRINTH

After his eyes had adjusted to the gloom in the cave opening, Alex spotted a shimmering force field a few feet away, similar to the afterlife entrances he'd seen in Lamanai. He sidled over to it, hesitating for an instant before shoving his hand in. Little blue sparks jumped all over his skin, causing him to reflexively yank his hand out. When he realized he was unharmed, he stepped through then waited for his sister to go through. But when she started pounding on the force field, he stepped back through and asked, "Can't you enter?"

"Does it look like I can pass through," Deborah replied in a frustrated tone. "This is just like Lamanai and Romania. You can get through, but I can't. The ankh must be doing something that allows you in."

"Hold my hand, and we'll go in together," Alex said.

"Are you sure? You always say you freeze when you touch a spirit."

"I can stand holding your hand for a few seconds," Alex replied. Ensuring he had a firm grip on her, he stepped through the force field again. It was like the first time, with the same blue sparks jumping all over his skin as he passed through. But no sooner had he taken a step away from the entrance than he lost his grip on his sister. When he looked back, she was still on the outside, with a pained look on her face.

He quickly stepped back out and asked, "Are you okay?"

Deborah shook her hand and said, "I'll be all right in a minute. But, you'll have to go on without me because whatever that is, it won't let me through. And since you'll be on your own, please be careful."

Alex didn't reply. Instead, he stared at the force field, looking as if it would provide a solution. After what seemed like an eternity to Deborah, he looked up and said, "I'm tired of always charging into the unknown on my own, and I'd appreciate it if you'd stick with me a while longer."

"I'll help any way I can, but I can't get through that blasted barrier," Deborah said.

Alex jumped back through. "I have an idea, but I'm hesitant to mention it because you'll think it's crazy."

"It can't be worse than other things you've done," Deborah replied.

"Oh, you'd be wrong about that."

"Okay, now you're starting to scare me. How do you propose getting me through that thing?"

"I told you; I want you to come with me as I have no desire to face what's inside alone. So please don't freak out when you hear what I have to say." Alex paused, then blurted out, "You could possess me. You know, just long enough to get through."

Deborah's jaw dropped, and it was some time before she could reply. "That is so creepy, on so many levels."

"I know it's weird, but do you have a better idea? All you have to do is squeeze into my body. I'm sure you can do that. Besides, it'll only be for a couple of seconds."

Grimacing, she floated to the entrance and said, "I don't know." Deborah continued staring at the force field, which was invisible to her. At last, she sighed deeply and blurted out, "Fine. Let's get this over with so I don't have to think any more about it."

"I'm not looking forward to it either," Alex retorted as he stood up and walked to the force field. "So, let's do it."

Deborah nodded then passed into her brother's body.

The cold was so intense that Alex started violently shaking as soon as she'd possessed his body. He was about to pass out when he dimly heard her voice in his head telling him, "Go." In a dreamlike state, he stepped through. He immediately knew it didn't work as he felt an excruciating pain as his sister was ripped from inside him. After recovering from the shock, he stepped back outside and asked, "Now what?"

"This isn't going to work," Deborah replied. "I'm afraid you'll have to go on by yourself."

"You should know me better by now," Alex replied. "I can be very stubborn." He took off his Tilley, slipped the ankh over his head, and held it out to her, saying, "Take this and see if you can get through on your own."

"Didn't you say that Dad was afraid of it?"

"No. Grandpa said that the wearers have been uncomfortable with it. He never said it hurt anybody. Drove 'em a little crazy, maybe, but don't worry. You'll only have it on for a few seconds. When you get through, toss it out to me."

Shaking her head in disbelief that she was following one of her brother's crazy ideas, she grabbed the ankh necklace from his hands and slipped it over her head. Then, holding on to it with one hand, she tried going through again.

It went so smoothly that it took her a moment to realize she was through, whereupon she let out a shriek and tossed the ankh back through the force field. After he passed through the barrier, she exclaimed, "Bloody hell. That was weird. How can you stand wearing that thing?"

Alex shrugged. "It took a while to get used to all the strange things that happen, but it's saved my life multiple times."

"Yeah, but it's also nearly gotten you killed twice as much."

"Well, let's not argue about it now. Come on. I need to figure out what's going on in here fast because I need to return to the ship in a couple of hours."

Alex led the way through the outer chamber and into a tunnel where the outside light soon faded. He briefly thought about using Deborah's greyish-green glow to light his way but discarded the idea as he knew he had to lead. He then pulled out his flashlight and started down the twisting passageway.

Small openings off to the sides of the tunnel began appearing, but Alex ignored them as he pressed on until he came into another chamber, big enough that he couldn't see the far side. Keeping his left hand on the wall, he circled the chamber counter-clockwise but didn't find any more openings. Thinking he'd hit a dead end in the cavern, he turned and headed back the way he'd come. After what seemed like an interminable time, panic set in when he didn't find the opening where he'd entered.

He started jogging, running his hand along the wall, looking for any opening – but found nothing. A few minutes later, he tripped on an unseen rock and crashed onto the rocky floor.

"Are you okay?" Deborah asked.

Alex pulled himself to a sitting position and leaned against the wall. "I will be in a moment. I need to let the pain subside and figure out what's going on." He turned off his flashlight to conserve power and asked, "Am I imagining it, or did the opening we came through disappear?"

"I don't think you are," his sister replied. "I might have miscalculated the size of the room, but that rock you stubbed your toes on wasn't there when we entered. It's too big to have missed the first time around, which means this place must be enchanted and has changed."

"That's just great. But how are we going to get out of here?" Alex wailed.

"I don't know. Maybe…."

Alex shushed Deborah and whispered, "Did you hear that?"

"What?" his sister whispered back.

Alex reflexively held up a finger to stop her without thinking about how dark it was and said, "I thought I heard some faint whisperings from across the chamber." Hoping to pinpoint where the sounds were coming from, he cupped his hands behind his ears and listened. When he thought he had a fix, he got up and, using his staff for a crutch, limped in the direction he thought they were coming from, stopping every few steps to listen and ensure he stayed on course.

He'd only gone a little ways when Deborah whispered, "I don't hear anything. Are you sure you heard something?"

"I don't hear anything now, so maybe I was imagining them. But, since I have no idea how to get out of here, I thought I'd follow the voices – unless you have a better idea." Without waiting for his sister's response, he continued his slow trek across the pitch-black chamber.

He wasn't sure how far he'd gone when he felt a breeze blowing across him. He flipped on his flashlight and saw that he'd somehow left the chamber and entered a large passageway that split a few feet in front of him.

The whisperings seemed louder in the left opening, but thoughts about the Greek story of Theseus and the Labyrinth flitted into his head, making him wish he had a ball of string. Since he didn't, he decided to mark the wall. He searched around for a sharp rock, and when he found one, carved a deep X near the opening, then scratched an arrow to mark the way he was heading.

He was about to enter the left opening when Deborah blurted out, "Maybe we should split up here. I'm not as worried about getting stuck in here as you are, as I can pass through the mountain if need be. And I can move much faster without you. I think me looking around for an exit is our best chance at getting out of here."

"But, how will we hook back up?" Alex asked.

"Don't worry. Remember, I've tracked you down from thousands of miles away, so I doubt if I'll have any problem finding you in here. Trust me. It'll be all right. I'll take the other way and return as soon as possible."

He reluctantly parted from his sister and headed down the left tunnel while Deborah took the right one. Once again, he put a hand on the wall to ensure he didn't miss an opening and started walking. Every few minutes, he would stop, listen for the whispering, then scratch more marks into the wall and move on.

Alex was about to turn back when he came upon a side passageway where he heard the voices more clearly. He marked both sides of the opening, then turned in. A short time later, he came upon a pile of bones at the end of the passage. He picked one up, shuddering when he saw large teeth marks on it. Not wanting to see what had caused the carnage, he turned and hurried back the way he'd come from. But he couldn't find any of the marks he'd made. Thinking he'd missed the turn, he returned to the dead-end and found the skeletons exactly where he'd remembered them. Slowly retracing his steps, he ran his hands on both sides of the narrow path to see if he'd missed the turn. But as before, there were no markings in the tunnel.

Frustrated by what he thought were games from some unknown tormenter, he screamed in frustration. He instantly regretted the action as his voice echoed so loudly in the enclosed chamber that goosebumps popped up all over his arms. As the echoes faded, Alex pulled the ankh from under his shirt to seek its guidance and groaned when he felt it pulling him ever deeper into the labyrinth. Reluctantly, he stuffed it back under his shirt and followed the whispering further into the cave complex.

He'd taken only a few steps when he found a complete skeleton of some animal he couldn't identify – and then another, both having the same giant teeth marks he'd seen on the bones in the earlier pile. Despite his growing uneasiness, Alex pressed on until the passage took a sharp turn, and he discovered another large chamber with an overpowering smell emanating from it.

Fearing he was about to enter a veritable lion's den, he rechecked his ankh. Instead of warning him off, though, it continued tugging him forward. Hoping he wasn't making a fatal mistake, he stepped into the chamber.

His foot hit something slick, and before he could react, his legs slipped out from under him, and he found himself sliding down a chute. Seconds later he crashed onto a stone floor and lost hold of his staff. He watched helplessly as his flashlight skidded across the floor, then went out – leaving him in total darkness.

It took him several minutes before he'd recovered from the fall and was able to get on his hands and knees and start searching for his lost items. He found his staff rather quickly, but after several ominutes of frantic but fruitless searching for his flashlight, he sat back and tried picturing where he'd last seen his Maglite. When he thought he had an idea of where it was, he crawled forward and began feeling around. But after several more minutes of futile searching, all he'd found were bones.

With panic starting to set in, Alex expanded his search and was just about to give up any hope of finding his flashlight when he felt the familiar cool metal under his fingers. With a sigh of relief, he turned it on and flashed it around to see where he was. His spirits sank when he saw he was trapped in a small chamber, with the only way in or out being the chute he'd unceremoniously slid down a short time before.

Desperate to escape, he tried climbing but found it too steep and slippery. After a dozen tries, he gave up and slumped against the end of the chute, thinking his situation was hopeless.

Alex had no idea how long he sat in the dark, staring into nothingness, but he didn't stir until he heard faint murmurings above him. Unsure if they were friend or foe, he didn't make a sound until he heard a familiar voice call out, "Alex, are you there?"

Relieved at hearing his sister's voice, he shouted, "I'm down here. But I'm stuck. Can you help me out?"

He heard an unknown voice ask his sister, "He can hear you? How is that possible?"

An instant later, Deborah and a young girl dressed in a plain brown smock appeared a few feet away. The faint green-gray glow of the two spirits enabled Alex to see that the newcomer had jet-black hair and dark brown skin color.

"Who are you?" Alex asked the girl.

"My name is Ariadne, but why are you here? You two are the only people who have been foolish enough to enter this labyrinth for almost three thousand years."

"It's a long story," Alex replied. "But the short version is that I was out hiking this morning and felt compelled to explore this place. I wasn't sure what I was getting into when I entered, but it wasn't this."

"You made the worst mistake of your life coming here," Ariadne said. "You're stuck here with no way out."

"There's got to be a way," Alex replied.

Ariadne shook her head. "You'd think so. But no one's ever found one."

"But you're a ghost. You can pass through anything."

"I wish," Ariadne replied. She paused, then said, "Hold on a minute. I'll be right back."

She apparated a short time later, along with dozens of other ghosts. They crowded around and began clamoring so loud for Alex's attention that he had to clap his hands over his ears in a vain attempt to keep the noise out.

A distinguished-looking elderly man dressed in a chiton apparated and called out for silence. When everyone had quieted down, he said, "You've gotten to see him; now leave us. I need to speak with him in private." All the ghosts, except Ariadne and Deborah, immediately disappeared.

"Please forgive them," the man said. "They're excited by your arrival. By the way, I'm Ariadne's father, Minos, King of Crete. She told me you came into this cursed place of your own volition. Is that true? Are you here to rescue us?"

Alex shook his head. "I'd help you if I could, but I don't even know how to rescue myself. Besides, I didn't know you existed until a minute ago. As I told your daughter, I was walking through the gorge and got curious. And you know what they say about curiosity."

The king shook his head. "No. What?"

"It doesn't matter. It's just a saying we use nowadays." Alex pointed his flashlight to some bones on the floor and said, "Please tell me that these aren't human remains."

Minos looked away, leaving his daughter to answer. "Have you heard the story of the Minotaur?" Ariadne didn't wait for Alex to respond before she said, "In response to the Athenians killing my brother, my father waged war against them, won, and exacted a tribute of young boys and girls to be sent here every year to feed the Minotaur."

Horrified, Alex exclaimed, "You mean all the people down here died because of your dad's desire for revenge? That's sick."

Ariadne winced. "Be that as it may, the gods have a way of making people pay for their arrogance. After many years of this practice, a group of witches attacked and threw us into this place as punishment for what my father did."

"I thought some dude named Theseus slew the Minotaur."

"I don't know who that is," Ariadne replied. "All I know is that my father and I died, just as all those innocent victims did. Since then, the witches have stopped the human sacrifices, but they've kept the beast alive by feeding him cattle, sheep, and pigs."

"You mean it's still alive? How can something live that long?" Alex asked.

"I don't know," Ariadne replied.

"But why are you still down here? Except for your dad, it sounds like everyone else is innocent." You should have moved on by now," Alex said.

"I don't know why we can't move on. It's as if some magical spell has trapped us here. We've tried all sorts of ways to leave – but can't. But now that you're here, maybe you can lead us out the way you came in. No one has ever entered or exited from that way before. Maybe that's the way out."

Alex shook his head. "I can't find my way back. There's some enchantment or someone who keeps shifting passages and obliterating all the marks I've made." He paused, then said, "Wait. You're saying there's another way out?"

Ariadne nodded. "Of course. We all entered through the front entrance. But no one can leave that way because of the magical barriers. Plus, it's not safe because that's where the creature is."

Ignoring her warning about the beast, Alex asked, "Can you lead me to that entrance?"

"Of course. You were close before you fell down here," Ariadne replied.

"I can't get up that slide by myself, but if you pulled me up, I could. Then you could show me how to get to the front exit."

It took several attempts before the three spirits finally managed to pull Alex up to the main level, but once there, even though his teeth were chattering from their freezing touches, he felt like he had a new lease on life. Ariadne led him down the hallway and up a set of stone stairs that emptied into a vast arena-like area with windows high above. After being in total darkness for so long, the light coming in, though not very bright, was hard on his eyes. He stopped and shielded them until they adjusted, then looked up, hoping to discover a way out. The first smile in hours crossed his face when he saw circular stairs leading up to a narrow balcony set even with the bottom of a bank of windows across the room. In the middle was a large brown object inside a glass case.

A roar from across the room caused him to look away. He froze when he saw a monster, he thought could only exist in the fantasy world, emerge from an opening at one end of the arena. The beast stood over ten feet tall with an immense horned head that reminded him more of a smaller, hairy Abraxas than the famous man-bull of mythology. He briefly closed his eyes and shook his head in resignation as he thought of how he'd gone out for a short walk and run into the Minotaur.

CHAPTER 16

OH GOD, NOW WHAT

Diana had been excited when Elizabeth invited Sophie and her to Istanbul to meet with Hanim Fatma, the High Priestess of the Istanbul grove. For the first few days, she'd wandered around the city, soaking in the sights and sounds of the former capital of the Byzantine and Ottoman Empires while the elders were in meetings. However, as the days passed, with no news from either the meetings or Jane on where Alex was and what he was doing, she became increasingly worried.

Hanim's assistant, Nadia Lazar, was Diana's guide on the city tours. At first, Diana was in awe of her fellow Druid. Nadia was far more skilled in everything Diana had always prided herself on – like fluency in foreign languages and magical skills. She also knew Nadia was more involved with her grove's council of elders than any other girl in the order her age. But it wasn't just her skills and accomplishments that Diana was jealous of. Nadia was several inches taller, one of the prettiest girls in the order, and also one of the most popular, as her easy-going manners always enabled her to be confident around everyone.

Her envy soon turned to suspicion, though, when she noticed Nadia started asking more and more questions about Alex. At first, they'd seemed innocent enough, such as what he was like. But they gradually became more probing, causing her to wonder if Nadia was using her to get information on Alex to support the order's desire to eliminate him. After that, Diana answered Nadia's questions in the vaguest manner possible.

Several days after she'd arrived, Sophie called Diana into an emergency meeting with all the other Druids. She was one of the last to arrive and was surprised Elizabeth was in charge instead of Hanim.

When everyone had settled, Elizabeth said, "I recently got a call from a Brother Robert Stafford, the head of the Magos order, which is a small organization of warlocks with similar goals to ours."

Elizabeth let the ensuing commotion die down before she continued. "I met him a year ago when my grandson appeared in London, long after we thought he was dead. He approached me, sharing his concerns about my grandson, and said Lady Yvaine had turned a deaf ear to his warning."

"Excuse me. But if this Magos order takes in warlocks, why didn't they take in your grandson?" Sophie asked.

"Because they believe he's dangerous – like we do. Apparently, he has acted strangely around them, too. Anyway, he called to warn me that my grandson has turned up in Greece and destroyed the home of a friend of Lady Yvaine's as well as a roomful of magical objects, disappearing as quickly as he'd appeared. He's concerned my grandson is after something of ours now."

Diana smiled, wondering what the rest of the story was because she was sure both Elizabeth and Brother Stafford were suppressing essential information.

"What exactly does that mean?" Sophie asked.

"It means the Omphalos isn't safe," Elizabeth said. "It can't be a coincidence that he ends up in Greece right after breaking into our Scottish stronghold and destroying the Chintamani."

"What are you suggesting we do?" Hanim asked. "Lady Yvaine has been adamant that we don't harm the boy. And he managed to escape your search for him in Scotland."

"Above all, we need to protect the Omphalos," Elizabeth replied. "I've repeatedly warned Lady Yvaine about him, but she keeps ignoring me, which is why I've concluded that we must gain control of the situation. We can't let her indecision about him cause irreparable harm to our order. I say we remove the Omphalos from its current hiding place and take it elsewhere for safekeeping."

"I thought it was the best-protected object we have," Nadia said.

"It is," Hanim replied. "But, if what I've heard about him is half-true, then it isn't safe." She took a deep breath and stood. "If we do this, everybody should understand that we risk censure, possibly banishment if anything goes wrong."

Sophie slapped her hands down on the table and stood up. "Finally. It's about time we do something to stop that boy from destroying everything we've worked for."

All the women started clamoring in support of Elizabeth's proposal until Hanim called for order. When the room had quieted down, she turned to Nadia, who usually didn't have a vote in order matters, and asked, "What do you think?"

Nadia glanced at Diana, then defiantly lifted her chin and said, "I agree with the recommendation. I don't think we should leave it to chance and risk having him steal one of the Maqlû right from under our noses."

"Good. Then that's settled," Elizabeth said.

Diana was shocked and hurt no one had asked her opinion, especially since she knew Alex better than any of them. Working up her courage, she stood and said, "I don't think that's a wise course of action. If Lady Yvaine thinks he's safe, then let the object be. She's usually several steps ahead of us. And think of how many things can go wrong if we take it out of the most heavily guarded place in our order."

Silence descended over the room after Diana's outburst as the women glared at her for her heretical statement. But it lasted for only a few seconds. Then, like a dam breaking, the women burst into a shouting match, debating next steps – completely ignoring Diana's comments.

The next day, Diana and half a dozen other Druids stepped off a chartered jet in Crete and into two waiting helicopters. Despite her misgivings about the operation, Diana couldn't help but get excited over this new adventure, wondering where they were going as they flew over the rugged central part of the island and down to its sparsely inhabited southern side.

When they finally landed, Diana was surprised to see how desolate the area was. She followed Hanim and the others a short distance up a hill through rocks, dirt, and a few scrub bushes into a superbly camouflaged opening.

Diana shivered from the drastic temperature difference between the blazing hot Mediterranean sun outside and the cool interior. She followed the others down a flight of stairs and into a conference room where a half dozen middle-aged ladies were waiting for them.

One of the women approached Diana, motioned for her to follow, then led her through the winding corridors of what looked like an ancient underground palace with old frescoes and furnishings still intact. After storing her bags in her room, she followed the woman back to a state-of-the-art conference room with large monitors hung all around and laptops sitting in front of each chair.

Diana sat down and waited for the rest of her party to enter. When all were present, Hanim stood and said, "The day has finally come when we must move the Omphalos to protect it, as this location is no longer safe."

One of the women stationed in the Druid hideout countered, "But the Omphalos has been safe here for two thousand years. This place is so remote and well-protected that nobody could ever break into it, as only Lady Yvaine and a few of us stationed here can unlock the doors."

"That might have been true in the past," Hanim replied, "but we are facing the greatest threat we've ever encountered, which is why we must move it to Meteora, as it's much more easily defensible. But first, we must develop a plan to ensure no harm comes to the object during the move.

Confused by the constant references to the Omphalos, Diana raised her hand and asked, "Excuse me, but what is this object you're talking about?"

"I'm sorry," Hanim replied. "I forgot that you haven't had the training on what it is yet. Greek mythology thought it represented the navel of the world and was a communication device to the gods. But it's one of the Maqlû, and like the rest of them, we haven't cracked all its secrets. However, we believe it controls the fire element, as the last time anyone tried to use it – they spontaneously burst into flames."

Diana sat back, trying to imagine the object's power, while the rest of the women started developing a plan for moving it. They kept at it till late into the evening, breaking only so everyone could get a little sleep. The second day of meetings was much like the first. By early afternoon, Diana was ready to scream in frustration at seemingly talking in circles and going over details ad nauseam. She was starting to drift off when a roar that rattled the glasses on the table startled her awake.

Hanim and the women who guarded the Omphalos jumped up and ran out the door. Diana wasn't far behind and quickly caught up with the last of the guards.

As they raced down the corridor, Diana asked between pants, "What was that?"

"That's the minotaur that guards the Omphalos."

Diana's astonishment almost caused her to trip, but she managed to gasp, "The minotaur? That's a fairy tale monster."

The woman shook her head as she raced onwards, saying, "Sometimes, I wish that were true."

They soon passed Hanim and the other guards and ran in front of the pack. "What does that roar mean?" asked Diana.

"We just fed him, which can only mean one thing – there's an intruder."

"But I thought Hanim said there was no way anyone could get in here without one of you escorting the person."

"That's what we've always thought, but it's obviously inaccurate. It's disconcerting to discover that we have a break-in for the first time in my life, just as we're discussing security measures."

The woman rounded a corner and skidded to a halt, then quickly chanted a spell that opened a massive steel door. Diana could hear chains sliding off the backside of the door as the guard muttered under her breath, "Come on, come on, hurry up."

The others arrived just as the door was wide enough to let the guard through. Diana didn't hesitate and slipped in after her. The brightness of the palace hallways was in stark contrast to the dimness of the room she entered.

"Hurry, help me get this case off," the guard called to her. "We must secure the Omphalos and get it out of here."

Diana rushed over and helped lift a thick glass case off a large, rather ugly, bullet-looking object. Another roar reverberated through the room shaking the floor beneath her. Diana reached out to steady herself on a railing, and happened to look out the windows lining the back wall. It was a sight she couldn't ever possibly have imagined. Twenty feet below, on what looked to be a giant arena floor, was a beast that had to be the infamous Minotaur. She heard Hanim shouting orders, but she didn't pay any attention to the commotion around her, as all she could focus on was the sight of Alex facing the gigantic beast.

Sophie grabbed her hand and pulled her away from the window, saying, "Hurry, we've got to leave now."

As her mother dragged her away, Diana glanced back at the wall hiding the arena of death and tried telling her mother that Alex was in the Minotaur's cage, but she couldn't make a sound.

The next hour went by in a blur. Diana barely had time to grab her gear before one of the guards rushed her outside. She then watched as the women used every spell they could think of to seal the monster and Alex inside the ancient palace. The dust was still settling around the entrance from the tons of boulders the Druids had used to seal the entrance when two helicopters arrived.

Thinking she'd never see Alex again, Diana stumbled into one in a daze.

CHAPTER 17

THE MINOTAUR

Alex caught a glimpse of motion out of the corner of his eye. Temporarily forgetting about the monster in front of him, he looked to the windowed area above and saw Diana staring down, a look of horror plastered on her face. An instant later, she was gone, as was the object he'd seen inside.

A deafening roar caused him to drop his staff and clap his hands over his ears, driving him to forget all the questions flitting through his mind about what Diana was doing there as he focused on the more pressing issue of how not to end up being another skeleton on the floor. Without thinking, he grabbed a nearby bone and threw it at the beast. It sailed wide right. Picking up the largest bone he could find, he aimed for what he hoped would be a sensitive spot. But his throw bounced harmlessly off the beast's thigh.

Realizing fighting the monster with sticks and stones was futile, Alex tried flanking it, hoping to reach the opening on the far wall. He'd taken only a half dozen steps when the Minotaur leaped over him and cut off his escape. Alex reversed directions, but the beast, swiping at him, hooked one claw into his backpack and lifted him off the floor as if he were no more than a feather. Hovering ten feet in the air, Alex wriggled free of the straps and landed on the floor with a thud that took his breath away.

Scrambling to his feet, he dashed towards the balcony stairs. Fear lent him speed, and he got to the steps a second before the beast's tail crashed into the wall, missing him by inches. He raced up the steps and reached the balcony just as the creature wrapped its arms around one of the support columns and pulled. The balcony shuddered forcing Alex to grab the hand rail to prevent falling into the monster's clutches. Seeing the door leading away from the arena a few feet away, he ran over, but any hope of escape vanished when he saw chains crisscrossing both sides of the door. He briefly thought about trying to head back down and make a mad dash across the arena and hide in the labyrinth, but he doubted he'd make it. And even if he did, he knew he wouldn't last long in the maze.

Another roar echoed through the room, followed by a loud wrenching sound. The next instant, Alex fell to the grating as the Minotaur ripped away the stairs, leaving the balcony hanging precariously.

More out of frustration than believing he'd get an answer, Alex shouted, "What have I done to you? Leave me alone."

He was surprised when he heard an answer in his head, *"Never. You're like all the rest of the human race. You fear what you don't understand. Your kind has kept me caged here for millennia as nothing more than a glorified guard dog."*

"I haven't done anything to you," Alex shouted back.

The Minotaur jumped and caught the balcony, tipping it even more precariously. The beast's head appeared above the half-destroyed terrace. Looking straight into Alex's eyes, it licked its lips.

Knowing he had to do something to avoid dying, he did the only thing he could think of – he ran across the balcony's short space, leapt onto the beast's head, and started running down its back.

The Minotaur tried reaching behind it with one arm and managed to rake Alex's side. Trying to ignore the pain, Alex ran down the monster's back and jumped when he was a couple of feet above the floor. As soon as his feet hit, he sprinted for the opening. But the Minotaur, once more, jumped over him and blocked the way.

Despite the blood flowing down his side, Alex tried to concentrate on how to escape his predicament. Spotting the staff, he ran over, picked it up, and charged. Distraught by the situation, he barely noticed the power surging from the ankh into his hands as he swung the gnarled piece of wood at the Minotaur. For a fraction of a second, he had the impression it changed form into a double-headed hammer. The next instant, his staff slammed into the beast with such force that the creature flew across the room and crashed into the far wall before crumpling to the floor.

Alex winced when he heard it whimpering in pain. "I didn't want to hurt you," he shouted, "but you forced me to defend myself."

"Please, be done with it and put me out of my misery."

The beast's plaintive plea caused Alex to recall painful memories of a similar encounter long ago with a black dragon. In a quiet voice, he replied, "I can't do that."

The Minotaur wearily opened one eye and stared at Alex. *"You can hear me?"* it asked.

"We wouldn't be having this conversation if I couldn't. You know, maybe if you weren't so all-fired anxious to kill me, I could help you as I did with Abraxas."

The Minotaur tried sitting up but failed and slumped back to the floor. "You know her?" it asked.

"I had a similar run-in with her a couple of years ago," Alex replied. "Like you, she tried to take her pent-up frustrations out on me. But we got along once she realized I wasn't trying to hurt her."

"I don't understand. Are you saying you'll help me get out of here?" the Minotaur asked.

"I would if I could, but I have no idea how to get out. And besides, there's no way I could help you – you're much too big for me."

The Minotaur roused itself and said, *"I'll be fine in a bit, but you pack quite a wallop. As for getting out – the problem is those women guards and their magic. I can show you the way out if you can eliminate them."*

Ariadne appeared beside him. "Aren't you going to punish him for what he's done to all of us?"

"No," Alex replied. "He's a victim like the rest of you and trying to survive like I am. Can you blame him?"

Ariadne huffed and disappeared.

Abraxas' family tree suddenly flashed in Alex's memory. He turned to the Minotaur and said, "Excuse me. Is your name Gugalanna by chance?"

"Yes, but how do you know that?" the beast asked.

"Abraxas dumped all sorts of information into my head when she adopted me into her weyr. I might not know how to access all the information she shared, but I'm sure you're a dragon. And if I'm right, I can't help but wonder why you haven't used your magical abilities to escape?"

"I've tried, but the witches' power has been too great. They force me to stay down here where they feed and water me so I can guard their precious object."

"I saw someone who could help us get out of here," Alex said. "But I need your help getting through that door up there."

The Minotaur struggled to his feet, walked over to below the door, then leapt onto the mangled balcony. Grabbing the chains on the outside of the door, he yanked, snapping them as easily as if they were pretzel sticks. Gugalanna threw the chains onto the arena floor, then threw his shoulder into the door, shattering the thick tempered glass. Shrugging off the shards, he attacked the inner chains until he had a clear path into the room where the Omphalos had rested for centuries. Then he jumped back to the floor and said, *"Get on. I'll take you up there so you can find your friend, but I'll stay down here until you tell me it's all clear. I have too many painful experiences with the witches to chance escaping until I know it's safe."*

Moments later, Alex jumped from the dragon's back onto the remains of the balcony and clawed his way to the shattered door frame. But his weight and movement caused the steel walkway to groan then crash to the floor. Teetering on the doorsill, with one arm flailing, Alex lunged forward and crashed onto the marble floor, knocking the air out of him.

It took him a minute before he caught his breath and was able to stand. Despite the shivers racing up and down his spine at the eerie silence pervading the old palace, he went searching for Diana and the other Druids. After several minutes of searching, he returned to the arena doorway and said, "Nobody's here. They're all gone."

He rushed to get out of the way as Gugalanna leapt up and shoved his immense body through the shattered doorframe. The hairy dragon looked hesitantly in all directions, listening for the presence of his former captors. Hearing and seeing nothing, he waddled through the old palace until he encountered tons of rubble at what used to be the exit.

Alex groaned. "Is this the way out?"

"I'm afraid it is. They must have sealed it to prevent us from escaping. Have patience, Little One. I'll soon have all these stones moved out of the way. But you'll have to leave the room so I don't hurt you."

"I'm tired of this. I just want to get out of here and catch my ride back to Athens," Alex screamed, slamming his staff against the rock pile to vent his frustrations.

The resulting blast threw him halfway across the entrance hall. A choking cloud of dust followed, sending Alex into a coughing fit. He pulled his shirt over his face to filter out the worst of the dust and stumbled from the room, seeking fresh air. When the dust finally settled, Alex tentatively returned to the entrance. A grin spread across his face when he saw daylight streaming through a gaping hole in the rocks.

Gugalanna nearly knocked Alex over in his mad rush to the outside. Alex followed him out and saw they were in a desert-like area high on a mountain overlooking the sea. And except for a large square concrete pad, there was no sign of habitation anywhere in sight.

"Where is everyone?" Alex asked.

"They took everything they'd stored here and ran when you entered the arena," Ariadne replied, startling Alex.

"Overcoming his surprise at the spirit's presence, he said, "But I wasn't going to steal anything. I just wanted to get out."

Her reply was lost in the cheers and shouts of joy as a horde of ghosts burst from the labyrinth. One by one, the ghosts floated into the sky, twinkling before they disappeared. Eventually only Deborah and Ariadne remained. "Thank you," the ancient Greek spirit said.

"For what? All I did was blow things up again," Alex replied.

"But you did more than that. You shattered the spells that kept us from leaving that hellhole. And because of that, you've freed thousands of blameless souls, enabling them to move on. We won't forget you." Before he could reply, she planted frozen kisses on both cheeks and disappeared.

Deborah wearily said, "I'm heading to the netherworld to rest. I can barely keep my eyes open." And in the blink of an eye, she, too, was gone, leaving him with only the Minotaur for company.

"I, too, must *thank you for freeing me,*" Gugalanna said. *"If you need my help, come to Mount Olympus. Seeing how you were able to get out of this prison, you'll know what to do once you're there."*

Then he spread his wings and began flapping them, sending clouds of sand swirling, forcing Alex to cover his face. When the dust had settled, Gugalanna was gone. It was several minutes before Alex stirred and looked around to figure out where he was. Using the sun as a guide, he figured he was still on the southern side of Crete. With a sigh, he started down the mountainside, hoping he wasn't too far away from his starting point that morning.

But he'd only gone a short distance when a dizzy spell hit him, reminding him of the injury he'd sustained in the arena. He found a nearby rock and sat down, then pulled his medical kit from his pack and began working on his shredded side.

CHAPTER 18

WHAT YOU LEAVE BEHIND

After bandaging his side, Alex looked around to get his bearings and was surprised to see how high the sun was in the sky. He knew he'd been underground for at least a couple of hours and thought the sun should be closer to setting than it was. Assuming it was just another oddity in his life, he heaved himself off the rock and looked for an easy way down the mountainside. Even though he didn't know exactly where he was, he knew he'd headed north from Agia Roumeli that morning and then turned west to enter the labyrinth. So he figured, all he had to do was reach the shoreline and turn left.

The way down was much rougher than he'd anticipated, as every step painfully reminded him of his wound. It was also much slower going than he'd hoped, for the sun was dipping close to the horizon by the time he'd reached a ledge overlooking the shoreline. That wasn't what worried him, though. There was no town in sight, and he was sure he should've been able to see it.

Alex inched close to the edge, looked down, and saw there wasn't any beach he could walk along – even if he could climb down the precipitous slope safely. Figuring he'd gone further into the labyrinth than he'd first estimated, he continued heading east along the ridge. The plateau eventually turned inland, and after another half hour of walking, he could faintly see a town's lights twinkling in the distance.

He kept going for some time until he spotted an old goat track. Breathing a sigh of relief, he headed down. But it wasn't an easy path, as several times he had to turn around and use his hands to slow his descent. He eventually made it to the shoreline, then used the lights from the town to guide him safely over the last stretch.

The town was small enough that he quickly found a hotel and checked in. But when he showed his passport, the desk clerk did a double-take before holding the picture next to Alex's face. "You're alive," she said. "We've had search parties out looking for you. Your friends went back to sea and planned to stop at towns along the coast to see if you'd wound up in one of them. Hold on. I must call the police and tell them the news."

Alex was confused. "But that can't be. I just got a little sidetracked up in the gorge today."

The woman shook her head. "It's been two days since you disappeared." After a quick call, she turned back to Alex and said, "The police want to interview you and determine what happened. So, make yourself comfortable."

"I don't understand what the big deal is," Alex protested. "All I did was explore a cave. But I'm here now and fine."

The clerk waved to a seat in the lobby. "Please, have a seat. It won't take long."

She was wrong, as it was after midnight before the authorities were done asking questions. When he finally got to his room, he was so exhausted that he plopped on his bed and promptly fell asleep.

A banging noise on his door the next day came all too early. At first, he ignored it, wanting to sleep more, but whoever was at the door was too persistent to let him stay asleep. He splashed water on his face and was only half awake when he answered the door and found Jean Paul and Francis standing in front of him.

The questions came at Alex so fast that he didn't have time to answer them. Jean Paul finally calmed down enough to say, "We're sorry. We should never have let you wander off. Why don't you get cleaned up, then come down for breakfast before we take off."

"Where are you going?" Alex asked.

"We're taking you back to Athens and dropping you off at the airport," Jean Paul replied. "You need to go home. No more of this gallivanting around."

Alex's first instinct was to argue with his Haitian friends by telling them what had happened in the labyrinth. But he decided against it since he wasn't sure what the significance of those events was. At last, he said, "You're right, as left to my own devices, I'd surely find more trouble." Then, he waved them out of the room and got cleaned up.

When he finally came down for breakfast, the two Haitians started peppering him with questions making it difficult to eat. When he didn't provide them with many details of all he'd been through, they ended their grilling and focused on discussing their plans to leave. A short time later, they were underway.

Early the next morning, they arrived in Athen's harbor. The three remained silent on the drive to the airport, and it wasn't until they were all standing uneasily outside the taxi, uncomfortable with saying goodbye again, that Jean Paul broke the silence. "Again, I'm sorry for leaving you like that on Crete. I'll never forgive myself. And yet, here we are doing the same thing – leaving you behind."

"It's okay," Alex replied. "And just so you know, I'm not sorry about being left behind, even though there were a few hairy moments when I thought I'd never return. But it's all good now, and I have to thank you for everything – getting my tickets and bringing me here. It makes things much simpler. And since I don't know when or if I'll see you guys again, good luck." He hugged them, then watched them get back in the taxi and head back to the harbor.

As he was about to head inside the terminal, he saw a motorcycle swerve in front of a heavily laden truck, forcing the truck driver to slam on the brakes causing boxes to fly off. The biker sped off without looking back.

A tall, dark, slender young woman in her mid-twenties, wearing old work clothes and boots, got out of the truck and surveyed the mess. She brushed her dark hair off her forehead and got to work moving the boxes out of the road.

Alex stood and watched as the woman worked with a big smile – as if it was what she wanted to do. Her soft, melodious voice floated across the way, acting on Alex like a siren calling him. Forgetting about everything else, Alex walked over and asked, "Can I help?"

The woman stopped working, gave Alex a big smile, and said, "I'd appreciate that."

Alex hopped into the back of the truck and started restacking the boxes she handed up. They worked steadily while the woman kept singing one cheerful song after another. When they'd finished strapping down the load, Alex jumped out and headed back towards the terminal, saying, "Have a great day, ma'am."

The woman stopped singing and said, "Thank you for your help, young man. If you'd hold on another minute, I'd like to pay you for all you've done."

Alex turned back and shook his head, saying, "No thank you. You've already paid me with your smile and your singing."

The woman's merry laugh caused Alex to flush in embarrassment. "That was probably the nicest compliment I've ever had. Thank you. Can I at least buy you lunch? I don't know about you, but I'm famished."

Alex looked at the terminal, then back to the woman. "Do you know what time it is?"

Looking at her watch, she told him. He slapped his forehead and said, "Where has the time gone? I've missed my flight."

"I'm sorry. I didn't realize you were in a rush."

"It's not your fault. I wasn't paying attention. But don't worry, these things happen to me all the time. I'll catch the next one."

The young woman looked at Alex's torn clothing and said, "I'm Agnodice Florence and am not taking no for an answer. I can see you're not the type to take handouts, but I can assure you this isn't one. Call it a business lunch then, because I have a proposition for you. And your name?"

"Alex Scire, ma'am."

The woman laughed and said, "Ma'am makes me sound too old. Call me Agnes. That's what my friends do." She motioned to the truck and said, "I need to move this out of the way. Hop in and we'll check on flights at lunch."

When they'd finished eating lunch an hour later, Agnes turned serious and said, "Here's the deal. I'm with the Red Crescent Society and am part of a convoy that is supposed to take aid to some refugee camps. My assistant has come down with the flu and can't make the trip, but I need someone to help me. And since you've already shown you're willing to work, how about it? The pay is miserable, but in addition to starvation wages, you get uncomfortable lodging and food that is, well, let's just say, it's nutritious. What do you say?"

"Where are these refugees from?"

"All over. They've come from poverty and war-torn areas around the Middle East and North Africa, seeking an opportunity to make a new and better life for themselves. Some even come from as far away as Afghanistan and Pakistan."

"But why are they coming to Greece?" Alex asked. "No offense, but I didn't think Greece was one of the more prosperous countries in Europe."

"No offense taken. And you're right. It isn't one of the wealthier countries. It's just that Greece and, to a lesser extent, Italy are physically the closest to many of these refugees' home countries. In addition, the xenophobes throughout Europe close their borders to the refugees, leaving Greece to deal with most of them even though we don't have enough resources to keep up with the demand."

Alex surprised himself by considering her offer. He put his hand over the ankh surreptitiously, and discovered it felt warm against his chest – neither excited nor worried – almost hopeful. All the recent events had seemed so haphazard that he couldn't see how this offer fit any pattern, yet he knew it wasn't random. He briefly wondered what Diana or Jane would recommend doing, but memories of talks with his grandfather, encouraging him to seek out his purpose in life, pushed his doubts out of his mind and drove him to say, "How can I turn down such a generous offer? But I've got to call my grandfather and let him know what I'm doing."

She handed him her phone and sat back, observing him closely as he talked. When he hung up, he said, "Let's go."

"I'm surprised he'd let you go," Agnes said.

"He believes the Great Spirit moves each of us differently." As he got up to follow Agnes, he groaned.

"Are you all right?" she asked.

"Yeah, I got a scratch the other day."

She'd noticed the rips in his shirt and the dried blood when she'd first met him but had chosen not to say anything. "Has anybody taken a look at that?" she asked, nodding her head at the streaks of dried blood on his shirt.

Seeing where she was looking, he said, "I bandaged it up the best I could and am sure it'll be fine. It looks worse than it is."

Agnes studied him, trying to understand the young man sitting across the table. She gave up, and after paying the bill, took him back to the truck and had him remove his shirt. She gasped when she saw the size of the rake marks after taking off his hastily wrapped bandages. "What in the world happened to you?" she asked.

Alex knew he couldn't tell her the truth, so all that came out of his mouth was, "Uhm…, you wouldn't believe me if I told you."

She shook her head and quietly said, "You've got too many secrets. But, as long as you're not wanted by the law or doing something illegal, I'll be quiet." When Alex didn't respond, she went about quietly and professionally, cleaning and bandaging his wounds before giving him some antibiotic medicine.

Alex started reaching for his worn-out t-shirt, but Agnes yanked it away before he could grab it and said, "No you don't. This thing is so tattered and filthy that I'm worried it'll cause an infection if you put it back on. Hold on while I grab a shirt. I think I have one that looks like it'd fit you."

When they finally took off, Agnes drove to a large graveled area near the docks and parked behind several other cargo trucks. As soon as she'd shut off the engine, she jumped out and ran towards a small group of people standing nearby and was soon hugging and crying in delight at reuniting with some old companions.

Alex stood by the truck, feeling out of place, and was surprised when she waved him forward. When he reached the group, he realized that Agnes was the youngest looking by far of the lot. She introduced Alex and told them how she'd found him. A short, swarthy-looking older man with a full silver beard stared at Alex and said, "He doesn't look old enough to be doing this type of work. Did you check his papers?"

Agnes bristled and said, "Have I ever given you cause to question my judgment? I'll personally vouch for Alex, Khalil. If you have a problem with that, you can find a replacement for me, too."

Khalil stepped back and held up his hands, knowing he'd crossed the line with her. "No, I was just saying that he looks too young. This work is not for the faint-hearted. He'll see some pretty harsh conditions, and I'm concerned about him, that's all. Once we leave here, there's no turning back."

Alex looked around, and, trying to sound more confident than he felt, said, "Don't worry about me. I'll do my part."

Khalil accepted defeat and stopped arguing.

Trucks continued streaming in for the rest of that day and the next, and Alex quickly discovered that Agnes hadn't been kidding about what he would experience. When he wasn't pulling guard duty to protect the supplies, he tried sleeping in the cab of his truck. The food wasn't much better as the humanitarian aid workers ate some of the canned goods they carried, saving the best food for the refugees.

After lunch on the second day, Khalil, who Alex learned was the convoy's leader, gathered everyone together. The grim look on his face said he didn't have good news. He got straight to the point. "There has been another big quake in the northwestern part of the country. Geneva has asked if we'd take some of our supplies there. Of course, we'll have to redistribute loads to ensure whoever heads up there has the right mix of supplies."

He paused for a moment, surveying the people around him. "Before any of you volunteer, I want you to know it'll be a long, hard run. The quake has closed many of the roads up to that area. Running water and electricity will be scarce. And it'll be dangerous, with aftershocks and crumbling buildings. The refugee camps will be a cakewalk in comparison. And I don't know how long you'll be gone for, but I need three teams of volunteers."

Alex saw the twitch in Agnes' arm as she thought about volunteering, then watched as her arm slowly sank to her side while she stared at her feet. A silence hung over the group for several moments as no one volunteered. Knowing he was the reason she hadn't spoken up, Alex raised his hand and said, "I'll go if someone will take me."

Agnes looked sharply at Alex, then turned to Khalil and stuck her hand in the air. "I'll take him."

Two more teams quickly volunteered, and the group dispersed. Khalil stayed behind until only Alex and Agnes remained with him. He put his rough weathered hand on her shoulder and said, "I apologize. You did choose wisely. Now go, but be safe."

He handed her a packet and said, "Here are the directions and necessary papers. You'll need to get going as soon as we get your loads redistributed because, as you know, every hour counts."

Agnes nodded, put her hand behind Alex's back, and steered him to the truck. An hour later, three vehicles pulled out and headed north.

CHAPTER 19

PAY ATTENTION TO YOUR ENEMIES

In the rush to move the Omphalos, none of the Druid leaders had thought to ask who the intruder had been. It wasn't until they were flying over the central mountain chain of Crete that Diana managed to work up the courage to ask her mother, "Why did we leave so quickly? I would've thought we would try to stop the intruder and leave the Omphalos where it was."

"We're not worried about whoever the intruder was," Sophie replied. "The Minotaur will take care of him. What drove us to move the Omphalos was our concern that if one person could break through our barriers, others could, too. We need to regroup and build better barriers around it."

"Has anyone ever survived an encounter with the Minotaur?" Diana asked.

Her mother shook her head. "That's why our order placed the Omphalos there in the first place. It's been an impregnable fortress for over two millennia. I saw you glance down into the arena. Did you notice who the intruder was?"

Diana nodded.

"And?"

Diana grimaced in response, causing Sophie to gasp.

Overhearing the conversation, Elizabeth shouted over the rotor's noise, "Are you sure?"

Diana nodded.

"This shouldn't be a surprise," Sophie said. "It's what we feared."

"But how did he get in there?" Hanim Fatma asked, "There's only one way in, and he didn't come that way. I checked our security camera footage and verified that I was the last person to enter through the front doors."

"Well, obviously, there's another way in," Elizabeth responded. "But that doesn't explain how he got through the labyrinth? No one has ever made it through there. Ever."

"When it comes to your grandson," Sophie said, "never doesn't mean what you think it means. And the sooner you accept the fact he managed to penetrate our defenses, the safer the Omphalos will be."

Diana stared out the window for several moments before she turned and asked, "What's next?"

"We do what we planned," Elizabeth replied. "We go to Meteora and bulk up our defenses."

Diana lost interest in the conversation as the numbness from seeing Alex in yet another impossible situation overwhelmed her. She tried convincing herself that if he could survive everything he'd experienced to date, he could extricate himself from the mess she'd seen. But the sight of the monster attacking Alex was like nothing she could have imagined. She feared that even if he could figure out a way to beat the beast, survival might be worse, as he would probably starve to death, sealed forever in the underground palace of King Minos.

Despite her fascination with UNESCO sites, Diana was down in the dumps and barely paid attention when they finally landed atop one of the giant stone pillars in Meteora. Instead of taking her bags inside the Druid safehouse with the other women, she absent-mindedly walked over to the side and looked down. She wished she hadn't, as her acrophobia quickly sent her reeling away from the side. Diana found a boulder to lean against and stayed there until her head stopped spinning, and she could look out over the awe-inspiring views of the valley to the other rock pillars.

She continued gazing over the valley until Hanim called out, "Diana, you need to come in now, unless you know the incantations to open these doors. Otherwise, you'll be stuck outside tonight."

Reluctantly, Diana followed the Istanbul Grove's High Priestess inside. As soon as she passed through the well-hidden bronzed doors, Hanim shut them, then chanted an incantation before lowering thick metal beams to seal them in. After double-checking the security of the doors, she said, "Follow me. We have a ways to go before we reach the Omphalos's vault."

Hanim led Diana down a well-worn granite pathway deep into the middle of the pillar until they finally entered the main living area, which had a state-of-the-art entertainment center, library, kitchen, living, and dining room. A hallway off to one side led to a dozen bedrooms. But what caught Diana's attention was a giant steel door in the center of the back wall with more inscriptions similar to the ones she'd seen on the outer door. "Where does that go?" Diana asked.

"That's where we've secured the Omphalos," Hanim replied. "That steel door is over two meters thick, with our most powerful spells protecting it. No one will get through it."

Diana didn't think any more about it and after a light dinner went to bed. Too restless to sleep, she got up around midnight and wandered around the Druid's hideaway, trying to dispel her memories from Crete. She eventually decided to go outside and was glad she'd asked Hanim to teach her the spells to get in and out through a small, well-hidden secondary door.

A gentle breeze wafted over the promontory, making Diana wish she'd worn a sweater. Because of the chill, she nestled inside a group of boulders, hoping to get a great view of the stars. But the lights of Kalabaka, hundreds of feet below, dimmed the stars' brilliance. With a sigh, she crossed her arms to stay warm and let her thoughts drift.

Her peaceful state of mind lasted only a few minutes. Diana wasn't sure what caused the uneasiness that suddenly descended over her, but she could feel it. She looked around, hoping to discover what had caused her senses to start tingling, but found nothing unusual. Silently cursing her poor hearing that couldn't help her identify the source of her unease, she'd just concluded that she'd imagined it all when she saw a giant figure moving towards the entrance doors.

Diana froze and helplessly watched as the intruder thrust a staff at the doors and chanted something in a language she didn't recognize. An energy stream burst from the crystal at the end of the giant's staff and smashed into their hideaway. The clash between the two magical forces created a fireworks show so blinding that it forced her to look away. Seconds later, a thunderous explosion blew the doors asunder, knocking Diana backwards. It took her a few seconds to recover from the blast and look up. But her heart sank when she saw the unknown giant disappearing into the Druid hideout.

Snapping out of her daze, she struggled to her feet and followed him, but he was out of sight by the time she got to the destroyed doorway. She ran down the steps towards the central room, hoping it was all just a bad nightmare. Halfway down, the lights went out, plunging the stairwell into darkness. She stopped and chanted a light spell, but as the flames sprang to life, she heard a series of small explosions down in the living quarters, followed by a powerful blast that shook the floor beneath her. Diana dimly heard screams, then silence. Freaked out by what was happening below, she stumbled and fell, causing the light in her hand to go out.

Her clumsiness saved her life, as a few seconds later, the unknown attacker rushed past her.

Diana lay unmoving in the stairwell for some time. When she finally collected her wits, she stood, chanted another fire spell to light her way, then headed down to the central room, where she froze at the sight of the carnage. Her hand-held flames gave off just enough light to see several lifeless bodies lying around.

In a tentative voice, she called out, "Hello. Is anyone here?"

CHAPTER 20

TO UNLEARN WHAT IS UNTRUE

"Why have we come to Delphi instead of going to Crete?" Jane asked Lady Yvaine. "Ye know that's where Elizabeth and all the others have gone. Aren't ye worried about them going rogue?"

"I am, but right now, I'm more concerned with understanding what Alex is doing. I keep thinking about what Hellwain said after the Loch Ness incident. She suggested we focus on the question of what's driving Alex – not stopping him. Which leads me to wonder why he came to Greece? Was he looking for one of our hideouts? If he was, how did he find Meteora so quickly, then suddenly leave without doing anything there?"

"Those are good questions, but perhaps he found something more interesting than our hideout."

"What do you mean?" Yvaine asked.

"Well, when I first met him, his only agenda was helping his sister move on. He usually had no plan, and his actions were seemingly random – even after he got close to one of the objects. But he's gradually become more focused on destroying the Maqlû. Which is why I think the question we should be asking right now is whether he's wandering or focused. But ye still haven't answered my question of, why are we here in Delphi."

"I'm sure you've heard of The Pythias – the famous ancient Greek seers, the High Priestesses of the Temple of Apollo at Delphi," Lady Yvaine replied. "Well, they were essentially doubles for the real Pythia, who has lived here for thousands of years. She's a bit of a recluse and created the Oracle of Delphi routine to hide her real identity and keep her from having to deal with people, while still influencing nations with her prognostications. The Pythia I know is the person who came up with the most famous prophecies, like her utterance to Croesus and her suggestions to the Athenians to count on their navy in their wars with Xerxes. I hope she's still here, so I can find out if she knows anything about Alex. Although, I'm not sure if she'll talk to me, since we didn't part on good terms."

They wandered around Delphi like the other tourists for some time, allowing Yvaine to temporarily forget about their mission. But as they came back down from the top of the archeological site, she stopped in front of the Temple of Apollo.

"What are ye looking for?" Jane asked.

"Some sign of Pythia's home. If it were me, I'd have my entrance far away from a busy place like this." She pointed to a cliff line above a stand of trees off to the left and said, "Like up there."

Yvaine chanted a misdirection spell on the same guard Deborah had distracted, allowing the two to slip into the trees without anyone noticing them. After wandering around the mountainside for nearly an hour, they found a giant pile of loose rocks. "This looks fresh," Jane said. "Do ye think this is what Brother Stafford was referring to?"

A voice behind them said, "Have you come here to gloat?"

Yvaine whirled around and saw a woman standing a few feet away wearing a white ankle-length dress and a large red shawl wrapped over her head and shoulders. The voice sounded familiar, but she couldn't place it. "I'm sorry. Do I know you?"

The woman stepped forward and flipped the shawl off her head. Even then, Yvaine had a hard time identifying her. At last, she hesitantly asked, "Pythia? Is that you?"

"Who else would you expect to see here? Were you hoping, perhaps, that I'd died," she asked, waving her arm towards the rubble. "Isn't that why you sent him here?"

"I have no idea what you're talking about. But I can assure you, whatever our past differences were, I mean you no harm," Yvaine replied. "In fact, we came here to ask you for help determining if you've seen a certain young man around here. He's of medium height, dark skinned, and wears his hair in two long braids."

"I know who you're talking about," Pythia said sarcastically.

Lady Yvaine was disconcerted by Pythia's response. "Oh." She shifted from one foot to another, trying to figure out how to proceed. At last she decided on being direct. "Brother Stafford contacted a member of our organization and said he'd caused a ruckus down here, but he wasn't very forthcoming with details."

"Hah. I bet he wasn't. I still can't figure out if Enkidu meant for all this to happen, or if he's as shocked as I am. You never know with him."

"What exactly did happen?"

"Enkidu thought it was a good idea to bring the boy here. But then he left him alone, and your protégé wandered off, found the front entrance to my home, and…," she waved a hand at the rubble and added, "then he broke in and destroyed everything, including all the magical objects I have collected."

Yvaine gasped. "Even the Cup?"

"No, thank Gaia. I kept it in a separate location, or he'd have destroyed that, too. Technically, though, he didn't destroy all the items. He took one."

"That doesn't sound like him," Yvaine replied. She grimaced, then said, "Oh no. I don't like the sound of this, which is why I hate to ask, which one?"

"You really don't know?" Pythia replied.

"Of course not. Why would I be here trying to learn what happened if I knew?"

Pythia's brows arched up. "He took Mjölnir."

"How can that be?" Yvaine responded. "No one can move it."

"That's what we all thought," Pythia said. "But at least I have the satisfaction of seeing you as bewildered by this as I am."

Yvaine hesitated before saying, "Since you have been more forthcoming than I expected, I feel it's only right to share something with you. This isn't the first time he's destroyed magical artifacts. Last month, he found the hiding place for the Chintamani Stone and destroyed it. And I believe it's not the only one of the Maqlû he's destroyed."

"I assumed that, which is why it will be the last object he destroys," Pythia said. "I've sent Erra after him – and he's never failed me."

Yvaine paled. "But that's a death sentence."

Pythia sniffed. "I know. Why would you expect anything different after what he's done?"

Seeing the hard glint in Pythia's eyes, Yvaine realized it was no use arguing. She turned to Jane and said, "Come on. Let's go." Several hours later, they arrived in Istanbul.

CHAPTER 21

ONCE MORE UNTO THE BREACH

The aid convoy left Athens and headed east on the south side of the Gulf of Corinth. The going was much slower than Alex had expected, as the big trucks they were driving were so old they had to stop several times for the drivers to fill fluid reservoirs that were perpetually leaking.

Alex didn't talk much at first, as he was too interested in watching the landscape change from farming land to hills and then to mountains. Agnes kept quiet until she couldn't take any more of the silence and asked, "I thought all I'd be doing was taking you on a quick run to one of the refugee camps. I never planned on taking you this far. So, why did you volunteer to go on this mission? You heard Khalil; it's not going to be an easy journey. The only things I can assure you are that it's hard work, harsh living conditions, suffering, and death. Quake zones are not for the faint-hearted. Heck, I don't even know if we can reach our destination. So, if you're trying to be macho, tell me now. I'm sure I'll be able to find someone to fill in for you."

Not knowing how to answer, Alex decided to play dumb and reply, "I'm sorry. Did you say something?"

"I know you heard me," Agnes said. "You have a certain look when you're trying to come up with a reply to avoid questions. Are you running from something you've done, or from someone?"

"No, but what would you say if I told you I was running towards something?"

"I don't know. But you still didn't answer my question. Why did you volunteer for this?"

"Over the last few years, when I haven't been running for my life, I've been deciding what to do next using wild-ass guesses to guide me," Alex replied. "My best decisions, though, have always come when I decide to help somebody, as good things always seem to come from those choices – not just for others, but for me and my goals. Plus, I've found it's always worse to do nothing, than make the hard choice and press on."

A raised eyebrow forced him to add, "Plus, I saw you start to raise your hand when Khalil asked for volunteers and figured you didn't say anything because of me. I also figured you would've found a way to go with or without me."

"Guilty as charged," Agnes laughingly replied. "Do you mind my asking how old you are? I've been trying to guess your age because you look really young."

"I'll be seventeen in October."

Agnodice hit the brakes and pulled over to the side of the road. She turned to Alex and said, "Seventeen! What are you doing running around here on your own? I thought you were at least twenty. You're too young for this work. I'm going to have to send you back on a bus."

Alex looked into the mirror on his side and saw one of the people from the last truck running forward to see what was wrong. Knowing he only had seconds before Agnes would announce his fate, and not quite knowing why he felt so strongly about going on, Alex said, "Look. I know you don't know me that well, but I've learned to trust my instincts. I can't explain it, but I feel I need to be on this trip."

She was about to reply when their coworker came up and asked, "Is there anything wrong?"

Agnes looked at Alex's pleading eyes, then turned and replied, "No. I got something in my eye and pulled over. I'm ready to go on now."

When they were moving again, Alex said, "Thank you. I won't let you down."

"You better not." Under her breath, she muttered, "If anybody finds out, I'll be in big trouble for taking a teenager along."

"Well I won't tell anybody," Alex said. "Besides, why shouldn't I be able to help? There are children in war zones all around the world, as well as the quake area we're going to."

"True, but bringing children and teenagers to those areas is too traumatizing for them."

"And it's not for adults?" Alex retorted.

"It's different for us. Adults have had more time to build coping mechanisms. What I don't understand is how your grandfather can be comfortable with you going off on your own at your age."

"He's seen too many of my ancestors ruin their lives because they shied away from the challenges they faced, including him," Alex replied.

Not knowing how to respond, Agnes lapsed into silence.

A short time later, they crossed over the Rio-Antirrio Bridge at the mouth of the Gulf of Corinth and stopped for lunch. As they returned to the trucks, Agnodice saw Alex heading towards the passenger side and said, "Uh, uh. Time to switch. It's your turn to drive. We need you to be able to handle all sorts of situations that might come up."

Alex's eyes bugged out, and he replied, "I don't have much experience. I've only driven this big of a vehicle once in Haiti. Other than that, I've only driven old pickup trucks while bucking hay."

"Well, there's no better time to get some road experience than now. Get in."

"I don't have a driver's license," Alex said. "What if the police stop us?"

"We're on a mission of mercy. I can talk my way out of this if there's a problem. Besides, I can't drive all day then go right to work. I need a rest now and then, and you need practice. So, now's as good a time as any."

Alex grimaced and headed for the driver's side. It was rough going at first, but Alex was soon grinning in delight as they sped down the highway.

Sometime later, he felt the ankh sending him a warning signal. He didn't see anything wrong, but he trusted the ankh and pulled over to the side of the road.

"What are you doing?" Agnes screamed.

Alex held up a hand to silence her so he could focus on the ankh thumping against his chest. Instead of answering her when she repeated her question, he jumped out and ran ahead, ignoring the cars honking as they whizzed by. Alex heard her approaching and thrust his hand out to stop her. Before any of the others could reach them, a loud explosion, followed by a rumble deep beneath them, shook the ground. He waved everyone back, then stepped onto the highway and started waving at cars to stop. Another rumble knocked him to his knees just as a car passed. He watched in horror as it disappeared into a giant split in the ground that opened only yards away.

Agnes quickly joined his efforts to stop traffic and called for the others to join her. Two more cars ignored them, both disappearing into the newly opened chasm before they got the first vehicle to stop. When she was sure it was safe, she called for the other members of the convoy to help.

For the next few hours, Alex was busy acting as an extra pair of hands, helping the rescue workers and paramedics when they arrived on the scene. The sun had already set when the convoy wearily turned around and headed back the way they'd come, looking for a place to rest and a new path north.

They'd only gone a few miles when Agnes glanced at Alex and asked, "How'd you know? Could you sense it? Because I didn't feel anything until the big jolt."

"Remember when I was talking about my decision-making? Well, I should have also said that many of my biggest decisions are based on hunches."

Agnes shook her head and said, "You're the strangest person I've ever met."

CHAPTER 22

ONE WHO WALKS IN

The relief convoy checked hotel availability at the next couple of towns, but it wasn't until the third town that they finally found available rooms. After a late dinner, they headed straight to bed as they planned to leave at dawn the next day to resume their journey to the quake zone.

While the group was finishing breakfast the next morning, Agnes said, "Rather than go all the way around on the main highways, I've been thinking we could take the shortcut through the mountains. Once we get to Trikala, we can cut north and reach our destination in a few hours."

One of the women replied, "That'll take us back close to where the quake was yesterday. If there are any problems going that way, we'll have to backtrack and lose hours, if not a whole day. Plus, we'll be on a narrow, twisty road for much of the way."

"But, if everything works out, it cuts our trip by hours and could mean the difference between somebody's life or death," Agnes replied.

The woman shrugged. "Just saying. I'll follow you."

"All right. Let's get going. Ensure you bring enough snacks because I don't plan to stop very often."

Once they were underway, Alex asked, "How long will it take to get to where we're going?"

"Probably all day," Agnes replied. "We're going from one side of Greece to the other before we turn north again. And the way over the mountains isn't that quick." She barely spoke until they stopped a couple of hours later for gas, a bathroom break, and food to go.

When they got back into the truck cab, Agnes looked ruefully over at Alex and said, "I'm sorry about being grumpy earlier. I'm frustrated we're not already there, as I've been to too many disaster-torn areas. Not only are these supplies critical, but one of our members is a licensed nurse, and the rest of us have first responder training. We can make a difference, but only if we're there."

As they made their way through the mountains, Alex gradually grew less talkative as a feeling of dread crept over him. It became almost painful as soon as they turned north and headed towards Kalabaka. At first, he thought it might have something to do with unfinished business at the site where Chrysophylax had left him when he'd first arrived in Greece. But as they got closer and the ankh seemed to be bouncing off his chest – he knew it was some new type of danger.

The pressure grew until he spotted a road sign showing the exit to Meteora and shouted for Agnes to pull over. She slammed on the brakes and pulled over, looking expectantly at Alex.

"I know I promised to go with you to the end, but I need to get off here," Alex said.

Agnes looked at him as if he was crazy. "I'm not letting you off here. It's practically the middle of nowhere."

"I'm sorry, but I really need to get to Meteora," Alex replied.

"Why didn't you mention it before?" Agnes asked.

"Because I didn't realize I needed to go there until I saw the sign. I know it doesn't make sense to you, but my friends and grandpa understand how I think and act, even if they'd try to talk me out of it like you will."

"Is it that you can't explain why you want to make this course change, or that you won't?" Agnes asked.

Subconsciously holding a hand over the ankh, Alex replied, "A little of both. But if you try to stop me, know that I'll figure out a way to come back – one way or another."

Agnes glanced at him, then began drumming her fingers on the steering wheel. Seconds later, she growled and got out of the truck. "Stay here."

She was gone a few minutes before he saw the other two trucks pull back onto the road and pass. "What's going on?" Alex asked.

"I'm taking you to Meteora," Agnes replied.

"Why? You've got much more important things to do than help me," Alex said. "Besides, you don't know me that well, and I'm breaking my promise to you."

She stared ahead, eyes unblinking, her jaws tightly clenched. Finally, she started up the truck and pulled onto the road. When she finally spoke, her words were very measured. "I knew there was a reason for your showing up like that in Athens."

"I didn't plan on any of this."

"I believe you. Call it women's intuition or whatever you like, but I knew there was something about you the day we met. Maybe it was the look on your face, or maybe it was how you started helping, causing you to miss your flight. I don't know why I believe in you, but I do. Besides, I owe it to you. You saved my life and others by stopping us before that quake hit."

She stopped talking as she made the turn to Meteora, then followed the loop road connecting the monasteries. Agnes kept looking to him for guidance on where they were going, but all he did was look up at the rocks towering overhead. He finally had her stop in a woody area in the middle of the loop, far from any of the monasteries' entrances.

Agnes got out and looked up at some of the area's tallest, most inaccessible pillars and said, "Are you sure this is where you want me to drop you off? There's nothing up there. The monasteries are on almost every other rock around here except the one you're looking at."

"I know, right." Alex leaned against the truck so he wouldn't fall backwards as he looked up and said, "I was here recently but was dog-tired when I came down, so I'm not entirely sure this is it. But, I've learned to trust that the Great Spirit will help me." He paused, then added, "I feel like something bad has happened here, and I need to check it out."

"What's this all about?" When she didn't get an answer, Agnes said, "I can't leave you here in the middle of nowhere. Let me lock the truck, and I'll go with you."

"I'll be fine," Alex said. "Besides, you have much more important things to do and should get going as a lot of people are counting on you up north. But I want to thank you for helping me. I couldn't have gotten here without you."

Agnes waved his argument aside. "I'll be there soon enough. Besides, the other two trucks in our convoy have the most urgent supplies and skills. I was just leading the group and am not critical to the immediate work there."

Alex didn't hear what she said as he looked around for a way up. He spotted what looked like an animal path cutting up through the short, shrubby trees in the area and felt sure it was the same path he'd come down on when he'd first arrived. Assuming Agnes was getting ready to head north, he shouldered his pack, smashed his Tilley on his head, and, gripping his staff, set off into the trees.

Agnes ran after him, but she'd only gone a short ways into the trees when she hit an invisible force field that knocked her backwards and caused her to cry out in surprise.

"Are you all right?" Alex called out as he ran back to her.

Agnes got up and rubbed her butt. "Yeah, but I didn't see that one coming. What's going on?"

Figuring the ankh had enabled his passage through an invisible protection spell, Alex stopped short of the force field, trying to figure out what to say and do. The uneasiness he'd been feeling for some time got worse as he looked towards the top of the pillar. Deciding he'd probably need her help up above, he said, "You'll need to snuggle up with me if you want to get through."

When Agnes didn't move, Alex stepped completely through the magical barrier and motioned her over. "Come on. I'm pretty sure it'll be okay this time."

"What the heck is going on?" Agnes asked, with a slight tremor in her voice.

"I know this is all a little strange," Alex replied. "But there's a hidden world of magic all around us that most people never see. Someone made a protective spell to keep out unwelcome guests for where we're headed."

"Where are we going? And what's there?"

"Well, I think we need to go to the top of that rock pillar," he replied, pointing straight up. "As for what's up there – I have no clue. But like that quake, I have a feeling that someone up there needs our help." Seeing she was about to ask a question, Alex said, "I can't answer all your questions, but suffice it to say that this is one of the hunches I was telling you about. And I've learned to trust them. I know none of this is what you were planning to do today, but I fear I'll need your help. Will you come with me?"

Agnes couldn't believe it when she nodded.

Alex smiled in response and said, "Get as close as you can and wrap your arms around me."

"Hold on. If you're right, I'll need my medical supplies." Agnes ran to the truck, grabbed her kit, then ran back. She tentatively stepped behind him and loosely wrapped her arms around him.

"You're going to have to get a lot closer if you want me to help you get through," Alex said.

Agnes nestled closer and said, "How are you doing this?"

Ignoring the question, Alex said, "Okay, prepare to step forward when I move. I'm going to test this, though, before I plunge in." He leaned forward and stuck his hand slowly into where he could see slightly hazy air. The familiar blue sparks lit up his arm, causing Agnes to jerk back.

Alex stopped moving and said, "Trust me. If you're going to get through, you've got to stick to me like glue. It'll only take a second, and it won't hurt."

Agnes snuggled closer and moved with him slowly through the force field, shrieking in surprised delight when they'd passed through. "That was cool. How did you do that?" she asked.

"No time to explain. We've got to get up there," Alex replied, nodding towards the top of the giant rock column.

"I should have mentioned this before, but won't we need climbing equipment?" Agnes asked.

"It should be okay, as I'm pretty sure there is a path to the top. It'll be tough going at times, though, but you can do it. Besides, think of the views we'll have from up top."

When they reached the base of the pillar, though, Alex realized he'd come down a different way, for in front of them were hundreds of shallow, narrow steps going up the rock. Despite the daunting climb ahead, Alex felt he was still on the right path. Taking a deep breath, he started up.

Alex had always thought he was comfortable with heights, but the steps up the pillar were something else, as they were much steeper than anything he'd ever climbed. And that wasn't the worst part. On his left shoulder was a rock wall. But there was nothing but air on his right shoulder – and the ground far below. The first time he paused to rest, he made the mistake of looking down, which caused a wave of vertigo to hit him. To make it worse, his dizziness caused him to keep tripping, nearly causing him to fall off the column before he caught himself.

Neither spoke for the entire ascent, as both focused on making the strenuous climb and avoiding a deadly fall. It wasn't until they were near the top that the stairs turned inward and headed up inside a narrow fissure, giving them relief from the unnerving view hundreds of feet below.

When they finally reached the top, Alex spotted a bench, not knowing it was the same one Diana had been sitting on when Erra had attacked, and headed to it for a welcome break.

Agnes plopped down beside him, panting, and said, "I hope we find an easier way down because I'm not sure I've ever been that scared in all my life."

Alex's response was to reach into his pack and pull out two chocolate power bars. Offering one to Agnes, he ripped open the wrapper and scarfed it down, hoping it would calm his nerves. As he was catching his breath, he looked around and felt his gut clench when he spotted a pair of blackened and twisted thick metal doors. Forgetting Agnes's presence, he rushed to the entrance and plunged in.

"Are you sure this is safe?" Agnes asked as she ran to catch up.

"I'm rarely sure of anything," Alex shouted over his shoulder. "But I've got a bad feeling about what happened here." He stopped when they'd gone so far down inside the column that the light from outside had almost disappeared, making it hard to see where he was going. Hastily pulling a flashlight out of his pack, he resumed his descent. When he reached the central room of the Druids, he stopped and surveyed the damage, shocked by what he saw. Holes pockmarked the walls while several blackened and twisted doors lay on the floor. But it was the dark reddish-brown spots that drew his attention.

It was some time before he could pull his eyes off the gruesome sight and notice that the ankh was pulling him to where one mangled steel door hung at a cockeyed angle. He glanced in and felt a trace of something familiar. But seeing nothing in the room, he turned to Agnes and said, "I'm sorry. This has been a wasted trip, as there's nobody here."

CHAPTER 23

THE OMPHALOS

"We can't leave here without checking to see if anybody's hurt," Agnes said.

"There's no one here," Alex replied. "You saw the doors. And those aren't rust stains on the floor – they're blood. We're trespassing on who knows whose property, and there's no telling what will happen if whoever did this comes back and finds us here. I'm telling you, we need to get out of here now."

Agnes grabbed his arm and spun him around. "You were the one who said we needed to come here."

"I know, and I'm sorry to drag you up here for nothing, but I had to check it out. You can see I was right that something happened up here. I was just wrong on timing. Now, let's go since we can't do anything here."

"You're taking this too calmly. Did you expect to see this?"

Alex took a deep breath and said, "Let's talk about this outside. I need some fresh air." Without waiting for her to respond, he headed up the steps. When he got outside, he sat on the bench and stared numbly at the valley below.

Agnes sat down beside him and asked, "What do you think happened?"

"I'm not sure, but I probably had something to do with it."

"Don't be ridiculous. You've been with me the last two days. There's no way you could've caused this."

"Well, I might not be directly involved, but I caused this somehow. You see, I never meant to come to Greece, but I happened to end up right here. On this rock. I didn't know anyone lived here at the time, but my unexpected visit must have scared whoever lived down here." He held up a hand to stall her protesting. "One thing led to another, and a few days ago, I wound up in Crete, where I surprised a bunch of women who ran away as soon as they saw me. I can't be sure, but I'd bet almost anything they came here with a valuable object. Then this happened – because of me."

Agnes frowned in disbelief. "There's no way people would run from you."

"I wish that were true. But if you don't believe me, how do you explain what's happened so far?"

"I can't, but I can assure you that you're unfairly blaming yourself for what happened here. You didn't do this. *You* didn't do anything wrong."

"I try to tell myself that, but I scare people sometimes because I get into too many strange situations. I know you've looked at me funny several times – like after the quake hit and when we got here. And before you ask. No. I can't see the future. At most, I have uneasy feelings about stuff. My grandpa said it's because I grew up in a forest and learned to listen to nature more than most." He paused, then scrunched up his face and said, "Switching subjects, a strange thought just hit me."

"What's that?"

"Well, this is going to sound strange, but you remind me of some other people I've met over the years. Which is why I can't help but wonder who you really are. And don't tell me you're just an aid worker."

"I'm nobody," Agnes replied. "I probably resemble someone you know. I get that a lot."

"No. It's the way you've gone out of your way to help me. There have been several people who popped into my life at key points and helped me in ways I couldn't have imagined before meeting them. You also have an 'old spirit' thing going on like the others, although you're the easiest one to talk to. In fact, I can't believe I've told you as much as I have. I just hope you'll forget most of it. Or at least not think I'm crazy."

"Thank you, I think," Agnes replied. "But if you think I popped up unexpectedly, how do you explain you appearing out of nowhere at the airport?"

"Na, na, na. You're trying to avoid my question."

"It's hard to know what you're talking about unless you explain who these other people are."

"Well, these two Haitians have helped me a few times, including saving my life. They're the ones who brought me back from Crete and dropped me off at the airport." He paused and studied Agnes for a bit before saying, "I know this sounds crazy because I don't see how all of you can be linked. It's just your actions and temperaments are similar."

Agnes gulped and, in a faint voice, asked, "Was one of these Haitians tall and thin and did all the talking while the other was a short taciturn type?"

"Yeah. You know Jean Paul and Francis? They're super nice guys and have saved my hide more than once."

"I've met them," Agnes replied hesitantly. Changing the subject abruptly, she said, "Right now, though, let's focus on the immediate situation – I'm starving. Let me see if I can find something for us to eat. Then, we need to head down before it gets dark. It'll be enough of a hair-raising descent, and I want to see where I'm going. We can discuss next steps when we return to the truck and have had time to process what we've seen here."

After she'd disappeared inside, Alex wondered why her hands had started shaking at his mention of Jean Paul and Francis. But he didn't have time to come up with an answer as a wave of cold air rushed over him. A second later, his sister and Ariadne apparated a few feet away, holding a large, blunt-nosed bullet-shaped object with raised decorations all over it – the same thing he'd seen in Crete.

Both ghosts had an odd mixture of fear and excitement plastered on their faces. "I'm glad you're still okay," Deborah said. "It must be some new record for you staying safe this long after one of your riskier adventures."

Alex couldn't respond as he was fighting the ankh to prevent it from pulling him off the bench in its excitement to get at the artifact. When he finally controlled it, he asked, "What is that?"

"It's the Omphalos," Deborah replied. "It's one of the Maqlû I studied about but never thought I'd see, much less hold. There were rumors our order had it in some super-secret hideaway, but I never heard where it was."

"How'd you get it?" Alex asked.

"After you escaped from the labyrinth, I followed Grandma, Diana, and the other Bandruí here and watched as some giant destroyed this place." A pained look swept across Deborah's face. She dropped her eyes and, in a sad voice, said, "I tried fighting him with my magic, but it didn't faze him."

"Who was it?" Alex asked.

"I don't know. But he was, but he was the biggest man I've ever seen," Deborah replied. "He used some magical staff to blow open those doors over there. And all we could do was watch in horror as he destroyed and killed. We couldn't even help those hurt in the attack."

"It wasn't either of your faults, Sis," Alex said. "If anybody's, it was mine, because I caused the Bandruí to leave their fortress in Crete and come here."

"You can't blame yourself either. Besides, there's no way you could have stopped him," Ariadne added. "When all of our other efforts failed – we did the next best thing – we followed him to Delphi and stole the object back. And here we are. The question now is, what will *you* do with it?"

"We'll deal with the object in a moment," Alex replied. "I want to know why you didn't move on with all your friends, Agnes. My sister and I have a theory on why she hasn't, but you? I didn't do anything to stop you, did I?"

"Of course not," Ariadne replied. "I chose not to move on because I want to make sure what happened to me never happens again. Your sister said you could eliminate the Omphalos, so here I am. But the question remains. What do we do with it?"

Alex picked up his staff and told Deborah to set it on the ground. Then he stepped over to the Omphalos and, with all his might, swung his staff at the object. He hoped it would change into the short-handled, boxy-looking hammer he'd seen twice before, but all that happened was his staff rebounded off the stone. Despite hitting it repeatedly, nothing happened. Exhausted from his futile efforts at destroying the Omphalos, Alex threw the staff down and plopped back onto the bench.

Agnes came out carrying two lunch plates just then and, seeing Alex red-faced and sweating, sitting in front of the strange, elaborately carved stone object, asked, "What happened while I was below?"

"Uh…." Alex wasn't sure how to reply. He'd already told her far more than he ever intended and was surprised he wasn't more uncomfortable with his disclosures. A faint whooshing sound hit his ears, and he looked up. An instant later, a gust of wind knocked him and Agnes over. When he looked up, Gugalanna towered over him.

"Come, Little One. I must get you away from here immediately."

"Is…is…is that a…a dragon?" Agnes asked, trying to get over the shock of seeing the fabled creature towering over her.

Alex's face turned beet red. "Surprise. I told you there was a hidden world of magic. Well, a few dragons are still living on Earth, although they're pretty good at hiding from humans. This is Gugalanna. Gugalanna, meet Agnodice."

"There's no time for introductions or explanations, Little One. The man who wrecked this place is coming for the Omphalos and will be here soon. Climb on and sit at the base of my neck. Grab whatever you can to hold on because I'm going to fly you away."

Alex ignored the surprised look on Agnes's face and said, "I'm sorry, but we're both in danger if we don't get the heck out of here."

"Hurry. We must leave now as he's not far behind me," Gugalanna said.

Alex heard the whup whup of helicopter blades getting steadily closer and hesitated for a second before shoving his pack at Agnes, grabbing her hand, and saying, "Take this and come with me."

The sandwiches she'd just made flew to the ground as she stumbled after Alex, trying to hold onto him. When they reached Gugalanna, he let go of her hand and clambered onto the dragon's back. Then he extended his hand and pulled Agnes up behind him.

Remembering the smell of Gugalanna in the arena, Alex was pleasantly surprised when he discovered the dragon had taken a bath. He settled down on the dragon's neck, laid the staff in his lap, and told Agnes, "Put my pack on and hold on tight to my staff. I can't afford to lose it, and it'll be something you can grab onto."

After some brief squirming around, Agnodice slipped on his pack then settled in snugly behind him.

Alex turned to Deborah and motioned for her to bring the Omphalos to him. He wrapped one arm around the object and, with his free hand, grabbed a handful of Gugalanna's long, shaggy hair. Alex bent low over the dragon's neck and said, "I'm ready. Let's go."

Seeing Deborah and Ariadne floating nearby, he said, "Sorry. Got to go. Bad guys coming." Before he could tell them anything else, Gugalanna stood up and started running towards the edge of the pillar, flapping his wings. The dragon leaped and dropped like a rock for a hundred feet before he started climbing. Within seconds, they were soaring into thick, billowy clouds.

The wind whistled past them, blowing away Alex's scream of delight and Agnes's shriek of terror.

CHAPTER 24

LIFE AND DEATH THEY ALLOT

As soon as Gugalanna leveled off, Alex could feel Agnes's arms relax and asked, "Are you all right?"

"I will be when we land," Agnes replied. "Aren't you afraid?"

"Only when I think about it. So, just try to forget about how high we are, relax, and try to enjoy the experience. And trust that Gugalanna will take care of us. Besides, our biggest problem will be figuring out how to stay warm. We've got a sunny day, and he's giving off a lot of heat, but the air is chilly up here, especially with the wind."

"Have you done this before?" Agnes asked.

"Only a few times, so I'm still getting used to it."

"How is it that you know about dragons? I thought they left Earth a long time ago."

"Most did, but a few chose to remain, either by choice or because they were trapped, like Gugalanna here," Alex replied. "There are also a few dragons and dragonets that come here from time to time."

"You've met one of those Ryujin pests?" Gugalanna asked. *"What was it doing here on Earth?"*

"What's with you big dragons always looking down on the Ryujins?" Alex asked. "One of them, Sadie, helps me occasionally, just like you have. The only difference I see is that your kind is a lot bigger."

"Sadie? Are you on a first-name basis with one of those things? Does she listen to anything you say?"

Alex chuckled. "I'll admit it's hard to understand what she's trying to tell me most of the time, but she's saved my life more than once."

"Who are you talking to?" Agnes shouted. "It sounds like you're having a one-sided conversation."

"Oh, I'm sorry," Alex replied. "Dragons communicate via telepathy. Gugalanna was asking me about a little dragon I know."

"Did you find out where we're going?"

"No, it didn't cross my mind to ask," Alex replied.

"Are you always this slapdash – going with the first person who shows up?" Agnes asked.

"Hey, I went with you."

"That's my point. And look where we're at."

"This is different," Alex said.

"How?"

"From my perspective, things have worked out," Alex replied. "Just look at this stone bullet-like thing I'm holding. I didn't know it at the time, but I've realized this is what I was looking for when I came to Greece."

"But you were taking a big chance trusting me. You didn't know anything about me," Agnes said.

Alex shrugged. "I get a gut feeling about whether I can trust someone. And so far, it hasn't led me astray."

There was a long silence before Gugalanna said, *"Tell your friend I'll drop you off wherever you like. After that, I plan to go home without any more delays."*

Skimming over the clouds nearly three miles above the ground, Alex asked, "Do you think it's safe to return to Meteora now? Agnodice was on the way to help some quake victims, and she needs to get to her truck."

"We could check, but if he spotted me while he's up in the air in that flying contraption, he'd catch us, as he can outfly me," Gugalanna said.

"What do you think, Agnes?"

"Think about what? You'll have to catch me up on the other half of your conversation."

Alex half turned his head and said, "Is it worth the risk of returning now so you can continue to the quake area? Whoever attacked that place had a helicopter at their disposal and is much faster than we are. If they're still around that pillar, we're done for."

"I'm not cut out for this type of life," Agnes replied. "I used to think my life was dangerous, but this is a whole nother level."

"Is there any way of determining if it's safe to return, Gugalanna?"

The dragon's answer was to dip one shoulder and make a slow turn until they leveled off and headed back the way they'd come. They'd only gone a short ways when Gugalanna angled down and landed on a remote mountaintop.

Her teeth chattering, Agnes took no time slipping down to the ground, where she backed away from the dragon towering over her, but Alex stayed on top of Gugalanna to ask, "What are we stopping here for?"

"I already took a huge chance rescuing you in daylight, but I had cloud cover and was landing on top of one of the rock pillars, far above the ground. I'd suggest we wait till dark before we return, as it's not worth risking our lives to save a couple of hours," Gugalanna said. *"We should be fine then."*

Chilled from their flight, Alex slipped off and helped Agnes build a fire. As they warmed up, Agnes looked at Alex and asked, "What's really going on? You seem to live in a fantasy world – one that the rest of us can't see."

Alex pointed to the Omphalos and said, "I can't tell you everything, in large part because I don't understand it myself, but things like this magical stone are what it's all about. A lot of people desire them and are willing to do just about anything, and I mean anything, including killing, to get them. I've seen the trouble they cause and have made a vow to do everything possible to remove them as a temptation."

"You mean destroy?"

Alex nodded. "But, they're tough to destroy. I've already tried busting this up but had no luck."

"But, why does it have to be you?" Agnes asked. "You said you're only seventeen. Surely someone else can do it."

"It doesn't have to be me, but no one else has been willing to try. Mostly because everybody wants to use these objects for themselves. Some delude themselves into believing that they will use them for good, but you saw what happened back there. I'm sure all that death and destruction was because of a desire for this thing."

"So, what are you going to do with it?" Agnes asked.

Alex chuckled.

"What's so funny?"

"I was thinking of what my friends would say to my answer. They'd just roll their eyes because they know I don't work off of detailed plans. I usually just go with the flow – trusting that things will work out – like you showing up, or Gugalanna appearing just in time, and my sister stealing this object."

"I've been meaning to ask where you found that," Agnes said. "I know you didn't have it when we climbed that rock. And I know there was nobody up there. So, how'd you get it?"

Alex grimaced trying to determine how much to tell Agnes, eventually deciding that since she'd accepted all his other strange explanations, it couldn't hurt to share one more secret. "My sister and her friend brought it. So, unless you can see ghosts, you wouldn't have been able to see them."

Agnes shook her head and said, "My, aren't we full of surprises."

Alex was glad when Gugalanna interrupted their discussion by saying, *"I think it's safe to return."*

Looking up, Alex realized they'd been talking so long that stars were beginning to appear. He stood and helped Agnes put out the fire before climbing back on Gugalanna's back with his staff and the Omphalos.

When they got close to Meteora, Gugalanna flew even higher, chilling Alex and driving him to lay on the dragon's neck to get its heat. They eventually leveled off when they were almost four miles above the ground and began circling, looking for any signs of danger. Seeing none, Gugalanna started a circular descent that made Alex a bit queasy as they sailed round and round, ever downwards, at a dizzying rate until they finally landed a few feet from the truck.

Alex got down and stood beside Agnodice. "You should get going in case that guy comes back."

"I can see now that I was nothing more than a glorified taxi driver for you," Agnes said. She held up her hand to stop him from protesting. "That's not meant as a dig. It's reality. You've said some pretty odd things in our time together, trying your best to avoid answering my questions, but I'm starting to understand why you can't tell me. Heck, I'm not sure I want to know. But I do understand that you have some destiny to follow. So, go. And do what you must. I'll be fine."

"Say your goodbyes, Little One. We must go while we can."

Alex stuck out his hand and said, "Thank you for everything you've done for me, Agnes. I couldn't have gotten this far without you. And besides, you have much more important tasks than to drive me around right now.

There are lots of people counting on your help, so you better get going."

With tears streaming down her cheek, Agnodice ignored Alex's hand and engulfed him in a hug, holding him tight for so long that he started getting uncomfortable.

Sensing his discomfort, she released him and headed to her truck. She was about to open the door when she dropped her hand and came running back to Alex, where she held out his pack and said, "I almost forgot about this." Before he could reply, she ran back to her truck and started it up.

Alex watched as Agnodice drove away and briefly thought about running after her truck and telling her he'd changed his mind. But he swallowed the lump in his throat and turned to Gugalanna.

As the truck's lights faded from view, Ariadne and Deborah appeared. "You need to leave now. That giant has been scouring the area all day, and it looks like he's headed back," Deborah said.

Alex looked at Gugalanna and asked, "Do you mind?"

The dragon snorted in reply, *"Need you ask?"*

They were soon in the air, with Gugalanna weaving in and out of the rock pillars, working his way north towards the mountains in the distance. He popped over a small ridge, then headed for a taller mountain with a rocky slope jutting out far enough that it provided cover from the Meteora complex. As soon as they were on the backside, Gugalanna started rising in elevation. Alex stuck his head into the dragon's long hair to stay warm and bury his emotions as he left safety behind once again.

CHAPTER 25

NIL DESPERANDUM

When Lady Yvaine arrived in Istanbul, she was shocked to see the Bandruí in a zombie-like state. Knowing she had to snap them out of their depression, Yvaine corralled Elizabeth and Sophie and barked, "Conference room, now." Turning to Susan Picotte, the American Indian woman who was the order's head medical officer for the Mediterranean region, she asked, "How many casualties?"

Susan winced and replied, "Half a dozen women are dead, including Hanim. And another half dozen are seriously injured. Their wounds are such that I've brought in burn specialists from the local hospitals to help us tend to them. And before you get upset about bringing in outsiders, know that I trust these women. I've worked with them before and can assure you they are some of the best in their field."

"Do what you think is right, and let me know what you need," Yvaine said. "We owe it to those women to do everything we can. Will you need Jane to help?"

Susan shook her head. "If I weren't bringing in outsiders, I'd want her. But, I think her methods and age would cause too many questions we don't want to answer."

"I understand and thank you for all that you're doing. I know they're in good hands."

As Yvaine headed away, she paused and said, "Diana, I want you there too." Surprised at being included, Diana headed after her mother and had just sat down when Jane slipped in and took a seat in the corner. Lady Yvaine kept them waiting for over ten minutes before she strode in, a thunderous look on her brow. "Who decided to move the Omphalos?" She stared at Elizabeth, then moved on to the other woman in the room, even stopping on Diana for several agonizing seconds.

At last, Elizabeth said, "It was Hanim Fatma's and my decision. We got reliable information that my grandson had arrived in Greece and was coming after the Omphalos instead of returning to his home in Colorado."

"I knew he was in Greece, as Jane and I met him in Meteora," Yvaine said. "But neither of us thought he was a threat. What made you think you needed to move the Omphalos?"

Elizabeth's eyes grew stormy. "You're forever protecting that boy. You were the only holdout at conclave last year when everybody else wanted to exact the death penalty on him for being a warlock. None of this would have happened if you'd done your duty."

"How dare you blame me for this fiasco," Yvaine stormed. "You and the others decided to move it. Not me. If you'd left it alone, it would still be safe, and no one would have died."

Elizabeth exploded. "And how do you explain my grandson finding our hideaway in Crete and coming in through the back doors?" She smiled seeing the shocked look on Yvaine's face. "Because either he's mastered the art of materializing through solid rock, or he found his way in through the labyrinth. If we hadn't taken the Omphalos away when we did, then he would have surely destroyed it. And since we all took an oath to defend the Maqlû, we would have been oath-breakers to let him do with it what he did to the Chintamani Stone. Is that what you want?"

Taken aback by Elizabeth's disclosures, Yvaine said, "Nobody told me he was involved. But I don't see how he could have gotten through the labyrinth with all our safeguards. Did he survive the Minotaur?" Yvaine asked numbly.

"Who knows?" Elizabeth replied. "Logic would say he didn't since no one else has, but we're talking about my grandson."

Lady Yvaine plopped into a nearby chair, putting her head into her hands. When she finally looked up, she addressed her question to Diana. "You're close to him. How could he do such a thing?"

"Alex didn't steal the Omphalos. I was outside our hideaway in Meteora when it all happened and saw who took it. The man was literally a giant with what looked like a wizard's staff – you know, like the ones you see in movies," Diana said. "As for how Alex broke into the labyrinth, well, your guess is as good as mine."

"A giant of a man you say? How large?"

"I didn't get a good look, because it was dark both times I saw him. But he looked to be eight to ten feet tall. He was huge," Diana said. "Why? Do you know him?"

Yvaine stared out the window and, in a faraway voice, replied, "I knew someone who matched that description, but I thought he died ages ago." She snapped out of her reverie and added, "I'll take responsibility for identifying the attacker. The rest of you should take some time off. Do whatever you need to do to grieve those we've lost."

"I know what I need to do," Sophie said. "And that's catch that boy. He had to be in league with our attacker. Otherwise, how do you explain his presence in Crete?"

Jane spoke up. "None of us can explain that. But I believe Diana - he didn't attack us in Meteora. Which means there's someone else trying to steal the Maqlû, requiring us to be more vigilant than ever. And if Alex has found two of our hideouts, what's to say others haven't."

She paused, then looked at Yvaine. "I've been thinking about this and would bet almost anything that right now, he's pursuing whoever took the Omphalos. Heck, he might already have taken it back. I suggest we send a small group of us back to Meteora, see if he returns, and learn what we can. And I, for one, am willing to go."

CHAPTER 26

THROUGH THE LOOKING GLASS

As much as he wanted to look around, Alex was afraid to loosen his grip on Gugalanna's hair as they were several miles up and still climbing. When they finally leveled out, Alex worked up the courage to look back to see if anyone was pursuing them. Seeing nothing, he relaxed his grip and asked, "Are you excited to be going home? How long has it been?"

"Almost four thousand years. But I have to tell you that I'm a little nervous because a lot can change in that time, and I don't know what to expect." Gugalanna paused, then, in a rush, said, *"I'd like you to come with me. I know it's a big ask, but our species argued about the Maqlû long before I came to this planet. I'd like you to come with me since your perspective vastly differs from what my kind has discussed."*

"You're asking me to go with you to your home planet? As in another solar system, thousands of light years away? How would we get there in my lifetime?"

A rumble from deep within Gugalanna told Alex the dragon was laughing at his question. *"You've already experienced what it's like to travel through space,"* the dragon replied.

"Huh?" Alex muttered.

"I'll let you in on a little secret about dragons. Not only do we communicate via telepathy, but we can read strong emotions in others. When we first took flight, I saw memories of your ride on Chrysophylax flash through your mind. That dark hole with the pinpricks of light you went through – that was a wormhole,"

"But that was only from Scotland to Greece," Alex replied. "It's nothing compared to space travel."

"Distance is irrelevant as wormholes essentially change the fabric of the space-time continuum and shorten the distance between two places. Some are like the one you recently traveled in, while others are like walking through a door – you go through the portal and come out instantly at the other end."

Alex didn't say anything for some time. At last, he said, "One thing I don't understand, is why did your species come here in the first place, especially considering what happened to you."

"Because of the object you carry – and others like it," Gugalanna replied. *"Twelve thousand years ago, a group of progressive dragons, including myself, got the High Council to agree to a program that had a few of us come to this planet, bringing some of the Maqlû. Our intent was to speed the transition of your species from hunter-gatherers to an advanced, peaceful, disease and poverty-free civilization.*

"Alas, it quickly became clear that humans couldn't handle all that power and knowledge. Some of the humans we trained revolted and stole the objects. I, and others, stayed on Earth to help undo the damage we had caused. But then, humans turned on my kind and began killing or imprisoning many of us. King Minos was one of those whom we trained. He used his magical object to capture and imprison me. Those women you saw when we first met were even more powerful. They overthrew Minos and became my long-term captors. But right now, I need to know if you'll accompany me. If you want to stay on Earth, I'll understand and find a place to drop you off near civilization."

"What do you expect from me?" Alex asked.

"After seeing the damage those objects have wrought on this planet and having undergone my own trauma because of that which you hold, I want the other dragons to become more active in helping me undo this mess. Your personal experience with the Maqlû would help me present a case to the High Council for intervening in human affairs so we could collect and destroy those things."

"You've thrown a lot at me, but I'm not ready to decide about anything except food, warmth, and sleep, and not in that order. Could we land someplace and talk about this some more?"

"We're not far from the portal that will take me home," Gugalanna replied. *"Could your questions wait till we're there?"*

"No. Because I can't keep going on like this. I'm so tired that I'm about to drop and can't decide about your request."

"I apologize, Little One, for not thinking about your needs in my haste to return home." Gugalanna banked into a looping downward spiral, looking for a place to stop. A few minutes later, he landed in a small clearing at the top of a narrow, forested valley. As soon as the dragon had folded his wings, Alex jumped down and started beating his arms to warm up.

"Gather some firewood, and I'll start a fire so you can warm yourself," the dragon said. *"The heat should quickly warm you, if you use me as a backstop."*

"Can dragons breathe fire?"

The low rumbling sound emanating from Gugalanna's belly sounded suspiciously like laughter. *"Hardly. Remember, I told you we taught humans how to control the elements? The fire that seems to be emanating from our mouths is just us pulling enormous amounts of heat out of the air around us and turning it into fire."*

Alex, who'd been gathering wood, dumped it on the ground, then selected a few smaller pieces and set them up in a teepee fashion. As soon as he pulled his hand away, the wood began to crackle and burn. Getting close, Alex stuck his hands out to warm up, then slowly turned around, trying to roast his chills away. When he'd finally gotten warm again, Alex searched inside his pack for some snacks and water, then sat between Gugalanna's front legs while staring at the dancing flames, as he tried to figure out what he should do.

When he'd finished eating, Alex said, "I understand what you're saying, but I don't see how I can help."

"I know how hard it has been for my species to find the Maqlû after the Atlantians stole them, but it seems you have a knack for it, as evidenced by the one you have with you," Gugalanna said. *"That gives you instant credibility, which should help convince the High Council to mount a concerted effort to find and destroy the rest of these objects. If we're successful, no one will ever have to go through what I have again, and we can remove the cause of some of the violence here on Earth."*

"Just how far is this planet of yours?" Alex asked.

"A little under 1,300 light-years." Seeing the blank look on Alex's face, Gugalanna added, *"Almost 8,000 trillion miles."*

"Are you sure this wormhole will work, because I don't see how anyone can go that far since nothing can go faster than the speed of light? And with that distance, I'd turn to dust long before we arrived, or die from lack of oxygen."

"Even though a lot of scientists believe you can't go faster than light – they're wrong," Gugalanna said. *"For*

instance, galaxies beyond the observable universe appear to be moving faster than the speed of light. It's a paradox that no one has adequately explained yet, but don't worry. We'll be using a tethered wormhole that will get us there almost instantaneously. And as for oxygen, you'll be fine. I'm not sure how it works, but apparently, the wormhole sucks in enough air to provide our needs for the short time we'll be in it."

"Will we need some type of starship to go through it?" Alex asked.

"No. Think of yourself as a mass of atoms. When the portal opens, your body will be sucked in. The portal at the other end of the wormhole acts as a magnet and pulls you through. Besides, my species has been traveling through wormholes for millennia without protective gear."

"Are you sure it'll take us to the right place? There was this one time in Romania when I stepped over a creek and felt like I'd entered a different world. But, what was even weirder was when I left, I ended up a thousand miles away and had somehow lost almost a year, even though it had only been a couple of days to me."

"That sounds like you stumbled into some sort of space-time distortion," Gugalanna said. *"But don't worry about this trip. I've made it many times and have always had the same experience. It'll only take a few minutes once I get it open."*

"How did your species figure out how to make the wormholes?"

"We didn't. They already existed when we began to explore space. We know they're not naturally occurring phenomena, but we don't know who made them or when. And as for time distortion – don't worry about it. You'll enter at one end of the wormhole and exit at the other end

a short time later. Whoever built them had vastly superior technology than we do. If they hadn't existed, we would never have left our home planet of Berellus."

Alex shook his head. "I've done some crazy stuff, but traveling across the universe is a different ballgame. Do you mind if I sleep on it?"

"Take your time. I've been gone this long, so a few more hours won't make any difference."

"One other thing. Shouldn't we be worried about someone seeing you? We can't go gallivanting around because people will freak out if they see a flying dragon."

"Don't worry," Gugalanna replied. *"We'll travel at night, and I'll use a glamour spell that bends light so people won't see us. Now go to sleep, and we'll talk in the morning."*

When Alex woke up, it was still dark, and his backside was cold. He tried snuggling into Gugalanna for warmth but found he was missing. Alex jumped up and looked around for the dragon but didn't spot him. Just when he was about to go in search of him, he heard a beating of wings, followed a few seconds later by Gugalanna.

"Thank God you're still here. I thought you'd deserted me."

"I apologize if I worried you. I went hunting – and no, it wasn't humans. I just had a couple of sheep. Besides, I'd never desert you. I owe you for freeing me from slavery. But that leads me to the big question. Have you decided what you're going to do yet?"

Alex looked at the Omphalos sitting a few feet from where the fire was, took a deep breath, and shook his head.

He could hear the dejection in the dragon's voice as Gugalanna said, *"I understand. I'll take you someplace closer to civilization, but I can't drop you off in a city or anything."*

"You misunderstand. I was shaking my head because I was telling myself that I'm crazy for thinking of going with you. After all, what's a little space travel after everything else I've experienced."

"That's wonderful. Are you ready to go, because I can't wait to go home?"

"What about people seeing us?"

"We'll be fine. It'll be dark for a little while longer, and we'll be going over remote terrain. We should be safe with the clouds, darkness, and my glamour spell. Besides, in a couple of hours, we'll be gone."

"Then hold on. I've got to take care of a little business, then have something to eat," Alex said. "By the way, what will I do about food on your planet?"

"We're mostly meat eaters, but we have fruits and other nutritious plants, so don't worry. You won't starve. But we need to get going and take advantage of the darkness. Just let me know when you're ready."

Half an hour later, they took off and headed in a northeasterly direction just as the eastern sky started to lighten. "Going through the wormhole won't hurt, will it?" Alex asked.

"No, but everyone has a different sensation. Just try to relax because we're not far from the portal."

"Where is it?"

"On Mt. Olympus," Gugalanna replied.

"The same mountain that was home to the ancient Greek and Roman gods?" Alex asked.

"Yes. Given our powers and the fact that we used the mountain as our primary opening to and from your world, it makes sense that they created imaginary gods with powers like ours."

A short time later, they reached the flanks of Mt. Olympus, and Gugalanna started circling the mountain, looking for the portal he hadn't seen in millennia. *"You should be aware that the portals are fickle, and we may have to wait for hours before I can open it,"* the dragon said,

Alex thought about sharing his discussion with Chrysophylax on the same subject but decided to keep it to himself, since he wasn't sure what would happen.

Gugalanna suddenly pulled up and hovered, staring intently at a spot less than ten yards away.

"Are you sure this is the right place? It looks like it's only rocks and snow…." Alex's sentence trailed off as he saw the rocks slowly moving apart and a pinprick of black appear. He watched in fascination as a mechanical iris slowly drew back the sides of the mountain, showing a dark hole with tiny pinpricks of light inside.

"I didn't expect it to open this quickly, so hold on. We're going in," Gugalanna roared.

For the first second, it felt like flying on Earth. Then something seized Alex and yanked him forward, making him feel like he'd left his arms and legs behind. The eerie sensation lasted only a few seconds before all parts of his body seemed to catch back up with his torso. Whatever was happening, it felt like Gugalanna had disappeared, and he was alone, floating freely in space.

The stars, just pinpricks of light before entering the wormhole, ranged from tiny red dwarfs to giant blue ones. He figured he should pay attention to what he was doing rather than look at them, but he was too awed to take his eyes off the fiery balls of gas as they zipped by. They went faster and faster, twisting and turning as if they were on a giant slippery slide, eventually causing the stars to look like a stream of colored lights.

He began enjoying himself so much that he was disappointed when they burst into another world where the oppressive heat and humidity made it hard to breathe.

Sensing Alex's discomfort, Gugalanna said, *"It'll take time to adjust to this place as it's much warmer than most places on Earth. You'll also feel sluggish here, as our planet has about 30% greater mass than Earth, thus making the gravity that much stronger."*

Wanting to take his mind off his discomfort, Alex looked around and saw they were amid seven giant mountains that ringed a huge valley over 20,000 feet below. His sightseeing abruptly ended when Gugalanna let out a deafening roar, forcing Alex to clap his hands over his ears. When the sound of the dragon's call stopped reverberating, Alex lowered his hands and asked, "Now what?"

"I just announced our arrival. Now we wait for someone to escort us to the High Council chambers, where the elders will determine if they'll accept you as a guest."

"Wait a minute. You never told me I had to go through some inspection. What happens if they don't like me? Will someone gobble me up or kick me back into that wormhole we just came through?"

"Relax. Although visitors are rare here, they're not unheard of; at least, that's how it used to be. They'll want to understand your purpose for visiting, but it should go smoothly after all you've accomplished. And since I was the one who asked you here, I'll do the talking."

"How long will that take?" Alex asked.

"I don't know. It could be days, weeks, or months before they see us. It depends on the High Council's mood. We live such long lives that it's rare for anything

to happen speedily. But I believe they'll rush their deliberations along because of the object you brought."

"Months! I can't be gone that long as I never told my grandpa I was leaving. And besides, I lost almost a year last time I did this type of thing."

He didn't get a reply as a loud bugle echoed through the circle of mountains. A moment later, a dark green dragon, slightly larger than Gugalanna with a large ruff, burst through a gap between two peaks directly across from where they were and flew towards them. When she was a hundred yards away, the green dragon stopped and said, *"I am Vasuki, and I've come to take you to the High Council. Please follow me."*

"I thought you didn't expect them to come this fast," Alex said. "This isn't giving me a warm and fuzzy feeling."

"I don't know what to say, as I never expected to see the High Council this soon.

They flew out of the ring of mountains and towards an immense cliff off in the distance that towered thousands of feet into the air. Vasuki dipped and headed straight for a large opening in the middle of the cliff face. Gugalanna followed her in and landed seconds after her.

It took a few moments for Alex's eyes to adjust to the dim lighting inside. When he could finally see, the sight took his breath away. Perched almost twenty feet above them on a rock ledge that curved around the chamber over fifty feet away were half a dozen dragons peering down.

"Bring forth the accused," boomed a voice in Alex's head.

CHAPTER 27

TWO FORCES

"You lied to me," Alex screamed.

"This isn't what I expected," Gugalanna replied, half-hopping, half-flying towards the High Council. Voicing his outrage to the dragons above him, he screamed, *"I demand to know why my friend and rescuer is on trial here. He's my guest."*

"Much has happened since you've left, Gugalanna," said the shimmering green dragon in the middle of the council, who was the same size as Vasuki but without the ruff. *"We've outlawed all humans because they've caused too much damage to our kind – instigating insurrection on Earth, then hunting us down. They're a lawless species, full of violence and greed. We cannot allow them to contaminate our culture. This trial is to decide what to do about that creature you brought with you."*

"But, Gaia, he's done nothing wrong. He freed me." Pointing to the Omphalos Alex was holding, he added, *"And he spirited this object away from Erra – you know, the giant Atlantian who participated in the revolt? Most importantly, although he doesn't know how to do it yet, he intends to destroy the object, as he has three others. I support that goal, so I convinced him to come here to get your help in finding the other Maqlû."*

A murmur among the high council members followed, allowing Alex the chance to study the dragons towering over him. He'd always thought humans were diverse, but the dragons made human diversity look lame.

On the far left was a seven-headed bronze-colored dragon with tiny wings extending off each neck. Next to him was a blue dragon with wings so large Alex thought they must scrape the ground when she walked. But it wasn't her size that made her fearsome-looking – it was the large ruff behind her head with a series of needle-like spines spreading beyond her neck. Next in line was a large dragon, not quite as big as the blue dragon, but one who looked much more powerful. His chest was bronze colored, which highlighted his reddish-brown back and wings. What fascinated Alex the most about the dragon were the two horns sloping back from its head and the spiked club at the end of his tail, much like a stegosaurus. Gaia, the dragon who'd called the council to order, was in the middle, flanked by a huge dragon, nearly as big as Abraxas, with scarlet and black tiger stripes along its body and gold-colored eyes that seemed to spit fire. Next to him was the second smallest one of the group, a golden dragon with spikes sticking out around all sides of its neck. As fearsome as the other dragons appeared, though, Alex was most concerned with the dragon on the far right. He was the smallest of the group, half the size of Gugalanna, with tan and black scales and a single horn poking out of the middle of its head, giving it the appearance of a unicorn. But it was the malevolent look in its eyes – something he didn't see in the others, that scared him.

Alex finished studying the members of the High Council and said, "What type of justice is this? You act like you're superior to my species, but from my perspective, you're acting just like humans – condemn first, ask questions later. So how does that make you any better than us? You're just bigger. And as Gugalanna said, I didn't want to come here. I only did it at his request to add my voice to ask you for help destroying those horrible magical objects. I understand some of you were responsible for sending those things to Earth. Do you know how much harm you've caused by that decision? Aren't you going to hold yourself responsible for your role in the mess?"

Gaia replied, *"Are you done ranting? Like all humans, you have no patience."*

"I have no patience! Are you listening to yourself? You should take a cue from our human system and presume I'm innocent until you prove me guilty – of whatever you're going to charge me with."

"Silence!" Gaia roared so loudly that Alex had to clap his hands over his ears to block out the noise. *"We're the ones who taught you that concept thousands of years ago, or at least tried to. We're the ones who raised you out of the muck you once lived in. We gave you the knowledge to jump-start your civilization, saving you countless millennia of struggling to survive. And you come here acting as if we're doing you some disservice."*

"I said you're not being fair. I also said the Maqlû you sent to my planet have caused nothing but problems. I'm asking you to own up to your mistakes and help me fix the problem."

The sly-looking dragon on the far right interrupted and, in a seductive voice, said, *"You're right. I apologize for our rudeness of jumping into these proceedings. Perhaps we should introduce ourselves first. My name is Thoth. On your far left is Ladon, followed by Tintaglia, Vermitrax, and Gaia, the head of this council. Then Drakon and Glaurung. We have asked you here, and I emphasize the word asked, because we have banned non-terrestrials from coming to our planet after some rather unfortunate incidents with your kind. Your sudden appearance with one of the causes of the rebellion against us is unnerving."*

"I'm sorry for yelling at you," Alex said. "But meeting all of you hasn't been easy. You're intimidating. Especially since there's only been three dragons whom I've met that haven't tried killing me."

Tintaglia edged forwards and asked, *"Who are you talking about? I thought those who chose to stay behind have shied away from all human contact."*

"In general, that's true," Alex replied. "But, one way or another, they all seemed tied to those blasted magical objects. The first dragon I met, Chrysophylax, has saved my life more than once. He treated me a lot better than his mother, Abraxas, who tried killing me."

Drakon flapped his wings restlessly. *"What do you know about Abraxas?"*

"Only that she tried killing me on sight, even though I didn't do anything to her. By the way, is she all right? I know some human ghosts attacked her and hurt her badly. I tried helping her, but she flew off, and I never saw her again."

"If you're the human who saved her, then we owe you a debt of gratitude. You begin to interest me, Little One. Who else have you met?" Gaia asked.

"I didn't actually meet Kraken, which I'm glad of because he was pretty mad. But I would've joined him on the bottom of the sea if it weren't for Chrysophylax calming him down. I've also met Apalāla, who helped me find one of the Maqlû. And then there's Sadie."

One of the seven heads of Ladon asked, *"Who, Sadie?"*

"She's a Ryujin dragonet who has helped me a few times. But who I've met isn't important. What's important is that each of them has been supportive of me destroying the Maqlû, as those things have hurt your kind almost as much as they've hurt us."

"Which of the objects have you destroyed?" Thoth asked warily.

Alex cringed and asked, "Are you going to be mad?"

"Answer my question. Which ones have you ruined?" Thoth asked. *"They should've been indestructible."*

"Just the Palantir, Pair Dadeni, and the Chintamani Stone. But in my defense, two were accidents as I tried keeping them away from madmen who wanted to abuse their powers." There was a long pause before Alex said, "And if I live through this, I intend to take the Omphalos back to Earth and figure out how to destroy it, too. Then I'll seek out and destroy the rest of the Maqlû."

A silence descended over the chamber. Alex could sense a slight vibration in his head but had no idea what it was. He turned to Gugalanna and asked, "What's going on?"

"They're deliberating what to do next. I don't think they expected to hear what they did. And I'm sorry for getting you into this mess. I should have checked things out before asking you to come with me. A lot has changed since I was last here."

The buzzing stopped in his head, causing Alex to turn back and look at the seven dragons deciding his fate. They all looked as fierce and determined as when he'd first arrived, except for Glaurung, who caught him off guard by winking at him.

Gaia's voice unexpectedly popped inside Alex's head, causing him to jump. *"We, The Berellian High Council, have decided to absolve you of all charges, but you may not remain here. Traversing space can be wearisome, so we'll allow you to stay one day to recuperate before we send you back to your planet."*

"But what about the remaining Maqlû? Are you going to help us destroy them?" Alex asked.

"No. They can still be useful to us, so we're keeping the one you brought here," Gaia replied, *"Our judgment is final. We will send you back tomorrow. Vasuki will find a suitable place for you to stay the night. As for Gugalanna, it's our decision that no Berellian will ever return to Earth. Those still there are welcome to come home should they do so. Some decent examples of humanity might be left, but we don't care. Humans have caused us enough trouble over the years, and we never want to deal with your species again. Now go. Leave us in peace."*

"You're making a mistake," Alex shouted at them as Vasuki nudged Alex towards the exit. "I don't know how, when, or who, but these objects will come back to bite you. You'll regret ignoring them."

His last words wafted over the valley as Vasuki picked him up with her front claws and flew out.

CHAPTER 28

IN UNLIKELY PLACES

Vasuki unceremoniously dumped Alex on a narrow ledge a few hundred yards away from the portal he'd arrived through, before flying off.

Looking around, he saw he was several thousand feet above the valley floor on a steep, densely forested ridge. The trees on the mountainside were like nothing he'd ever seen on Earth, as giant redwood-like conifers intermixed with huge palm-like trees and fronds, large enough that they could swallow a person. He considered working his way across a cut in the mountain to the nearby portal and escaping Berellus before the dragons could return, but the underbrush was too thick, forcing him to give up before making it very far. With no way to escape his predicament, he set down his pack and staff, found a spot to rest, and waited for what was to come.

Between the emotional turmoil he'd just gone through and the oppressive heat and gravity, he grew sluggish, and before he knew it, he'd fallen asleep. He wasn't sure how long he was out, but when he awoke, he found food lying on a giant leaf a few feet away. It was mostly cooked meat, but wasn't anything he was familiar with. It did have an object that looked like a pear, some vegetable-like things, and some water in a large gourd. He hesitated for only a few seconds before gingerly trying some of the meat. Discovering it was some of the tastiest food he'd ever eaten, whatever it was, he dug in. As he ate, the shadows from the setting sun crept up the mountainside, slowly turning the western sky into a brilliant sea of orange. He was so looking forward to seeing how different Berellus' nighttime sky was from Earth's that he didn't hear the sound of flapping wings coming towards him.

Chrysophylax landed on the ledge a minute later and whispered, *"Hurry, get on my back. You need to come to my uncle's lab so he can talk with you. And we don't have much time as I must get you back before morning when Vasuki will come to send you back to Earth."*

Alex barely had time to grab his pack and staff before they were flying away. An hour later, they set down on a wide ledge on one of the mountains in the next range over from the portals. Chrysophylax didn't wait for Alex to slide down before he strode to a large opening and went inside.

A long reptilian dragon with a row of spikes down its back met them, an anxious look in his eyes. *"Did you have any problems? Did anyone see you?"*

"No, Uncle. I did like you told me. Besides, I got pretty good on Earth slipping into and out of places while following the boy." He twisted his long neck around and said, *"This is my Uncle Nabu. He was the one who sent the ankh to Earth centuries ago in an attempt to stop the misuse of the Maqlû."*

Nabu limped closer to Chrysophylax and asked, *"Where's the Omphalos? Even though I studied it for years, I've been looking forward to seeing it again."*

Alex, who'd been studying the cavernous workshop, giant tables, and strange-looking instruments surrounding him, snapped out of his reverie and replied, "The High Council took it."

"We must get it back and hide it," Nabu said.

"Hey. I don't have wings to get around, so don't look for me to snatch it back," Alex said. "Besides, aren't you worried you'll get into trouble if someone finds us together?"

"Go easy on him, Little One," Chrysophylax said. *"This has been a trying day for both of us. My uncle is our world's foremost scientist and has been trying to figure out how the Maqlû work since long before I was born. He even helped an Irkallan girl write a book on each of them. So, imagine how he feels at having one of the objects he's devoted his life to studying suddenly snatched away, just when he thought he'd get another chance to study it."*

Alex slid off Chrysophylax and walked over to Nabu. "Would the books you mentioned be metal bound with a steel rod spine and a bunch of concentric circles on the cover?"

"You've seen one of the *Sibylline Books?*" Nabu asked.

"A few, but I wouldn't worry about them as they're not very useful in getting rid of those objects."

"What do you mean? If you didn't use the books, how did you know how to destroy the Palantir?" Nabu asked.

"It was an accident. I was fighting with some ghost over it and happened to grab his magical staff and kablooey. It blew apart."

"And the Pair Dadeni?"

Alex cringed. "I was holding it, and it just spontaneously combusted. As for the Chintamani, well, that was completely on me. I didn't want a spirit to get it, so I threw it into a pot of molten lava."

"Have you tried destroying the Omphalos?"

"Yeah. I beat it with this magical staff I found, but the only thing that happened was my hands got numb from the reverberations."

"May I see it," Nabu asked, nodding at Alex.

"What, the staff? I don't know what you can learn about it as its powers come and go."

"I meant the ankh. You needn't hide it, as I studied it for ages."

Alex reluctantly pulled out the little looped cross and held it up. "I hope you know more about it than I do because it still mystifies me. It has guided me to the Maqlû, helped me talk to spirits, and even saved my life a few times. But it seems to have a mind of its own at times and often leads me into trouble."

"Interesting. No one who has ever worn it has talked about it that way. The Irkallan girl who found it believed that the same, unknown species who built the wormhole gateways also made the ankh and the Maqlû. But neither of us ever figured out its main purpose. It was the girl's idea to send the ankh to your planet in the hopes it would lead us to the Maqlû, which it has, although not in the way we expected. We used some of the equipment you see around you to track its progress as the girl believed the ankh would eventually find its way to its rightful owner, who would then help us retrieve the Maqlû so that we could safely guard them. We thought it would be your sister who unlocked the ankh's powers, but I lost all communication with it when you took it – which is when I sent Chrysophylax to your planet to learn what happened."

"You mean you are one of the primary culprits for turning my life upside down and driving my dad, grandpa, and my other ancestors crazy? Who is this person you partnered with to cause this mess?" Alex demanded.

"Her name was Sibyl," Nabu replied. *"I believe she died some time ago on Earth."*

"Sibyl! You mean that woman whose voice in my head keeps goading me forward, encouraging me to risk my life for those blasted objects? She's the one you partnered with?"

"You know her?" Nabu asked incredulously.

"A little. We talk once in a while, but she never shows herself. None of that's important, though. You still haven't explained why I'm here."

"I wanted to discuss what to do with the Omphalos and your cross."

"Just to be clear – you're not going to do anything with my ankh," Alex said. "I'm keeping it because I need it to find and destroy the rest of the Maqlû. But, since I'm here, I'm interested in learning what you know about it because, like I said, I'm still trying to figure it out."

Nabu sighed. *"Fine, but there's not enough time to tell you everything, as Chrysophylax will need to take you back soon. First, you need a little background. You should also understand that nobody knows when, where, or who made it. Sibyl found the ankh on her home planet of Irkalla and fled with it to here. The two of us joined up and started studying the Maqlû."*

"She arrived at a critical juncture in our species history, for after countless thousands of years of sedentary life, some of us were growing restless and left this world searching for some greater meaning to life. Gaia, the current leader of our High Council, was the one who discovered your planet. "The Ice Ages had just ended on Earth. There were no buildings, no farming, and no civilization. Mortality rates were astronomically high as your species was barely eking out an existence. So, she proposed a plan to jump-start your progress.

"She gathered some like-minded dragons, led us to your planet, and set us to work. We knew we couldn't teach everyone, so we selected the most promising humans and began teaching them how to plant crops and build homes in the Mesopotamian area of your planet. The results were rather spectacular. In 10,000 BCE,

humans were solely hunter-gatherers. Only four hundred years later, people had started farming and living in small villages.

"But from there, progress slowed as humans weren't ready to make bigger jumps in their evolution. So, we brought the most promising humans in our program to a remote island in the Atlantic Ocean called Atlantis, where we conducted more aggressive breeding and education programs.

"You're kidding. Atlantis was real?" Alex exclaimed.

"Indeed it was – just as many of your other myths were. Eventually, we achieved what we were aiming for – genetically superior humans in intelligence, health, and physical attributes. Then we began breeding those individuals to bring out specific abilities we thought would help humanity even more. When we felt we had reached the critical mass of talented humans, we endowed them with unnaturally long life, extraordinary intelligence, and the ability to manipulate the elements – or as you call it, magic – all in the hope they'd use these talents to help their fellow humans.

"Gaia's next step, though, was a step too far, and the downfall of the program. She proposed we loan the Maqlû to the Atlantians to help them progress even faster. But a group of humans banded together and stole the Maqlû because they thought we were holding back your species. Tragically, most of the humans we'd been training for ages died in a cataclysmic disaster caused by one of the objects.

"The situation became untenable for us when the Atlantians, who had escaped the cataclysm and having moved out into the populace at large, started hunting us down. It wasn't long before we stopped all our efforts and retreated to this planet. Thinking they could minimize the

damage, a few of our kind remained behind. But it was too late. Eventually, those who stayed gave up, too. We never made another attempt to help humans. The Council was shocked you'd met several of us – because the dragons who remained on Earth have shunned all human interaction."

"That's all fascinating, but you still haven't explained why you brought me here," Alex said.

"I'm getting to that. You see, I don't believe your species can ever rise above the mess you're in today. You will always be petty, greedy, and power-hungry, which leads to the constant wars your world undergoes. And the Maqlû only make the situation worse, which is why I beg you to find the remaining objects and bring them back here where I can safeguard them."

"But earlier, you said it was bad that the High Council had the Omphalos. Now you're saying you're glad I brought it and want the rest of the Maqlû. Which is it?"

"I don't want the High Council to have the Maqlû anymore than I want humans to," Nabu replied.

"How would it be different than the last time you had them?" Alex asked. "Your species wants the Maqlû, just like mine. But I've come to believe that no one should have them as they corrupt their owners. Which is why, one way or another, I will figure out a way to destroy the Maqlû, including the one your High Council took from me."

"I don't understand. If you don't trust us, why did you bring the Omphalos to Berellus?" Nabu asked.

"I didn't have much choice," Alex replied. "I'd just gained possession of it when Gugalanna asked me to come here and ask for help. I couldn't leave it on Earth, knowing a bunch of people were after it. And, since you guys had the objects for a long time, I figured it would be safe here. Plus, I thought one of you could tell me how to get rid of it."

"I agree with the boy, Uncle. We should help him destroy the objects, not bring them here. They're too tempting for either of our species," Chrysophylax said.

Nabu sighed. *"I hate admitting it, but I suppose you're right. The thing is, I don't know how to control those objects any more than you do. When I heard the Omphalos was back on this planet, my first instinct was to study it more, as I've never understood how any of the objects worked. It's why I helped Sibyl document everything we knew about each object – hoping we could someday control their powers. But we lost all that knowledge when the humans revolted and stole the objects and books. The only good thing that came out of all that was the knowledge that we put impenetrable safety features on the books so no one could use them."*

"Well, the books aren't impenetrable," Alex said. "But, if it makes you feel any better, they're not useful either. About the only thing they're good for are the maps showing the objects' general location."

"You figured out how to open them?" Nabu managed to stutter,

"Well, one at least. I saw a couple of others but didn't bother looking inside them as I figured they were more of the same. Now, if you would've put in a section about how to destroy them, then they would've been useful."

Chrysophylax interrupted the discussion, saying, *"Uncle, we need to leave soon to avoid anyone spotting us."*

Nabu shook his great head. *"You're right,"* he said. *"It's just that I'm still trying to get my mind wrapped around the situation. I have spent so much time trying to understand the ankh and the Maqlû, and now it seems to have been a waste of time as the boy's experience invalidates much of what I thought was true. But you're right. You must return to the portal so Vasuki can send you back to Earth. If you're not where you're supposed to be when she comes to get you, all hell will break loose."*

"That's it? This whole trip was a waste of time," Alex growled. "I wish I hadn't come here. Then, at the very least, I could've gotten a good night's sleep and not felt like I was going to be dragon chow."

As Alex was about to step up onto Chrysophylax's leg, Nabu said, *"Wait. There is one more thing, although I hate sharing this, as it goes against everything I've worked towards for the last few millennia. But I may know a way which would enable you to destroy the Omphalos."*

Alex stepped back down and waited expectantly for Nabu to proceed.

"I can't be positive, but Sibyl once thought that one could destroy the Omphalos by throwing it into the heart of an active volcano. As for how you destroy the rest of the objects – I don't know. My advice would be to find Pandora, if she is still alive. She would probably have the information you are looking for on how to destroy the Maqlû.

"And where can I find her?" Alex asked.

"That's the problem. The last place anybody saw her was in Atlantis. I fear she's been dead for centuries."

"Well, that's just dandy," Alex said sarcastically. "What you're suggesting is find a place that few believe exist and talk to a dead person. That doesn't sound like a recipe for success." Crestfallen he shook his head and added, "I wish you would've destroyed them when you had a chance. It would have saved so much pain and suffering."

"You sound a lot like Sibyl's friend. She believed, as you do, that we should have destroyed the Maqlû. Alas, she died in the Atlantis cataclysm with her object, known to your species as Pandora's Box, going with her to a watery grave. But enough of the history. You must go now. I will search for a way to help you, but I must be careful of the High Council members. Many have tried helping humans and now regret their actions."

Chrysophylax told Alex to mount. *"I'm sorry, Uncle, but I have to get him back. I know you wanted more time with him, but a journey begins with the first step. And that means getting him back through the wormhole."* They lifted off just as the cliffs on the far side of the valley started turning orange-red as the Berellian sun rose in the sky.

The opalescent dragon had barely flown out of sight when Vasuki appeared. The dark green dragon bellowed, "The boy is gone. Where is he?"

For the first time in his life, Nabu lied. *"I haven't seen him."*

With a roar, Vasuki took off and headed back towards the portals.

CHAPTER 29

ONLY THE DEAD

The deserts of Berellus were lifeless realms where no plant or animal life could survive the harsh conditions. Yet, on the smallest continent on the planet, in the middle of the largest desert on the planet, was a structure. It sat behind a ridge to shelter it from the prevailing winds that hurled bits of sand across the landscape so fiercely that it would tear apart any unwary traveler. The building – shack was a more accurate description, although sparsely decorated, had everything essential for a person's survival.

Only one person lived there – a man with wrinkled, leathery, ebony-colored skin, pepper-colored hair, and a hunched back. He had beady black eyes and a scar that cut across his face, giving him a Frankenstein-like look. His only visitors were an occasional dragon who would drop off food and other supplies that would last him until the next time there was a break in the almost constant sandstorms. There was never any communication between the man and his captors, as the supplying dragon would instantly take off after dropping the supplies, to avoid the storms.

He'd lived a solitary life in these harsh conditions for over three centuries when a dragon landed outside and shouted, *"We need to talk."*

"Unless you're bringing me some prime steaks and better reading material, go away," Gilgamesh shouted. "None of you have cared to talk with me for centuries. Why start now?"

184

"There has been a development that aligns our interests. And yes, I did bring some extra supplies, although no steaks."

Gilgamesh opened the door and looked out. It took him a moment to recover from his surprise. "Thoth? What are you doing here?"

"I told you there has been a development."

"Does the High and Almighty Council know you're here?"

"No. And I suggest you don't mention this visit to any of the supply dragons. We would both be in trouble if anybody found out I was here – but you more than me."

"I understand your meaning. Get to the point," Gilgamesh replied. "Why are you here?"

"A young human arrived on our planet recently, bearing one of the Maqlû and asking us to help him find and destroy the remaining objects," Thoth replied. *"He claims he's already destroyed three."*

"Ah. That explains why I've been feeling older all of a sudden. You've got to stop him. If you don't, all hell will break loose."

"Relax. We've already confiscated the object he brought and will keep it here. And you can rest assured we will never support him. He's playing into my hands by reopening the discussion on the Maqlû. It's the opportunity I've been waiting for. With a bit of persuasion and a dash of fear-mongering, I'm sure I can get the High Council to back an expedition to recover the remaining Maqlû."

"Do you know why the boy is so hell-bent on destroying them?" Gilgamesh asked.

"He believes they've caused too many problems on Earth," Thoth replied.

"What have you done with the boy? Have you disposed of him?"

"No. The High Council wants nothing to do with humans or the objects and is sending him back to Earth."

"I can't believe you're sending him back to where he can continue his wanton destruction of the most precious objects in the universe. What madness is this?" Gilgamesh screamed. "You can't let him destroy the remaining Maqlû while you do nothing to stop him. Remember, your kind wanted the Maqlû just as much as we did. What are you going to do about it?"

"Nothing. This is where you come in. When I talked about sending an expedition to Earth to retrieve the objects, I was thinking about you," Thoth said.

"How?" Gilgamesh threw his hands out and pointed at the stark landscape. "You've seen to it that I can never escape this hellhole. I wouldn't survive a day in the desert surrounding me. Either I'd die of dehydration, or more likely, the wind would flay me alive. And even if I could escape from here, I'd need a way back to Earth – through one of your wormholes, which your kind would never allow me to use."

"That's all true, unless you had someone helping you – someone who could carry you off this continent to one of the portals," Thoth replied.

Gilgamesh narrowed his eyes. "What's in it for you? You aren't doing this out of the goodness of your spiteful dragon heart."

"I would expect to split the Maqlû with you. You go back. Stop the boy. Find the remaining objects, and call me. I'll come and retrieve my share and let you go on your merry way. We need never meet again after you do that."

"How can I trust you'll follow through on your end of the bargain?"

"I don't need all the Maqlû. I just need a couple to eliminate my enemies on the High Council. However, to ensure you follow through on your end of the bargain and don't double-cross me, I'll put a tracking bracelet on you that will monitor your movements and kill you if I find you ever try to cheat me. I hope you're smart enough to see it would be a win-win if we work together. I could care less what you do after we part ways, though I assume world domination is your goal – like it is mine. Do we have a deal?"

Gilgamesh studied Thoth, trying to determine what the catch was. At last, realizing he didn't have any other option except to die in the hellhole he'd been living in for centuries, he said, "Deal. How soon do you think this could happen?"

"I do not have your escape plan finalized yet because I wanted to see if you were open to this deal before I made final arrangements. But our meteorologist forecasts that there will be a window of opportunity to return here in about two weeks. So be ready. Do you need me to get anything ready for your escape?"

Gilgamesh shook his head. "Food, water, and a way off this god-forsaken planet are all I need. I'm glad you finally came to your senses and enlisted my help. I always thought you had it in you because you had a different perspective than the others of your kind."

"I don't know if I should take that as a compliment," Thoth said.

"From me, it's a compliment. But, if this is to work, you better get going, for I feel a major sandstorm coming." Before Thoth could say anything else, Gilgamesh ducked back into his shelter.

CHAPTER 30

DARKNESS IS YOUR CANDLE

Diana had thought the flight from Greece to Istanbul was quiet, but the return flight to Meteora was more somber than anything she'd ever experienced. She wasn't sure how much of it was dread at going back to the scene of the catastrophe, and how much of it was the blistering scolding they'd had from Lady Yvaine for losing the Omphalos. Even Jane, the least discomposed of the group, was quiet during the trip, although she kept looking over as if she wanted to talk about something.

Diana spent the first few days in Meteora helping clean and repair the damage from the attack and was pleasantly surprised at how therapeutic the work was as it helped her slowly wash away her mental wounds. But it wasn't until the end of the week, at the end of a long, tiring day, that Jane finally approached Diana as she sat on a boulder overlooking the brightly lit valley and sat beside her. Neither said anything for a while, but Diana was comfortable with that state as she feared Jane had morphed into Lady Yvaine's enforcer rather than being her friend.

After several minutes of silence, Jane couldn't take it any longer. "Aren't ye going to talk to me?"

"Why should I? Neither you, nor Lady Yvaine, were here, or on Crete when everything happened. Yet you both blamed us for screwing everything up."

"Whoa, whoa, whoa. Back yer horses up. I never said anything against ye, or the others. And besides, no one expects ye to stop two high priestesses from doing what they want. But I'm dying to know how ye think Alex found the hiding place of the Omphalos. From what I understand, it should have been impossible."

"Did Lady Yvaine send you?"

"Of course not. I'm trying to figure out what's going on and what we should do about it," Jane replied.

"What *we're* supposed to do about it? Look at what's happened. Alex is dead. The Omphalos is gone. And the order is in an uproar. And you think we should do something about this mess. Are you crazy?"

"I'm not saying we have to fix anything, but at least we need to understand the threat and do what we can because Lady Yvaine isn't thinking ahead. She's been so focused on the breakdown of discipline that she hasn't talked to the one person who might have the key to what happened – ye. Which means she has only part of the story. So, what really happened in Crete?"

Diana looked out to one of the monasteries on a neighboring pillar and said, "There's not much to tell you. At first, all they were doing was planning how to move the Omphalos safely. But, like here, they didn't bother listening to anything I said."

"So far, that's what I've heard. But how in the heck did Alex know where the Omphalos was? And how did he break in? I can't figure it out."

"Obviously, he came in through a back door no one knew about," Diana replied. "There was no way he could've gotten through the front doors as we had two guards posted there round the clock, and they never saw him. Plus, those doors were heavily enchanted. I saw Hanim placing the enchantments on the doors here, and they were of a nature that was far more powerful than anything I've ever seen. Besides, who would purposely go through the arena where the Minotaur kept guard? I asked everybody about the back door, but nobody knew about it – except him."

"Lady Yvaine admitted she'd heard about it a long time ago, but she figured that if it existed, between the famous labyrinth of Greek mythological days and the Minotaur, that she didn't need to worry about that entrance."

"Did you know our order had imprisoned a beast in the arena?" Diana asked. "I felt bad for it because it looked furious at our treatment of it."

"No, I didn't," Jane replied. "I have to say this whole quest for the Maqlû keeps exposing a seedy side of our order that I never expected."

The two sat silently until Diana said, "Why would we need a beast like the Minotaur? The place is really remote, with enchantments and guards on the doors all the time." Diana shuddered. "Just thinking about that place gives me the creeps because of the piles of bones littering the floor of the open area below where they kept the Omphalos. It's also the last place I saw Alex. And I just don't see how he could have gotten out of there alive."

"So ye haven't heard?"

"Haven't heard what?" Diana asked.

"I would've told ye earlier that he made it out and called his grandfather a couple of days later, but ye were giving me such a cold shoulder earlier that I didn't dare approach ye."

"Thanks a lot for telling me now. I've only been thinking he was nothing but a pile of bones for days."

"I'm sorry. But like I said, I wasn't sure ye'd talk to me. Well, he did get out, which gets back to my question of what we should do next. Do we wait for him to show up, or do we take matters into our own hands?"

"And do what?" Diana asked. "That ankh thingy is controlling him. Who knows what it'll get him to do next."

Jane shook her head. "I don't believe that. The ankh helps and influences him, but it doesn't control him like it used to. If possible, I'd like to help him."

"I don't know if he needs us anymore. We've talked about whether he has others helping him, and his latest escapades seem to confirm that others are involved – people and ghosts we don't know about," Diana said. "If that's the case, he'll be too unpredictable to guess his next moves and will just have to wait until he shows up."

"Maybe not. One of our cameras down by the road caught him getting out of a Red Crescent truck a few hours after ye left here. He and the worker appeared to be heading towards the main trail up before the cameras went on the blitz."

"And?"

"I don't know what he did up here, but there was enough information on the video that I was able to track down the truck and the aid worker. She said she met Alex in Athens, and he volunteered to help a relief effort in a quake-hit zone in northwestern Greece. Along the way, he saved their convoy from another quake that collapsed the road they were traveling on. Then he convinced her to divert to Meteora, where the camera caught them. But they parted ways shortly after that, and she had no idea where he went. Now, both he and the Omphalos are missing, and we need to find them."

Jane was silent for a minute before adding, "There's one other thing I found odd. I think the aid worker was hiding something about Alex."

"Like what?" Diana asked.

"I'm not sure, but I got the impression she was covering for him, jest as we do."

"Interesting. But that leaves the question of which is the priority – the object or Alex," Diana replied. "If you were in his shoes, what would you be doing now?"

Jane smiled and started chuckling. "I have no idea. Besides, as I'm talking this out loud with ye, I'm beginning to think I asked the wrong question."

"What do you mean?"

"We've gotten lucky and guessed where he was a few times. But there's been jest as many times where he vanishes and pops up in some place we never expected."

"So? What are you saying? Do we go in search of him or the object?"

"I say we do nothing and wait for him to reappear," Jane replied. "I have a feeling that once he does, he'll lead us to the Omphalos."

CHAPTER 31

NOT AS WIDE AS YOU THINK

"I'm sorry about what just happened," Chrysophylax said as they winged their way back to the ring of mountain portals. *"I assumed my uncle wanted to discuss how to help you, not talk you into helping him."*

"It wasn't a total waste of time because I got to see another example of the power of the Maqlû."

"What do you mean, Little One?"

"Your uncle has been around those objects for a long time and seems to covet them as much as everyone else. Which means I can't trust anyone with them." Alex took a deep breath before blurting out, "I can't believe I'm going to say this, but is there any way we can steal the Omphalos from the High Council's chambers?"

"Are you sure you want to risk your life to get that object back?" Chrysophylax asked. *"It's a death sentence if they catch you, and I shudder to think what they'll do to me."*

"Would it really be that dangerous," Alex asked.

"I'm afraid so. Ever since the last dragon returned from Earth, we've become more xenophobic. And recently, it's gotten a lot more tense as there seems to be a power struggle going on in the High Council."

"Is there no way of stealing the Omphalos back?" Alex sensed the dragon hesitate before dipping one of his opalescent-colored wings and heading in a new direction.

"There's a chance of taking it. But we'll need speed and stealth," Chrys said. *"You can't speak to me mentally or verbally until you're safely in the wormhole, because someone might hear you. I also need you to focus all your*

thoughts on that object, as I'll use them to guide me to it in the dark. And one last thing. Hold on tight. I might be one of the smallest dragons on this planet, but I'm faster and more maneuverable than everybody else, so I'll fly into the High Council's chambers and grab it mid-flight before high-tailing it out of there."

Gulping down his fears, Alex closed his eyes and focused on the Omphalos. He almost yelped when he felt a sudden tug – not from the ankh, but an unexpected mental connection to the Omphalos. It had such a strong pull that all he could think about, all he wanted, was to hold the Omphalos once more. It was an all-consuming desire that drove everything else from his mind, including the cold from their flight. He was so focused on the object that he didn't notice they were at the cavern of the High Council until Chrysophylax broke into his thoughts and said, *"Hold on tight. We're going in.*

Chrys's warning broke the mental connection to the Omphalos and caused Alex to clutch the dragon as tight as he could with his arms and legs just before they went into a nerve-wracking high-speed spin that had Alex's legs flying into the air.

Just when he thought he was about to fall off, Chrys completed the spin and snatched the Omphalos. Alex slammed back onto the dragon and fought to stay on as Chrys flapped his wings mightily to gain speed. Then they shot out of the cavern, leaving Alex struggling to regain his hold.

Alex had barely settled down when Chrys whispered, *"We're not out of danger yet. I need you to keep your mind blank – driving everything from your mind. We can't afford to let anyone know where we are."*

They flew silently for the next half hour until they'd passed over one of the peaks forming the ring of mountain portals. As soon as Chrys had tipped forward to angle towards the gateway to Earth, he said, *"I'll drop you off at the entrance to the wormhole. Once it opens, all you have to do is step through, and it'll take you back to Mt. Olympus. But you'll only have about two minutes before it closes again, so don't hesitate."*

"Wait. You're not coming with me?" Alex asked.

"I can't. I've no idea how long it'll take for the portal to open since I don't know if our species history will be the better indicator of how much time it will take, or if my last experience with you will happen. But if you're to get off this planet safely with the Omphalos, then I have to be prepared to lead any pursuers away. I'm sorry. But it has to be this way for you to survive."

"What about you? Will you be safe?" Alex asked.

"Don't worry about me," Chrys replied. *"Now, get ready to jump off as soon as I land."*

Almost as soon as Alex's feet hit the ground, the portal slid open, and Alex could feel the ankh tugging him towards the opening. Smashing his Tilley on his head, Alex tightened his pack straps, picked up the Omphalos, and stepped into… a place that wasn't Mt. Olympus.

A second later, Chrysophylax came through the gateway, slamming into Alex and sending him soaring through the air for almost a hundred feet before he crashed back to the ground.

It took Alex several minutes before he regained his senses and was able to look around at where they'd landed. What immediately caught his attention was the total silence. It was eerily quiet, giving it the appearance that there wasn't any life on the planet. Even the light breeze blowing across the landscape made no sound, as there were no trees, bushes, or rocks to disrupt the air flow. The only living vegetation in sight were some ground-hugging grasses growing from the near-barren landscape. The only things that indicated life once existed were the gigantic crumbling city wall off in the distance and the large teardrop-shaped metal structure they'd come through, looking oddly like the top half of Alex's ankh.

"What is this place?" Alex asked.

Chrysophylax didn't respond right away as he gazed at the surrounding landscape. *"I don't know what world we're on. If I had to guess, it looks somewhat like the images I've seen in Nabu's old memories of the planet Irkalla before their world war."*

"What are you talking about?" Alex asked.

"Irkalla is Sibyl's home world, where my uncle believes the ankh and Maqlû came from. It appears possible that your ankh brought us to its former home."

"Are we stuck here?" Alex asked, with a touch of panic in his voice. "Because I'm freaking out. We're stuck on some unknown planet somewhere in the galaxy, and I have no idea how to get back to Earth."

Chrysophylax didn't respond for some time as he stared at the strange opening they'd come through. At last, he said, *"I don't know if it'll be as hard as you fear, Little One."*

"Why not?"

"Because I'm pretty sure that your ankh can activate the portals. Maybe, all you have to do is tell it where you want to go, and we go back through."

Alex answered with an inelegant, "Huh?"

"I've gone through the portals over a dozen times, and it has usually taken me hours to open them. But they open instantly for you. Tell me, did the ankh do anything strange before we made this jump?"

Alex thought back to just before they'd entered the wormhole on Berellus and replied, "Come to think of it, yeah. It was tugging at me. But I didn't pay any attention to it because all I could think of was how to get the heck off your planet."

"Then we might have our answer on how to get to Earth. All you have to do is tell the ankh wherever YOU wish to go. Show it who's boss."

"Well, it sounds crazy, but since I don't have a better idea, I'll trust your logic. Once we get back to Earth, though, what will you do? This planet looks too barren to survive, and you'd have to hide for the rest of your life if you stayed on Earth. Or, will you return to Berellus?"

"Since I'll be in big trouble if I return home, I'd like to stay with you for as long as it takes to destroy the remaining Maqlû. Besides, when I saw you disappear into the wormhole, I realized I have felt more alive on our adventures than at any other time in my life. It's exciting, and I don't want to go back to my old boring life."

"I can't thank you enough," Alex said, "as I feel much more comfortable when you're with me. But now, what do we do?"

Chrysophylax looked around at the barren landscape and said, *"I don't think we could survive here for very long."* Then he got to one knee and added, *"Leave the object and hop up. I'll carry it through the wormhole. All I want you to do is focus on getting us to Earth. Once we get there, we can figure out our next steps."*

Alex clambered up and looked for someplace to hold on, but Chrysophylax had no natural handholds as Gugalanna had. Sensing his discomfort, Chrysophylax said, *"Just grip my neck as tight as you can for now. When we reach Earth, we can rig up something to help you stay on."*

Chrysophylax picked up the Omphalos and headed towards the opening jutting from the ground. Unlike the ones on Berellus and Earth, there wasn't an iris – just darkness. He stepped in and was instantly on a steep, rocky mountainside.

"Do you know where we are?" Alex asked.

"I believe we've returned to Mt. Olympus on Earth," Chrys replied.

"Are you sure? That wormhole was nothing like the others I've gone through."

Alex could feel a rumble deep within Chrysophylax. "What are you laughing at?"

"You, Little One. Your comment suggested you were an experienced space traveler. It hit my funny bone. But right now, we need to get out of sight."

Before Alex could react, Chrysophylax launched off the mountain and plummeted towards the forest far below. Their descent was so steep that Alex thought he would slide off until Chrys caught a thermal and soared away from the mountainside. They rode the air currents ever higher until they crossed over the peak and headed northwest across an unbroken expanse of forest.

Although he'd only briefly been on Berellus, Earth's lower humidity and temperatures made the air seem bitterly cold. When combined with the wind, Alex's teeth were soon chattering. Luckily, they only flew to the next ridge before diving into the valley, where Chrysophylax found a small meadow with no structures or roads within miles, and landed.

As Alex hopped around, slapping his arms to warm up, he said, "I heard what you said about why you came with me, but I don't understand. Why are you willing to take on this much risk?"

"He doesn't talk about it, but my uncle still has nightmares about the Maqlû, and your actions have stirred up his old fears. Since he can't travel anymore, I came instead. Enough of that, though. Let's move on to practical issues. Do you have some rope or cord we could use to help you stay on me, at least until we can get someplace where we can find a better solution?"

"Let me check," Alex said. After rummaging around in his pack for a minute, he pulled out a survival bracelet, started unwrapping the nylon paracord, and soon had eight feet unraveled.

"It's not much, but it'll have to do," Chrysophylax said. *"I'll make sure to take it easy, though. Now, we need to discuss how you're going to destroy the object, although it doesn't sound that hard, as my uncle said, all we have to do is fly over an active volcano and drop it in."*

Alex didn't reply right away as he sat, staring at the forest surrounding them. At last, he shook his head and said, "It can't be that easy. For one thing, you might be able to survive flying over an active volcano, but I doubt I could. If the heat doesn't kill me, the fumes will. And more importantly, it's like that old saying, 'If it's too good to be true, it probably is.' Nothing has come easy concerning these Maqlû. Why should this time be different?"

"That type of thinking is one of the big differences between dragons and humans," Chrys said. *"Your kind often look gift horses in the mouth. We don't. We tend to look at things very logically."*

"I guess we can try it your way," Alex said. "Do you know where the nearest active volcanoes are?"

"Mt. Etna on Sicily is the closest and most active. Mt. Vesuvius is a little farther north, near Naples. Then there

are some volcanoes south of here, near Santorini. Are you thinking we just head for the nearest one, or should we target a specific volcano?"

Alex thought for a bit before he replied. "It's hard to explain, but I need to talk with my friends before we go further because I wouldn't have gotten this far without them. One can do magic, speak several languages, and knows tons of stuff. The other knows people and senses things nobody else can. Both have saved my life on more than one occasion."

"As you wish. Do you know where they are?"

Alex blushed. "No, but I'll find them – somehow. But right now, I need to make something to keep me safe on your back."

Studying his dragon companion, Alex realized his cord was too short to do anything more than make a single loop around Chrysophylax's neck, with just enough left to form a loop at each end he could hold onto when riding. When he finished, Alex said, "Okay, that's one issue temporarily taken care of, but there are a thousand more issues – like where are we going to get food."

"Don't worry about me. I don't need to eat every day. When I'm hungry, I'll go hunting. As for you, I could drop you off near a town before it gets light, then pick you up that night. Besides food and water, you'll need a coat and a more secure harness."

"Gugalanna said he uses a glamour spell to hide his flying around," Alex said. "Does that really work?"

"Somewhat, but I'm not comfortable with it. Human technology has greatly advanced since Gugalanna first came to Earth. Two of the biggest dangers are airplanes and people filming everything. I'll use a glamour spell, but I suggest we move around only at night. Our kind has

spent too long trying to erase our existence from your people's minds to screw it up now."

They talked through a myriad of details for the next couple of hours, such as navigating, how to carry the Omphalos, what the plan was if neither Etna nor Vesuvius would work, and what other precautions they needed to take to stay hidden. After one long pause, Chrys asked, *"What about the other objects? How will you find them?"*

"I don't know. This whole quest is so overwhelming that it's tough enough to address one thing at a time, much less think about the future. But enough of that. Right now, I need to get some sleep."

"Go ahead. I'll watch over you."

Using his pack for a pillow, Alex found a soft spot on the ground and curled up. When he woke, it was nighttime. A fire was crackling a few feet away, causing everything beyond its glow to seem darker than it was. It took him a few moments to clear the sleepers out of his eyes, but when he was fully awake, he noticed Deborah and Ariadne sitting on a log on the other side of the fire.

He sat up with a jerk and said, "How did you find me?"

"I haven't gone anywhere, Little One."

Alex turned and looked over at Chrysophylax. "I was talking to my sister and a friend who must have arrived while I was asleep."

"Your living friends must get frustrated when you speak to people they can't see."

"I'm not sure who gets more frustrated – my friends, or me," Alex replied.

"Are you talking to us?" Deborah asked. "Because I don't understand what you're trying to get at."

Alex furrowed his brows. "Let me get this straight. Chrys, you can't hear or see the two spirits here in camp?"

The dragon shook his head. "Deb, Ariadne, can either of you hear Chrys?"

Deborah shook her head and said, "That's not important right now. The bigger question is, where have you been? We looked all over for you but didn't pick up any trace of you until today."

"A dragon named Gugalanna, or as Ariadne knew him, the Minotaur, took me to his home planet to ask for help destroying the Maqlû," Alex replied. "But it was a waste of time. The High Council refused to help and sent me away. Chrys, who's helped me before, decided to risk censure and help me."

Deborah shook her head. "Unbelievable. You're sitting out in the middle of nowhere, casually talking about space travel, while sitting beside a dragon. But that's beside the point. What are you planning to do now?"

"Chrysophylax's uncle, Nabu, knows more about the Maqlû than anyone else. He says we need to throw it into an active volcano."

"You've got to be kidding!" Deborah exclaimed.

"I wish I were," Alex replied. "Chrys and I were talking about the plan earlier today and have decided our first step is to find Diana and Jane, then start checking out volcanos in Europe, starting with Vesuvius and Etna."

"Why can't you just dump it into any volcano?" Ariadne asked.

"I wish it was that easy, but I fear that would be too good to be true."

"At least there's one piece of good news," Deborah said. "We know where Diana and Jane are. They're in Meteora."

"What are they doing back there?" Alex asked.

"They're cleaning up after the attack." She hesitated before adding, "You should know that a few of the women think you took the Omphalos and are searching for you which means it's not safe to go see Diana and Jane."

"But I need to see them. I don't feel comfortable going on without their help, or, at the minimum, advice. Besides, no one will expect me to come to them."

"You're hopeless, you know," Deborah said. "It's like you have a death wish – always charging in where you shouldn't go."

"Believe me," Alex replied, "it's not what I like doing. It's what I feel I must do. Will you help me see them?"

Deborah sighed. "Fine. What do you want us to do?"

"Chrys and I will fly to Meteora when we finish talking, but I'll need one of you to let me know when Jane or Diana are alone outside so I can talk to them."

"What do you expect to achieve?" Deborah asked. "They can't keep running off after you as they've done in the past."

"I hate to interrupt, but if I'm to help, would you please catch me up on what you've been talking about," Chrysophylax said.

After Alex finished telling him about his conversation with the two ghosts, Chrysophylax said, *"There is an old saying among our kind that goes, keep your friends close and your enemies closer."*

"I don't understand. What are you saying?" Alex asked.

"You said you valued the advice and skills of your friends, but it sounds like there's no way their leaders would let them help you. Why not have your friends tell their elders where you're going and that you have the Omphalos? Since we'll only travel at night, I believe I can

stay out of their sight. Along the way, you could arrange for meetings or updates, and that way, stay in close contact with them and know what they're doing."

"That's a great idea," Alex said. "If we leave now, we might be able to get there before they go to bed."

Within minutes, he'd put the fire out, packed up, and slipped on the simple harness he'd made earlier in the day. An hour later, Chrys started a circling pattern several miles away from the Druid's hideaway, waiting on the all-clear signal. They only had to wait half an hour before Ariadne flew up and said, "If you hurry, one of your friends is outside by herself right now."

After Alex had relayed the information, the dragon turned towards the Druid hideout and glided towards the rock pillar. "You can't stay down there, as someone's bound to see you," Alex said. "How do I contact you to tell you I'm ready to leave?"

"Don't worry. I'll stay close enough that I can hear your thoughts. Just mentally call me when you're ready, and I'll come pick you up."

Deborah flew close and said, "Ariadne and I won't be able to carry you any distance, but in an emergency, we can get you out of there at a moment's notice. You better hurry, though. Diana's been out on the patio for a while and looks like she's getting antsy."

When Chrys landed a few seconds later, Alex jumped off, feeling like he was walking into the lion's den. He walked around a boulder and saw Diana looking out over the valley. He cleared his throat to announce his presence and said, "I didn't take the Omphalos."

Jane stepped out of the shadows and said, "We know ye didn't."

Alex pulled back, his senses on high alert. "Were you guys waiting for me? Is this some sort of trap?"

"Relax. "Our resident mind reader felt your presence a little while ago," Diana said.

Jane blushed, then hissed, "I don't read minds."

"I just meant you have an uncanny ability to sense things," Diana replied.

"Well, I'm sorry. It's just that I'm a little on edge after everything that's gone on." Turning to Alex, Jane said, "Diana and I have been expecting you and have been on the lookout for you every night since we returned."

"Why would you be expecting me?" Alex asked.

Diana smiled. "Somehow, you manage to rope us into your little escapades whenever you get in trouble. Since you got everyone in the order riled up, then disappeared, it seemed logical that you'd eventually come here. And we figured you wouldn't just stroll in in broad daylight. So, here we are. Do you have the Omphalos?"

"Chrysophylax is keeping it for me right now, but as I said, I didn't take it. My sister and a friend took it from some crazy warlock giant. I came to talk to you about it because I was looking for some help." Seeing how Jane and Diana were about to bombard him with questions, he gave them an abbreviated version of everything that had happened since Scotland.

"Are you kidding me?" Diana asked incredulously after he was finished. "You've been riding dragons and traveling to different planets since you ran away from us? Why couldn't you include us?"

"I am now," Alex responded.

Jane interrupted the discussion. "Enough of the chit-chat. We don't have much time before someone else comes out here. What's important is that we agree on what to do with the object. Are ye okay, Diana, with him destroying it? Because I'm willing to help him any way I can."

Diana hesitated before giving a weak affirmative.

"I'm surprised it wasn't an easier decision for you. Protecting the Omphalos trapped an innocent dragon, cost hundreds of souls their lives, and nearly killed me," Alex said.

"How could we know?" Diana replied. "I didn't know what was happening until the day I saw you there."

"But generations of your people did and never questioned it. After what you've seen, didn't you think it right to ask more questions about what your order is doing? Shouldn't you be eager to get rid of this thing?"

Diana bristled at the unexpected attack and said, "That's easy for you to say. You haven't lived through what our order has."

"Oh. And what about what happened to the American Indians," Alex retorted.

"Enough, ye two," Jane hissed. "Keep yer voices down, and let's get back to the main subject." She waited until Alex and Diana quieted down, then said, "We're out of time tonight. Someone will be looking for us any minute now. When and where are we going to meet next?"

"How about tomorrow night here, but an hour earlier? I need to know if you can convince your leaders to follow me," Alex said.

"Why do you want us to do that?" Diana asked.

"Because… I don't think I can do it without you. You plan better than I do, you have magic at your beck and call, and you've saved my bacon too many times to count. Plus, it was Chrys' idea to keep guys close, but keep my enemies, your order, closer. This way, I won't have to keep looking over my back wondering where and when your people will strike."

"We're in," Jane said. "But ye need to tell us where ye're heading and when and where we can meet."

"It'll need to be in some remote place so Chrys can get me close. Do you really think you can get them to come after me?"

"Are ye kidding?" Jane replied. "They'll be panting to get at ye. The only problem will be convincing them we know where ye're going without letting them know we're helping ye."

"That shouldn't be a problem," Diana said. "They'll believe you, Jane, if you do one of your mystical things. Maybe you can even throw your runes to make it look good." She turned back to Alex and punched him in the arm. "And don't you dare leave us again without telling us where you're going. You can't come flying in on some dragon no one can see, tell us a wild story about space travel and alien civilizations, and then disappear again."

"I promise. I'll be here tomorrow night, and you can meet Chrys," Alex said. "But, I need some things, like food, water, batteries, a coat…."

"It's summer in Greece. What would you need all that for?" Diana asked.

"It gets really cold, flying around at 20,000 feet with a strong wind blowing in your face. You should try it sometime."

"Promise?" Diana asked with a grin.

The doors opened, sending Alex scurrying around the corner. A few seconds later, Deborah and Ariadne lifted him off the top of the pillar and carried him down to the ridge behind.

It would have taken a sharp-eyed observer, who happened to be looking in the right direction at the right moment, to see a dragon flying away a short time later.

CHAPTER 32

FOUND AND LOST

Jane and Diana were waiting when Alex and Chrysophylax showed up the next night. "Did you get my grandma to agree to chase after me?" Alex asked.

Diana shook her head as she handed him a bag of supplies. "No. We couldn't be too obvious about what we wanted, so they didn't pick up on our hints. Based on your history of disappearing and showing up thousands of miles away from where you were supposed to be has given them a profound distaste for going on wild goose chases. They're not moving without concrete evidence of your location, which means unless we want to give away all our secrets, we're staying right here."

"That sucks," Alex replied. "I was counting on your help to destroy this thing. You two have the skills and common sense I lack. How am I going to get it done without you?"

"That's sweet of ye to think of us that way," Jane said. "But, ye've done fine on yer own."

"This is different. All the other times, I didn't have any plan. But this time, I have a clear goal, and trying to figure out how to achieve it scares me, as it feels like I'm walking into a lion's den on purpose. It was a lot easier when I was clueless and didn't know what I was doing."

"I figured ye'd be cold, so I made some hot chocolate for ye," Jane said while thrusting a mug of steaming cocoa towards him.

Alex held up a hand and said, "No, thank you."

"But I thought ye loved chocolate."

"I do, especially dark chocolate. But I don't like any hot drinks, including cocoa." The words had barely left his mouth when he was overcome with images of Jane's hot chocolate. It took him a couple of seconds before he remembered a similar craving and realize they were emanating from Sadie. But his shouted warning, "Watch out!" was too late. The little Ryujin dragon flew into Jane's arms and greedily started slurping down the steaming cocoa, causing her to throw the cup and dragonet up into the air.

"What is with yer dragon and hot chocolate?" she shouted.

It took a minute before Alex stopped chuckling and managed to reply, "What can I say? She likes hot chocolate. Based on the images I get from her, I wouldn't have any of that stuff around her if I were you. At the most, I'd suggest you bring out a bowl and set it down in the future for her to attack, as she seems to go crazy at the presence of the stuff."

Diana hushed them and whispered, "What's in the shadows over there?" Without waiting for an answer, she moved forward and gasped when she could make out Chrysophylax's shape. "Is that a dragon? He's beautiful. Can I pet it?"

"Chrys is a him, and he's not a pet," Alex replied testily. "He's ten times smarter than the three of us put together, has lived for centuries, and has probably forgotten more magic than you'll ever learn. In fact, his species were the ones who taught your order how to harness your powers."

Diana threw up her hands. "I'm sorry. I didn't mean to offend him. It's just that I still have to pinch myself to believe they exist. You said Nessie was a dragon, but it's hard to think of her as one.

"Tell her it's okay to touch me," Chrysophylax said. *"Her attitude is far better than we're used to from humans."*

Alex swung an arm towards Chrysophylax. "He said it's okay."

"I didn't hear anything," Diana said.

"It's because he communicates via telepathy."

While Diana ran her hand lightly over Chrysophylax's opalescent colored scales, Jane asked, "Can he read our minds?"

"I don't know. I haven't asked him that." Alex turned to Chrysophylax and asked, "Can you?"

"It's not that simple," Chrysophylax replied. *"Your thoughts are so chaotic most of the time that I tune them out and wait until you verbalize what you wish to communicate. I don't know how you can think coherently with everything rattling about in your mind."*

Jane chuckled.

Alex looked at Jane and asked, "Can you hear him?"

Jane pulled out the golden dragon necklace with a flaming red pearl inset Alex had given her in the Caribbean and replied, "Yes, and I think it's because of this. It thrums against my chest when he's speaking. But don't worry. I can't read your mind either. It's like what Chrysophylax said. Yer mind is just a bunch of chaotic noise to me."

Diana humphed. "It's unfair that you two can talk to dragons, but I can't."

Alex grinned. "But you can do magic, and neither Jane nor I can."

"Well, there is that," Diana said grudgingly.

"Save your grumbling for another time," Jane said. "We need to talk next steps, especially our immediate problem of figuring out how to get rid of the Omphalos."

Jane spotted the carved bullet-shaped stone between Chrysophylax's front legs and asked, "Is that it?"

Alex looked down at what she was staring at. "Oh, yeah. Gugalanna and Chrys have been carrying it around while I've been holding on for dear life on their backs.

"Unbelievable," Jane said. "I'm amazed ye're being so casual carrying around one of the Maqlû that our order has religiously guarded for centuries. Ye're being careless with it, and if ye're not careful, ye could cause big problems."

"What did you want me to do with it?" Alex retorted. "I'm stuck with it until I figure out a way of disposing of it in an active volcano without killing myself."

"What about the staff you're carrying around?" Diana asked. "It looks… uh, different."

She reached down to touch it, but Alex caught her wrist and said, "I wouldn't do that. It can be pretty destructive at times."

"Why do you have it then?" Diana asked.

"I found it in Delphi. It's some magical object, but I don't know what it is."

"Then why didn't you leave it where you found it?"

Alex didn't get a chance to reply. They'd all been so engrossed in the conversation that no one had noticed a helicopter approaching. Even then, nobody saw it until it was hovering overhead, and a giant bearded man came repelling down, sending balls of energy all around. Diana and Jane instinctively ran for the entrance while Alex climbed on Chrysophylax.

A blast at Chrysophylax's feet drove the dragon to start running to the edge while flapping his wings as Alex reached for his hastily made bridle. He'd barely settled down when Chrysophylax jumped off and flew away.

Alex heard a couple more blasts, but all he could think about was that he'd barely escaped with his life.

It wasn't until they'd climbed over the nearest ridge and plunged into the next valley that Alex realized the ankh was beating hard against his chest. A second later, he groaned and slapped his head with one hand.

"Are you all right, Little One?"

"Yeah. I just realized we left both the supplies and the Omphalos back there. Now, what are we going to do."

"We're living to fight another day. I should have known someone would try to steal the object. I'm sorry for not stopping the theft, but I was so interested in hearing what your friends had to say that I wasn't listening for approaching danger."

"It's not your fault," Alex said. "It's mine. I was so glad to see Diana and Jane again that I didn't notice anything else. At least there's some good news in all this. I don't have to worry about live volcanoes anymore."

CHAPTER 33
TAKE ONLY WHAT YOU NEED

Diana reached for the handle to go inside just as Elizabeth yanked the door open. Caught off balance, Diana stumbled forward. Her clumsiness saved her life, as one of the giant's fireballs passed through the space she had occupied a second earlier and hit the door to the Druid stronghold. Jane pushed Diana inside, then shoved the newly installed door shut just as a second ball of flames smashed into it.

Elizabeth slammed the steel bars into place and hustled the two girls down to the central chambers before shutting and locking the inner doors. Women came running into the main area, asking so many questions that it made it impossible for anybody to hear anything.

Sticking two fingers into her mouth, Elizabeth whistled loudly to get everybody to quiet down. Then she turned to Diana and shouted, "I saw the Omphalos. What was my grandson doing here? Have you been in league with him all along?"

The explosions had exacerbated Diana's hearing problems, causing her ears to ring and making it impossible to hear what anyone was saying. She turned to Jane and pointed to her ears, letting the older girl know she needed help.

Jane faced Elizabeth and said, "This is what Diana has been trying to tell ye – it wasn't yer grandson who attacked us and stole the object. It was that giant. Alex had stolen the Omphalos and was bringing it back when that beast of a man attacked again. I warned ye that I felt like that man was nearby. He must have been waiting for

Alex to return. But ye didn't listen. Well, now ye have yer proof of who wrecked this place before. Are ye happy?"

"Who is this man you're talking about?" Sophie shouted, trying to be heard above the din of explosions.

"I don't know," Jane replied. "Maybe if we'd listen to Alex for a change, instead of pursuing him, we'd be able to answer yer question. But not a single person in the order, except for Lady Yvaine, has tried listening to us since the beginning of this ordeal."

By this time, the ringing in Diana's ears had stopped, and she added, "You need to believe us, Mom. That's not Alex out there attacking us. It was the same person I saw attack us the first time – a real warlock. He was huge with a thick beard and rappelled from a helicopter. Alex ran away as soon as he saw that man. I don't know where he's going or if he's…."

Jane cut Diana off, saying, "I don't think now's the time to discuss who's to blame. Elizabeth, don't ye think we should be spending time preparing our defenses against that giant warlock?"

Elizabeth shook her head to clear it. "Of course." She then turned and started shouting instructions to the assembled women. A minute later, they had pulled every piece of heavy furniture into a wall in front of the door and had settled down to wait.

As the minutes ticked on, the deafening silence began to cause the women to fidget. At last, Sophie called out to Elizabeth, "Do you think he's gone?"

"I don't know. Go check the cameras in the security room to see if he's still out there."

Sophie came back a few minutes later and said, "I think we're all clear, as I didn't see any movement out there."

"Send someone else back to monitor the cameras, but for now, I'd rather remain cautious so he doesn't surprise us again," Elizabeth replied. After another half hour of tense waiting, she made the call to stand down but left the hastily prepared defensive fortifications in place.

Barely able to contain her rage, she stepped over to where Jane and Diana were quietly conversing and said, "You might be Lady Yvaine's pet, but I intend to pursue my grandson and take back the Omphalos no matter what it costs. I'm sure he was involved in this attack despite what Diana was saying. This incident has made it even more obvious he's a dangerous warlock. So, even though the High Council has decided not to take action against him, he has crossed the line too many times and must pay the ultimate penalty before he does any more harm to the order." She turned to the other women who'd edged in closer and, in a loud voice, said, "When it's safe, we're going to go after him. Anyone who doesn't want to be part of this is free to leave. There will be no recriminations."

"Lady Yvaine won't like this," Jane said.

"She hasn't been here and under attack as we have. Too many of us have already died because of my grandson, and it's my fault. As soon as I found out that he existed, I should have taken action to make sure he died from his injuries in the accident, just like my daughter and granddaughter. It isn't fair that he lived and they died. So, who's with me?"

Every woman's hand, but Diana's and Jane's, shot into the air. Sophie turned on her daughter and spat out, "You're coming with us – whether you like it or not."

Diana's lips pursed into a tight line. Then she shook her head and said, "I won't do it. This is wrong. If you took time to view the facts, you'd realize he's not our problem. We are. If we hadn't been so worried about him, we would never have taken the Omphalos, and we'd all be alive today." She turned to Elizabeth and said, "If you chase after him, I can almost guarantee you that more of us will die. And it'll be on your head."

"Diana!" Sophie exclaimed. "Don't you dare talk to your High Priestess like that."

Surprised by her temerity, Diana glared at her mother.

"That's fine, Sophie. I don't want a naysayer with us. It'll be better leaving her and Jane behind," Elizabeth said. "That way, they won't impede our actions." She turned to Jane and said, "We're leaving tonight to search for him. There's plenty of food here. But I want the two of you to make your way into town tomorrow and go back to Stormhold."

She turned to the rest of the Druids and said, "I don't want word of our plans to get out to the rest of the order until we've retaken the Omphalos, for we'll get nowhere if we try to get everyone aligned with this course of action. Besides, I know my grandson. He's very resourceful, so we can't afford to give him any chance of learning what we're doing. Nadia, I'd like you to make travel arrangements for us. They need to be flexible and discrete. Salome, I'd like you to handle the provisions and anything else you think we'll need. Ensure we can operate in any conditions because we won't have time to stop and get the equipment and gear we'll need wherever he heads. Now go. I want to depart in an hour. Sophie, I'd like you to plan our search for him. Now, let's get to it."

Everybody scattered, leaving Diana and Jane alone in the great room. "Now, what do we do?" asked Diana.

"What else? We wait till they're gone and go help him," Jane replied.

"But how are we going to find him?"

"Easy. We follow the path of chaos that will inevitably follow him. I need to call Lady Yvaine to tell her what's happened. Do you think ye can arrange a vehicle for us?"

"Neither of us is twenty-one yet," Diana said.

"Well, a little thing like that shouldn't stop us. Just use your magic fingers."

Diana smiled and pulled out her phone.

CHAPTER 34
WHAT WE OBTAIN TOO CHEAP

Chrysophylax set down in a small meadow miles away from Meteora.

"What are you doing?" Alex asked. "Shouldn't we be going after that monster?"

Chrys shook his head. *"He was using an object that greatly amplified his powers and I don't have enough magical ability to best him. And unless you do, we'll have to devise another way to get the Omphalos back."*

"Then what do we do? I've always been the person chased, never the chasee. I have no idea what to do next except…"

"Yes?"

"Nah, it couldn't be that simple," Alex said, talking to himself.

"What are you going on about?" Chrysophylax asked.

"A thought just struck me. I know Pythia lives in Delphi. And I know my sister and Ariadne stole the Omphalos from there. Could it be possible the warlock will return to Delphi with it?"

"Delphi used to be an influential part of the ancient world, and Pythia…" It was Chrysophylax's turn for his thoughts to tail off. *"I'm only a few centuries old and wasn't around when Pythia was so influential that kings would seek her counsel. My uncle believes she was the Atlantian who stole The Cup of Jamshid, which allows her to see into the future. If she had that ability, she would have had enormous influence, enabling her to control or manipulate other powerful people. So, I could see her*

directing the thief's actions. You said you've been to Delphi. Why did you go there?"

"A man named Brother Stafford, who I've met several times in some strange situations, talked me into going with him to Delphi so he could introduce me to Pythia. Well, one thing led to another, and I happened to find a place with a bunch of magical objects, and … there was an accident, and … that's where I picked up this magical staff. If you add it all up, it can't be coincidence."

"You're probably right. My guess is that all three of these people, Pythia, this Stafford of yours, and the giant warlock, are probably former Atlantians, which would make it logical for the warlock to return to Delphi."

A rumble in Alex's stomach drove him to say, "Do you think it'd be safe to return to Meteora tonight to get the supplies I left? I've only had one real meal in days and have been rationing my power bars since before that. I'll faint from hunger if I don't eat something substantial soon."

"I don't think it's smart to go back," Chrys replied. *"That Atlantian still might be looking for you, so returning would only be looking for trouble you don't need. It would be safer to drop you near a town to get supplies."*

Alex didn't respond right away. At last, he said, "I guess you're right that it would be a lot safer to find a town to get supplies in, but I need to see Jane and Diana and find out what they've been able to accomplish. And even though it might not be safe, I think there's a good chance the warlock is long gone. I mean, why would he hang around? He's retaken the Omphalos."

Chrysophylax was silent for a moment before replying, *"Then I guess we better get going. We've got a lot of flying ahead if we're to pick up your supplies and get to Delphi before morning."*

The next hour seemed to go by in a flash, and in no time, they were circling Meteora. They were about to fly in when Chrysophylax spotted a helicopter landing near the entrance to the Druid stronghold. It was only on the ground for a few minutes, just enough for a group of women to rush out and board, before it flew away, leaving the mountaintop deserted.

Half an hour later, they tried again. When they saw the area was clear of people and machines, they swooped in, snatched the bag Alex had dropped the night before, and glided out over the valley. When he was clear of the rocks, he turned southwest.

The eastern sky was just turning a light purple when Chrysophylax landed in a small clearing at the base of a cliff, far from any town. Alex slid down and immediately went for the sack Chrysophylax had dropped on the ground. Quickly rummaging through it, he pulled out an apple, one of the crushed loaves of bread inside, and some packaged meat. His hands were shaking from cold and hunger as he gobbled down the apple before turning his attention to making a thick sandwich. He thought about making a second one, but unsure how often he could get supplies, he held off and asked, "Where are we?"

"We're still some distance from Delphi. The delay at Meteora caused me to arrive too late to do anything this morning."

"What about a fire so I can warm up?" Alex asked.

"It's too risky. We can't chance a fire this close to civilization unless we hide in a cave. You should at least be thankful it's not the middle of winter."

"So, how do we watch what's happening in Delphi?"

"Let's hope your sister and her friend are following you. Now get some sleep because you won't get any tonight."

A yawn hit him just then, causing Alex to fluff up the coat Jane and Diana had put in the sack and lay down. It seemed like he'd barely closed his eyes when a wave of cold air washed over him. He blinked open his eyes and saw the sun was sending long shadows across the camp. Chrysophylax didn't seem to have moved from where he'd settled down earlier in the day, but something felt different.

"I'm glad you're finally awake, brother," Deborah said.

Alex rubbed his eyes and sat up. "I'm glad you're here, Sis, but where's Ariadne?"

"She's keeping an eye on the Omphalos," Deborah replied. "I don't know how you figured it out, but that giant bearded man, whose name is Erra, came straight there after taking it."

"Did you see anyone else?" Alex asked.

Deborah shook her head. "Nope."

Alex looked to Chrysophylax and said, "My sister is back. Let me get more information from her, and then we can discuss next steps." Alex turned back to Deborah and asked, "Where is the Omphalos? Can we steal it back?"

"It's in the same cave we found it the first time. But it's more heavily guarded than before," Deborah replied. "I'm guessing they thought you stole it the first time, so they have more enchantments protecting their place, plus a couple of guards outside. I don't see how you could get in there, but Ariadne and I might be able to sneak it out. There's only one catch."

"What's that?" Alex asked with a note of hesitancy in his voice.

"You'd have to be waiting somewhere close to the entrance, then swoop in, take out the guards, blow the doors open, grab the object the minute we emerge, and fly away."

"Oh, that sounds simple," Alex replied sarcastically. "How will we know when to come in?"

"We won't be able to steal the object without them noticing, and that'll be when the ruckus starts. We'll only get one shot at it, which means this has to work."

"What about you two? Do you think they can hurt you?"

"I don't know," Deborah replied. "Their magic is unlike anything I've ever seen. It's an ancient type and very powerful. But, we're willing to risk it to get the Omphalos out of his control."

Alex tried internalizing everything his sister had told him. Then he turned to Chrysophylax and relayed what she'd said. After explaining the plan, he asked, "What do you think?"

"There's going to be risk no matter what we do, but the less time they have to prepare their defenses, the better for us. One of the biggest unknowns is whether Pythia will spot the two girls. She has a reputation for being able to see spirits, but I don't know if she can see them the way you can or if there have to be some special circumstances. We'll have to assume she can. And Erra, well, you should know he used to be so violent and wild that the ancient Akkadians thought of him as the god of mayhem and pestilence. This is a perilous situation."

"I long ago stopped dismissing warnings about danger, so what can we do to minimize the risks?" Alex asked.

"We know what we're facing, and we have a plan. That's about all we can do for now," Chrysophylax replied.

Turning to his sister, Alex asked, "What about Ariadne?" "How are you going to relay all this information to her?"

"Right now, she's hovering a little ways away from the entrance, waiting for me," Deborah replied. "I'll update her before we go in."

Seeing the sun had set, Alex nodded to Deborah and said, "Borrowing a line from the old Western movies, let's saddle up." A few minutes later, they took off and arrived in Delphi all too soon. Alex watched as his sister dove down to where Ariadne was hovering then disappeared into an opening in the mountain.

Circling in the night, more than a mile from Pythia's hideout, made the waiting far more nerve-wracking than he'd thought it'd be. A faint explosion caused Chrysophylax to alter his path and head straight for the entrance.

More and louder explosions sounded, followed by a stray ball of energy shooting through the opening. Chrysophylax dropped his head and folded his wings, sending them into a steep dive. Bright flashes and loud booms, started coming faster and more furiously, followed by Ariadne popping out of the cave with the Omphalos and fly toward them.

Alex felt the wind howling around him as they plunged towards the cliff face. He saw his sister appear, backing out of the opening while throwing fireballs at the hidden occupants of the cave. Then she turned and flew after Ariadne as four people burst out of the mountainside, throwing energy bolts in all directions at their unseen thieves.

His heart stopped when he recognized Erra turn and point his staff directly at Chrysophylax. "Pull up, Chrys. We're not going to make it. They're going to kill us."

The opalescent-colored dragon ignored his warning and continued his death-defying dive. For a moment, Alex thought they would crash, but Chrysophylax pulled back, changing their angle of descent slightly, and headed straight for Ariadne. In the blink of an eye, the dragon snatched the Omphalos and passed through the spirit girl before pulling out of the dive. He started flapping his wings mightily to gain altitude and put distance between them and their foes.

But just as he thought they'd get away safely, two more people came out of the cave, aimed their staffs, and shot huge flaming balls of fire at them.

Everything was happening so quickly that Alex forgot about the ankh until he felt a familiar tingling sensation shoot through his arms and legs, surrounding him and Chrysophylax in a blue force field.

He felt a few shocks, which he assumed were explosions hitting the ankh's protective shield, but they faded, finally disappearing when they were a mile away from Delphi. Only then did he take the opportunity to look back. But it was too dark, and they were too far from Delphi to see anything.

Alex had no idea where they were going but trusted Chrysophylax implicitly.

CHAPTER 35
I'LL MEET YOU THERE

Diana waved goodbye to her mother, but all she got in return was a glower, which made her wonder if she'd ever have a good relationship with her again. With an aching heart, she watched the helicopter fade into the distance, then turned and went below to pack.

As she was pulling clothes from her drawers, she glanced up and noticed a dark spot inside her light. Curious, she got a chair to stand on, then reached over the open bowl to fish out the item. Her eyes flew open in disbelief when she realized what she held. Dropping it to the floor, she stepped on it, smiling at the satisfying crunch she felt under her foot.

Hurt by the subterfuge of her mother and the other Druid leaders, Diana went in search of Jane. When she finally found her, she grabbed one arm while holding a finger to her lips and led her outside.

As soon as Diana let go of Jane's arm, the older girl asked, "What's going on?"

"While packing, I spotted a listening device they put in my light. There's probably one in your room, too. They probably think we know where Alex is and what he's doing and have been bugging us ever since we returned," Diana replied.

"That's a safe assumption. But how do they think bugging us will help them, especially since they ordered us to return to Scotland?" Tapping her finger against her chin, Jane added, "Unless they think we'll ignore them and go after Alex."

"Okay, let's assume they're using us. That means they've probably planted bugs in all our stuff and have assigned someone to tail us," Diana said. "The question then is, what should we do." She began pacing back and forth across the rocky pillar, talking to herself sotto voce. "If we return to Scotland, we'll essentially be turning a blind eye to what's going on in our order and leaving Alex to the vagaries of fate. And I can't accept that. Since I doubt we'll be able to evade all the ways they're tracking us, we might as well be obvious and do as Alex suggested – keep our enemies closer. Maybe they'll let their guard down, and we'll be able to spot them. If we don't want them to hear something, all we have to do is get away from our stuff. Easy enough. But I just don't get why they won't listen to us."

"It's because they're crazy with fear, and unable to cope with all the changes going on," Jane replied."

"Intellectually, I get that. But it seems like it'd be a lot easier if they'd just listen."

Jane snorted. "They're human. They have the same frailties as everybody else, maybe more because they tend to overthink things. It's hard to see the women who raised us be so lost."

"But none of that is to the point. The real question is, what are we going to do."

"Ye're not going to argue that we return to Scotland?" Jane asked.

"Nope. My mom can't conceive of life outside the order. And when Deborah died, her hopes soared, because she thought that would mean I had a much better chance of becoming the next High Priestess of the Salem Grove. So, it's been hard for me to envision my life without what I've grown up with."

"Have ye ever talked to her about what ye've told me – of going off on yer own and having a business career and family?"

Diana shook her head. "She's ignored me every time I've talked about my dreams. And to be fair, I've changed my mind a lot. I guess what I really want is the option to have a life that is not bound by tradition. The problem is that I don't want to give up my magical abilities, which I'd have to do if I left the order. So, I don't have many options."

Both were quiet until Diana said, "Have you thought about how we find Alex?"

"I have, but it's more a hunch than anything else."

"Your hunches are usually better than most people's facts," Diana replied. "So, out with it. What do we do?"

"You know Alex. He can be pretty stubborn about things, which is why I'm guessing the first thing he'll do is track down that warlock and try to steal the Omphalos back. If he doesn't accomplish that, none of the rest matters."

"I agree, but you saw the magic of that giant warlock. The only time I've ever seen magic that powerful was in the caves under Lamanai. And that was with one ghost having one of the Maqlû, while the other had some magical staff. How's he going to defeat him?"

"He's got the ankh, his sister, and Chrysophylax," Jane replied.

"Do you think that's enough to get the Omphalos back? And if he does get it, what'll he do with it?"

"It seems unlikely he'll be able to steal it, but he's surprised us so many times that I wouldn't put anything past him. Your second question is easy, though. If he takes it, he'll try to destroy...." Jane's voice trailed off. "Which means...."

"Oh. Right. He's already told us how he thinks he has to destroy it, which limits the number of places we have to search."

"I don't know how many active volcanoes are in Europe or where they are. Do ye?" Jane asked.

"No, but give me a few minutes, and I'll do some research."

"Ye know, I never understood what Alex meant when he said he counted on ye to know stuff – until now. Can I do anything to help?"

"Maybe finish packing. Then you can help me when I'm ready. This should only take a few minutes."

True to her word, Diana had an answer in less than five minutes. Handing Jane a list, she said, "Here it is. I was surprised at how many active volcanoes there are in Europe. Not counting Iceland, there are over a dozen, with the most active being Mt. Etna in Italy. The most powerful one also happens to be in Italy – Mt. Vesuvius. Then, there is the line of volcanoes stretching from Greece to Turkey. But I wonder if he knows any of that."

"He might not, but Chrysophylax probably does." Jane began drumming her fingers on her dresser as she asked, "Which begs the question of which one will he head towards."

"They're about the same distance from here, but he's not one for beating around the bush – except when he's trying to hide something from us. I'm guessing he'll go to something he knows?"

"Then I think this is a perfect opportunity to apply Occam's Razor," Jane said.

"Okay, so Naples it is. He's not a big history buff, but I'm sure he's heard of the Pompeii disaster," Diana explained.

"Good point," Jane replied, "but that would indicate that he would head to Etna."

"You mentioned using Occam's Razor to figure out where he'll be. Yet here you are, adding in needless complexity. Are you saying you don't think he'll go to Vesuvius?"

"That makes sense, but the thing is, even though scientists consider Vesuvius an active volcano, the last time it erupted was… well, I don't know when, but it was a long time ago. And even if steam is coming out of the crater, I doubt it will do him any good. Which is why I think he'll conclude Vesuvius isn't what he's looking for and head south to a more active volcano, where lava regularly erupts – and that's Etna."

"That makes sense," Diana said.

They returned inside, where Diana went straight to her laptop and started typing furiously. After a few minutes, she said, "Okay, I've tentatively booked two tickets for us to Catania, which is at the base of Etna. But we need to get going because we have to go to Athens to catch the flight. There's one other catch, though. I'm not like Alex with his little trust fund."

Jane smiled. "Lady Yvaine has given me an expense account plus provided me with an identity that bumps up my age a little bit so I can get around on my own."

"Are you going to tell her what we're doing?" Diana asked.

"Of course. Well, at least part of it." Jane was silent for a moment, then started nodding as if she was in violent agreement with herself. "No, that's exactly what I'm going to do. She told me to keep an eye on Alex, and that's what I intend to do."

"What will you say about him probably wanting to destroy another one of the Maqlû."

Jane grinned. "I fear I might forget to mention that point when I talk to her."

When they were outside again, Jane said, "I've been thinking. Since Elizabeth has probably put tracers on our computers, gear, and phones, it'll be hard to be sneaky. Why don't we have some fun with this? Whenever we think they're listening, let's ham it up. Exaggerate the hell out of everything. Maybe we even talk about Alex's magical powers. Since they won't listen to us, why not feed the beast?"

With a gleam in her eye, Diana nodded and said, "With pleasure."

CHAPTER 36

QUESTIONS FROM THE HEART

Pythia watched in horror as Erra chased the Omphalos out of the cave, randomly shooting magical energy blasts at the invisible targets flying away.

When he finally slunk back in without the object, a stunned Erra asked, "What type of magic did that boy use to turn himself invisible?"

"I don't think he was using magic – at least not the way you and I know it," Pythia replied. "I'm guessing he used spirits to do his bidding."

"But how can he control spirits? Even you can't do that."

"I'm not sure. Maybe he has an innate ability to interact with the spirit world," Pythia replied. "I can only see spirits in the cup's waters, but I'm starting to wonder if he can communicate directly with them. Otherwise, how could he have defeated all the spirits I've sent after him, some with powerful magical objects."

"What happened to them?" Erra asked.

"That's just it. I don't know," Pythia said. "None have returned, while he continues to steal and destroy the Maqlû." She looked up at the giant warlock and said, "We must stop him before he destroys us and everything we've worked for. I no longer have the strength to pursue him, as I've been growing weaker since he started his unholy rampage. Will you go after him for me?"

"Of course, but how will I find him? I doubt he'll go back to Meteora."

"I might have a way. Come with me." Pythia went to her safe and pulled out the Cup of Jamshid. Setting it down on the table in the center of the room, she got up on her three-legged stool and stirred the silvery waters to life while chanting,

"Eyes of day, eyes of night

Let me see where he'll be."

Pythia held her breath, wondering if the cup would do her will – or act up again. She sighed in relief when the waters swirling around gradually coalesced into a picture of a mountain with a city spread out on its lower slopes. It stayed on the scene for only a few seconds before switching to a cone-shaped mountain. The second image lasted a few seconds longer before the cup went dark. Frustrated that the cup hadn't been more helpful, Pythia threw up her hands in disgust and screamed.

"What's wrong?" asked Erra.

"It's my cup. Ever since I had spirits kill that boy's family, my divination cup has worked only intermittently. And even when it shows me something, the images are often too confusing to interpret. For instance, I just asked it where the boy is, and it showed me pictures of two...."

"Two what?" Erra prompted.

Pythia didn't hear his question as she began drumming her fingers on the table while trying to remember where she'd seen the two mountains before. Suddenly, she slammed her hands down on the table, causing some of the precious liquid to spill out of her cup, and jumped up. "I've got it. I know where he's going. Well, at least I've narrowed down the places he might go."

"And...?"

"I believe he's headed for either Mt. Vesuvius or Mt. Etna."

"Why would he be going to volcanoes?" Erra asked.

"Why indeed?" Pythia lapsed into thoughtful silence. It was almost a minute before she made a sound, and then it was more of a wail. "No, no, no, no." She turned to Erra with a horrified look and said, "I fear he's taking the Omphalos to one of the volcanoes to destroy it."

"Which one?"

Pythia tapped her chin with one finger while thinking about how to respond. At last, she said, "If he is trying to destroy the Omphalos, he's probably thinking of dropping it into lava. However, he won't find much of that in Vesuvius, which means he'll have to go to Etna. That's where I recommend you go."

"How will I find him? If he can turn himself invisible, then I'll never be able to spot him," Erra said.

"I'm telling you, he can't make himself invisible," Pythia replied. "He's been using spirits to do his dirty work. No, if he's going to dispose of it, he'll carry it himself. I'd suggest you leave immediately because I have no idea what means of transportation he uses. Will you need any financial help?"

Erra shook his head. "I'll be fine. And this time, he won't escape me. I'll return here with the object in a few days."

"I have a couple of suggestions for you," Pythia said. "First and foremost, do NOT underestimate the boy. You tend to be single-minded, removing anything and everything from your path. But he's defeated many worthy foes, so don't think you can beat him with brute force alone. You need to be smarter than him. And second, know that the witches are our allies in this. They know him better than anybody else, have great numbers, and are furious with him. I'd recommend you go easy on the witches until you have the Omphalos. But then, do what you want with them because they want it as badly as I do."

Erra nodded and left without another word.

As Pythia watched her fellow Atlantian depart, she had a sinking feeling about the mission. She'd never seen Erra demonstrate planning skills, or subtlety, as he always barged ahead, using his magic and strength to shove obstacles out of his way. Hoping she wasn't being too pessimistic but wanting to cover her bases, she pulled out her phone and dialed the one person she knew who was as eager to rid the world of the pest as she was.

CHAPTER 37

MAGIC IS BELIEVING IN YOURSELF

Alex and Chrysophylax flew the rest of the night over country so remote that they only occasionally saw the lights of cities miles below. When they finally set down in a forested mountain area, just as the sky was starting to lighten, Alex asked, "Where are we?"

"We're in the arch of the boot of Italy," Chrysophylax replied before dropping the Omphalos with a sigh of relief. *"Oh, it feels good not having to carry that thing."*

"I'm sorry. I know it's big and heavy, but I was worried about hanging on to you and didn't think about how much of a burden it would be for you. I'll try rigging up something to make it easier for you to carry it. But why did you stop here?"

"I've been thinking about how to destroy the Omphalos and believe you should have multiple opportunities to select the right volcano. I don't remember all of them in the region, but I know most are in the Mediterranean in a fallen-down L-shape. We could start at Vesuvius, then, if that's not the right one, go to Etna. If that's still not the right one, then we could head east in a fairly straight line across a bunch of active volcanoes in the Greek Isles and Turkey."

"Let's do that, because I don't have a better plan. But, how far are we from Vesuvius?"

"About 300 kilometers, and about as far as I can go while carrying the object which means we should leave as soon as the sun sets. That would give us time to fly around Vesuvius and decide if it's the right place before it gets light tomorrow. Right now, though, we need to consider

our immediate needs. I know I said I don't need much food or rest, but I need both now. Do you think you could stay awake and guard the Omphalos long enough for me to go hunting and take a nap?"

"Of course. Go, do your thing," Alex said. "I'll watch the Omphalos."

Chrysophylax wasn't gone long, returning as the sun broached the horizon. As the dragon settled down, Alex asked, "Did you get enough to eat?"

"Yes, thank you. We're near the Mediterranean, so I gorged myself on fish. Now, if you don't mind, I'm going to rest."

Before Alex could respond, he heard Chrysophylax gently snoring. Shifting his gear and the Omphalos closer to the sleeping dragon, he began walking the camp perimeter, trying to stay awake. As the morning drug on, though, it got harder to keep going. He knew Chrysophylax hadn't slept in several days, but it wasn't like he'd gotten a lot of sleep either. And when he'd slept, it was usually fitful because his circadian rhythm was out-of-whack. That, plus his living conditions: infrequent meals, sleeping on the hard ground during the hot Greek summer days, and hanging on a dragon's neck for dear life in freezing temperatures at night, made it impossible to rest.

Alex was grateful when Chrysophylax finally woke up midday to take over guarding the object. He lay down and was instantly asleep. It seemed like he'd barely fallen asleep when a nudge woke him shortly before sunset. After a quick meal, he started packing up, but when he tried stuffing the Omphalos in his supply bag, it wouldn't fit.

He pulled everything back out and put on almost every piece of outer clothing, including his rain jacket and coat.

Then he stuffed as many other things as possible in every pocket before trying to pack the Omphalos again. Breathing a sigh of relief when it slipped in, he placed the bag's straps over Chrys's neck, wrapped the loose cords of the reins around his wrists, and climbed up. He'd barely settled down when Chrysophylax started flapping his way northwesterly.

At first, Alex sweltered with all the clothing he had on, but as Chrysophylax continued his ascent, he began enjoying the extra warmth and, for the first time, felt comfortable riding a dragon. But the warmth soon caused his eyelids to start drooping. With his eyes stinging from lack of sleep, he figured it wouldn't hurt to close them for a few seconds. Before he knew it, though, he'd fallen asleep.

Luckily, he jerked awake as he started sliding down Chrys' side. Scared that he'd nearly fallen off, Alex began humming to stay awake. But it wasn't long before his head drooped again. This time, though, he didn't wake up and slumped onto the dragon's back.

As he fell into a deeper sleep, his grip loosened, until he slipped sideways and fell off, jerking to a stop only when his thin homemade reins bit into his wrists.

Alex's eyes shot open. And thinking he was going to die, he screamed.

Chrysophylax immediately dropped his tail, threw his head back, and climbed straight into the sky, causing Alex to slam back into the dragon. Chrys dipped one shoulder so Alex could slide around his scaly neck, then leveled out when he felt a foot catch on his wing.

Still shaking with fear, Alex pushed himself back between the dragon's shoulder blades and clamped down with his arms and legs to ensure he wouldn't fall off again.

When he was sure Alex was secure on his back again, Chrys dipped into a shallow descent, landing on a rocky mountain slope above the timberline a short time later. He folded his wings and ducked into the forest, winding his way around until he found a small opening a hundred yards below where he'd landed.

"I'm sorry, Little One," Chrys said. *"I didn't realize I was pushing you too hard."*

"It's not your fault," Alex said as he started stripping off his extra clothing. "I was exhausted and dozed off. That was stupid and dangerous of me. I should have said something."

"We'll continue tomorrow night," the dragon replied. *"For now, though, get some rest. You must be at your best when we get to Vesuvius."*

"You're right. This thing," Alex said as he pulled the bag containing the Omphalos over Chrys's head, "has been around for millennia. It won't hurt to take extra time to do things right." He searched for a comfortable spot to lay down, fluffed his coat into a pillow, and was soon fast asleep.

Alex slept the rest of that night and half the next day. By the time they took off the next night, he felt more rested than at any time since he'd left Scotland, which now seemed like the distant past.

They reached Naples shortly before midnight and began circling the ancient volcano, gradually descending from over 15,000 feet to less than 5,000 feet in elevation, barely a thousand feet above the volcano's peak. Even though it was the middle of the night, the lights of Naples and the surrounding countryside lit the area, making it easy to see the mountain.

After the third circuit, Chrysophylax asked, *"What do you think? Is this the right place?"*

Alex hesitated before replying, "I don't think so. It doesn't feel right, but I can't figure out if it's because it's not the right place or it's crazy to see all these people living on the slopes of an active volcano. I mean, if it blew, tens of thousands of people would die. And they should know better, because it's happened before."

"The choices of where humans choose to live have always baffled me. But focus. Is this the right place?"

Alex started to put a hand over his chest to feel the ankh but realized he couldn't touch it through all the layers of clothing he was wearing. He closed his eyes, trying to sense if it was telling him anything. But there was no signal from it. Opening his eyes, he said, "Nope. This isn't it. You said Etna was the next place. How far is it?"

"It's a few hundred kilometers south of here. We'll get to the toe of Italy early this morning, stop for the day, then approach Etna tomorrow night." Without waiting for guidance, Chrysophylax dipped his right shoulder and headed south.

The next night, they flew south, over the Tyrrhenian Sea, reaching Sicily's northern coastline shortly after midnight. "How far now?" Alex asked as soon as they were over land.

"Not far. I estimate we have a little over thirty kilometers before we reach Mt. Etna," Chrys replied.

A short while later, the moon broke through the cloud cover, illuminating a large conical mountain that dominated the southern horizon. Shivers, that he hadn't felt near Vesuvius shot through Alex as they approached the giant volcano. But it was several minutes before he realized it was due to the ankh thumping against his chest. "This is it," he told Chrys.

"Are you sure?"

"Of course not. But last night over Vesuvius, my ankh was inert. It's acting weird tonight like it's fearful of this place – like it doesn't like the idea I'm trying to get rid of the Omphalos. Which probably means it's the right place."

"Has it fought you when you've destroyed the other Maqlû?"

"That's one of the strange things about the ankh. At first, it's eager to get to the Maqlû, but then it tries to stop me when I start thinking of destroying the object. But in the end, when push comes to shove, it has always helped me destroy the objects," Alex replied.

"That's bizarre," Chrys replied. *"Someday, you'll have to explain it better to me, but right now, I need to look for a place to set down close enough to that city in the distance that you'll be able to get supplies.*

They circled the city, which was much smaller than Naples, a couple of times before Chrysophylax said, *"It looks like the only landing spot close enough for you to get into the city is on the beach. So, even though I'm using a glamour spell to hide us, I worry about someone spotting me. It might work if I come in low and slow off the sea, and you jump onto the beach while I keep flying. Then, I could pick you up tonight in the same spot."*

"If I have to jump off, how will I get back on, especially with you flying?" Alex asked.

Chrysophylax made a sound like clearing his throat. *"Do you trust me?"*

"Yeah, but you make it sound like a scary question," Alex replied.

"I was thinking I'd grab you while I fly over the beach, then set you down someplace remote where you can climb on my back."

Alex thought about the large, sharp talons on Chrys's front legs. "Will it be safe?"

"As long as you don't squirm while I'm flying."

Hoping it wasn't more dangerous than flying with ghosts, he reluctantly agreed. "Fine. I need supplies, and this seems like the best way to do it. Since it's late, I'll find a hotel room, clean up, and get some rest before going shopping tomorrow. But how will we coordinate my pickup?"

"I don't need a watch to keep track of time, so meet me on the beach at midnight tomorrow. I'll swoop in as soon as you're ready for me."

Alex tossed his supply bag, staff, and pack off as soon as they swept in over the beach. Gulping down his fears, he launched himself off Chrys's back just as the dragon dropped the Omphalos. He hit the ground hard and rolled a couple of times before stopping. By the time he looked up, Chrys had disappeared into the darkness.

Wincing, he walked around on the beach, picking up his gear and the object before turning inland. Luckily, even though it was the middle of the night, he found a hotel room fairly close and, after a quick shower, fell into bed thinking it was a much better day than he'd expected.

Alex didn't wake until midday. After checking out, he found a storage locker and shoved his bag in, so he didn't have to lug his gear around all day. He was about to follow it with the staff when he rethought the idea, remembering how nobody could lift it. Not wanting to crush the thin sheet metal of the locker, he slammed the door closed, took the key, and headed outside. With nothing else to do for the next few hours, he decided to wander around and see some of the sites of the ancient city before getting his supplies later that day.

Overcoming his natural shyness, he started asking strangers for help and eventually found a middle-aged woman who could speak English. She suggested several choices, including a centuries-old cathedral, ancient Roman theaters, and a seaside fortress. Selecting the castle, he got directions and headed for it.

A little while later, he stood in front of an old lava stone fort with massive walls that reminded him of a smaller but taller version of Avila. Looking at the front gate, he was trying to decide whether to go in when a car stopped behind him, and he heard, "Alex? Is that you?"

He swung around and was surprised to see Diana hanging out the window of a car, with Jane behind the steering wheel. "Don't go anyplace," she said. "We'll park and be right back."

Alex only had to wait a few minutes before both girls were running towards him. Diana was the first to reach him and engulfed him in a hug. Jane didn't wait and wrapped her arms around the other two when she caught up.

When they finally disengaged, Alex asked, "What are you two doing here? Is anybody else here?"

Diana shook her head. "You think this is a coincidence? Hardly. We've done a lot of second-guessing trying to figure out where you were headed. Do you know how nerve-wracking it was seeing you fly off, knowing you were going after that warlock to steal the Omphalos back and not knowing what happened?"

"I'm sorry about all you've been through, but I couldn't stay."

"Did you get it?"

He nodded and said, "It's in a locker with the supply bag you filled for me."

Diana's jaw dropped. "You left one of the Maqlû in a public locker? Don't you realize how many people are looking for it? Why, anyone could steal it."

Alex grinned. "How's anyone going to know where it is? Heck, I'll struggle just to get back to it."

Jane gently gripped Diana's arm and said, "Relax. I'm sure it'll be okay. We should be grateful he reclaimed it, as I've been worried we'd lost it for good." She turned to Alex and added, "You can tell us all about your adventures over lunch, including how you got here."

Alex grinned. "Are you buying because I'm starving?"

"When aren't you?" Diana replied while looking around for a restaurant.

They found one nearby and discussed everything that had happened since Alex left Meteora. When they'd finished lunch, Jane asked, "What are yer next steps?"

"Well, the first thing is I've got to get more supplies. I was so hungry the last time I saw you that I ate up most of what you'd gotten me pretty quickly. And it's kind of tough to find an inconspicuous place to land and get things when you're flying around on a dragon. After that, I'm not sure. As I said before, I feel like Etna is the right place to destroy the Omphalos, but I have no idea how to go about it."

"Well, there's one thing about all this," Jane said. "Ye've become predictably unpredictable. How can we help?"

"Are you sure you want to get involved?" Alex asked. "I mean, I'm going to try to find some way into the volcano and drop the Omphalos into a magma pool. That sounds incredibly dangerous and stupid to me. I was hoping to fly over the top of it and drop it in, but Chrys said the magma pools are usually deep underground."

"Usually, he's right – except for when the volcano is erupting. We figured you'd have to find some way into the mountain. And if you do find a way in, the gasses might kill you, so we got you this gas mask," Diana said, handing him a package.

Alex took the bag and peeked inside. Shaking his head, he said, "You guys are amazing, but you can't come with me. It'll be too dangerous."

Diana's sapphire blue eyes flashed. "You don't understand. We're going with you no matter what you say. She took a deep breath and placed a hand on his arm, adding, "I can imagine what it's like having to worry about diving into volcanoes and looking over your shoulder to see if a bunch of mad witches and warlocks are coming after you. But, you need us. Besides, we're guessing your grandma and the others are already here, waiting for us to make our next move."

"What! Couldn't you shake them?"

"We've been keeping track of them by leaving a trail of breadcrumbs they could follow," Jane said, "because we don't want to be surprised by them any more than ye do."

Alex took a deep breath, before saying, "It's comforting to have you guys with me, but I need to think about it some more. I came here today mainly to get some supplies, and I still need to go shopping. But maybe we could have dinner and talk about it some more. Then we can go to where I'm meeting Chrys and finalize plans."

CHAPTER 38

ASCENT

Jane found a place to park her rental car half an hour before the designated rendezvous.

Reunited with his best friends, rested, warm, restocked, and with a full stomach, Alex found the waiting far more bearable than he'd expected. But his blissful state only lasted a minute before Jane turned to him and said, "I don't think this is the way to do it."

"What do you mean?" he asked.

"Well, for one thing, I don't think ye can destroy that object by flying over Etna and dropping it into the crater. Most likely, it'd land on rocks and be accessible to anyone willing to risk descending into the crater to pick it up. If ye think this is the right place to get rid of that thing, then ye'll need to find a way on the ground."

"I agree with Jane," Diana said. "You need a different plan. Do you have any other thoughts on how to do it?"

Alex stared into the growing darkness for a minute before finally saying, "I knew things were going too smoothly to last. Wait here. I'll let Chrys know there's a change of plans. Then, if you don't mind, I'd like a ride up the mountain. I'm unsure where to go, but my gut tells me it's up there."

Without waiting for a response, he got out and walked down to the beach. He didn't have long to wait until he heard Chrys' voice in his head. *"Are you ready, Little One?"*

"There's a change in plans, Chrys. I don't think dropping the Omphalos into the volcano from the air will work, so I'm going up the mountain with my friends to find another way in. But, I'd appreciate it if you could stay close so you could help me if needed."

"Are you sure about this?" Chrysophylax asked.

Alex took a deep breath and let it out. "It's the right thing to do, although I couldn't have gotten this far without you. Now, go hide someplace where you'll be safe. I hope to see you soon."

Saddened at the thought of his dragon friend flying away over the Ionian Sea, he trudged back to the car. After getting in, he said, "He's gone. Now, if we're going up the mountain tomorrow, I'd like to get a good night's sleep and be on our way by dawn. The hotel where I stayed last night was nice and close by."

"We guessed ye'd come here to Catania, but didn't know when, so we already have a couple of rooms," Jane said. "Ye can have one." She started the car, and they discussed plans for the next day on the way to the hotel.

Dawn came all too soon. The ride up Mt. Etna was quiet, as all three were either lost in thought or still waking up. They'd just left the outskirts of the Sicilian city when Deborah and Ariadne appeared inside the car, both with frantic looks on their face. "What's wrong?" Alex asked, overcoming the strange sight of seeing the two ghosts floating inside the front seat.

"Everybody's coming for you," Deborah replied breathlessly. "Grandma and almost a dozen Bandruí arrived in Catania by plane a few minutes ago. And, that beast of a man we stole the Omphalos from, along with two henchmen, just arrived at the train station. Since they know you're here, I'm sure they'll all be coming up the mountain soon after you."

"I figured they'd come, but I hoped to have a little more breathing room," Alex replied.

"Are you talking to your sister?" Diana asked.

"Yeah. Deb and Ariadne showed up and said your order, that warlock, and a couple of his goons are heading our way."

"How can you be so blasé about the danger you're in?" Deborah asked.

"I'm not, but at least I don't have to keep looking over my shoulder every few minutes wondering if they're near," Alex said. "Besides, I'm more worried about surviving the volcano than them."

"I think you should be more worried about your pursuers," Diana replied. "You have to avoid them to get where you're going. And we can't keep driving around this mountain because there's only so far we can go before we have to turn around and come back down. We could easily become sitting ducks."

"Diana's right," Jane said. "The question now is, where to?"

Alex pulled the ankh out from under his shirt and stared at it. At last, he said, "I feel like we're getting closer, so let's keep going."

Once they left the city, the landscape quickly changed. Initially, vineyards spread over the hillside, taking advantage of the rich volcanic soil. But as they went higher, the vineyards slowly gave way to more sparsely vegetated rocky areas where trees and plants tried to establish themselves in the debris from old lava rivers and ancient volcanic craters.

The higher they climbed, the steeper the slope became, requiring more and more switchbacks and causing Diana to go pale. Seeing her discomfort, Alex suggested they pull over at the next available spot.

Jane found a pullout a little ways up the road and parked. Alex got out and was studying an immense lava flow when he heard a crunching sound behind him. His nerves were so on edge that he jumped and whirled around, ready to flee. He felt goofy when he saw it was only Diana.

"I wanted to thank you for noticing my distress and doing something about it. I don't know how much longer I could've lasted. All those turns were too much for me."

He smiled and said, "No problem. But I have to tell you, I've had several experiences over the last year that have given me a new appreciation for how miserable one can get with motion sickness."

Both were silent until Jane joined them and said, "Ye know, it's okay to be nervous about what's ahead. In fact, it would be unnatural if ye weren't."

"Who says I'm worried?" Alex replied.

"I've been watching ye since we stopped and know yer troubled by something. What is it?"

"The ankh is tugging me to cross that lava field."

"But there's nothing down there but rock," Diana said.

Alex pointed to a small tree-covered hill in the middle of the lava field and said, "I think it's urging me to go towards that." He bent over the railing and looked down, then added, "My problem is that I don't know how to get down there. Where's a dragon when you need them?"

"Didn't you say your sister and Ariadne are here?" Diana asked. "Maybe they could lift us down."

"No, no, no. I can't let you follow me into the middle of a volcano," Alex said.

"We didn't ask what yer thoughts on the subject were. Just ask them if they'll help," Jane replied.

Deborah drifted over and said, "No need. We've been listening to the conversation. If we can lift you, then of course we'll help."

Alex went to the car, pulled out his pack and supply bag, then started reorganizing the contents. "What are you doing?" Diana asked.

"My sister said she and Ariadne would try to lift us down, so I'm getting ready. I want to keep my hands free, so I'll use my pack to carry the Omphalos, plus the little bit of food and water I can cram in and leave the rest of my supplies in the car. If you still plan on coming with me, I suggest you figure out the minimum you need to carry and get ready. With all those people after me, I can't afford to sit around and wait."

Within minutes, they were ready. As soon as Alex slipped his pack on, Deborah and Ariadne each grabbed an arm and lifted him over the fence and through the trees on the other side. Almost immediately, they started dropping. Worried they would crash, he screamed, "Can you slow down?"

"We're trying," replied Deborah. "We should have tested to see how strong we were."

When they were only ten feet above the lava field, Deborah shouted, "Lift harder, Ariadne."

Alex hit so hard that his legs crumpled. Dazed from the hard landing, he could hear his sister anxiously asking if he was all right. He waved his hand to indicate he was okay and pushed himself up. "Do you think you can get the girls down here safely? Diana's about my size but won't be carrying as much weight as I am. But Jane is bigger than me."

"It wasn't your weight," Ariadne replied. "I felt something pushing you down here."

Alex pulled off his pack and pulled out the Omphalos. He immediately dropped it when he felt it giving off a strange vibration. Looking up, he said, "Sorry about that.

It feels like it's anxious about being down here, almost as if it knows I'm trying to destroy it."

"That sounds so weird," Deborah said. "But, I've been around you long enough not to be surprised at what happens."

He picked it up and slowly turned, holding the magical object like a compass. When he faced the forested hill in the middle of the lava field, the Omphalos started shaking but quieted down as he turned away. After shoving it back in his pack, he said, "Yep. That's what it was."

"Can you handle it?" Deborah asked.

"I should be able to. But you better hurry and get Jane and Diana. I want to get across that open area without anybody seeing us."

Minutes later, the party of five set off across the lava field.

The going was a lot harder than Alex thought it would be. When he'd looked down on the lava from above, it looked much smoother than it actually was. Deep furrows every few feet required them to jump across or climb down into and back out of the crevices. Even on the flat stretches, the hard lava rocks strewn all over made it difficult to walk across.

Half an hour in, Jane suggested a break. All three gratefully knocked some of the loose rocks away and sat down.

"Are ye sure we're going the right way?" Jane asked.

Alex nodded. "The Omphalos is acting like a little kid who doesn't want to go where I want it to, so all I'm doing is going whichever way it doesn't want me to."

"Can I touch it and feel what you're talking about?" Diana asked.

"I don't think you should. Like I said, it's acting weird, and I'm afraid of what it might do."

"What about you?" Diana said. "Why are you safe with it?"

Alex patted the ankh underneath his shirt. "I have a defense mechanism."

Wanting to get out of the open and into the forested hill ahead of them as quickly as possible, Alex got up before he felt rested and was about to lead them onward when he heard the distant thwop-thwop sound of an approaching helicopter. Without looking up, he grabbed his bag and ran across the lava field as fast as he could, crying, "Hurry. We've got to get out of sight before they see us."

They didn't make it, but to Alex's relief, the helicopter made only a single pass overhead, then headed back in the direction it came. As he slowed to a walk, he heard Diana cry out in pain. He turned and, seeing she was holding her ankle, rushed back to her, reaching her just as Jane did.

Jane knelt beside Diana and gently removed her shoe and sock, grimacing when she saw it was already turning a light shade of blue. Without looking up, she said, "She's twisted her ankle pretty badly and can't go any further until I bandage it up. Even then, I'll need some help to move her because she won't be able to put any weight on it, especially on this ground."

Diana waved Alex away. "I know what you're thinking, but I'll be fine. Go, do your thing, and get rid of it. Jane can get help, or if my read on that helicopter is right, my mom and your grandma will be here soon."

Looking to Jane to appeal Diana's stubbornness, Alex said, "I'm not leaving her behind."

"Ye swore ye'd destroy that thing," Jane replied. "So go and do it." Without giving Alex a chance to argue, she reached into her pack and pulled out her first aid kit.

"I agree with them," Deborah interjected. "Go. Ariadne and I will stay here and airlift Diana and Jane back to the car."

Alex hesitated, then told the girls what his sister had said.

Jane sighed. "I wish I had the same ability as yer sister to influence ye. But I'll take her up on her offer. And since she can hear me, I'll be able to instruct them on what to do. Now go. I doubt if ye have much time before one, or both, of yer pursuers will be here."

Alex slung his pack on and headed for the forested hill. Several times, he looked back at Jane and Diana alone on the slope, but each time, the ankh pulled him forward. He paused to rest when he finally reached the tree line, but as he caught his breath, he heard a pair of helicopters approaching.

He watched as they set down near Jane and Diana and disgorged half a dozen women. Part of him wanted to wait and see if one of them would help Diana, but he pushed on, knowing time was of the essence.

Unsure where he should head, he skirted along the lower edge of the hill and was relieved to find it was much easier to walk on than the lava flow. He'd only gone a short distance when he heard Sibyl inside his head saying, "I've been listening to your plans and believe I've discovered a way into the volcano. Just keep going, and you'll spot Sadie. She'll show you the way in."

He looked around for his mysterious ghost whisperer but, as usual, didn't spot her. Alex was still looking for her when he stepped onto squishy ground cover and fell into a hidden hole. He landed hard, a few feet below ground level. Dazed by the fall, it took him a minute to recover and notice Sadie had appeared on his lap.

The little dragon nudged him towards what looked like a lava tube sloping down into the mountain. Hoping he'd stumbled into the way he needed to go, he pulled out the Omphalos and noticed it was fighting him as if it wanted to get out of the hole.

Convinced he was in the right place, he stuffed the object back into his pack and was about to crawl into the tunnel when he felt the ankh vibrating against his chest. He hesitated, trying to decide whether to ignore the little cross, or trust his gut that something was going wrong.

Guilt won out.

He rose up in the hole and looked outside. His stomach did a flip flop when he saw three men repelling from a helicopter – and one of them was the giant who'd stolen the Omphalos.

CHAPTER 39

A BLAST FROM THE PAST

Elizabeth looked out the helicopter's window at the barren lava field below and wondered what had possessed her grandson to come to such a god-forsaken place. It had been easy to track him using the listening devices she'd planted in Jane and Diana's gear, but somehow, he'd always managed to stay one step ahead of them despite all the resources at her disposal – until now.

Spotting two of the figures she'd seen in their first pass, Elizabeth ordered the pilot to set down. As soon as the landing skids touched, women began pouring out of the two helicopters. Elizabeth had just gotten out from under the whirling blades when Sophie met her and said, "Jane and my daughter are a few hundred yards away, but there's no sign of your grandson."

"I'm sure they can tell us something of his whereabouts, so let's get moving," Elizabeth replied.

When they reached the girls, Elizabeth looked at Diana's bandaged ankle and asked, "What happened? Did my grandson cause this?"

Jane shook her head. "No. She has a severe ankle sprain. This terrain is tougher to walk on than it looks, so I'd advise ye to be careful where ye step."

"It serves you right since both of you disobeyed me in Meteora," Elizabeth retorted.

Jane stood up and stepped towards the older woman. "Jest a reminder. I don't report to ye. I report to Lady Yvaine, who has tasked me with keeping an eye on yer grandson. And since ye deserted Diana, I brought her along to keep her safe."

Sophie pushed through the assembled women and glared at Jane. "Well, you didn't do a good job of it." She looked down at her daughter and said, "As for you, I'll deal with you when I get back to Stormhold, where I expect you to be waiting."

"Are you just going to leave me here, Mom?" Diana asked in a shocked tone.

"You made your bed. Now lie in it," Sophie replied.

Diana's jaw dropped as she'd never seen her mother so uncaring. "You don't know what you're getting into, Mom. You should quit while you're all still alive. Otherwise, this manhunt of yours will end in disaster."

One of the women at the back said, "The only one who's risking anything is your boyfriend. He stole the Omphalos, and now he's going to pay for it."

Diana's face grew red and she practically stuttered as she spat out, "He's not my boyfriend."

Jane laid a hand on Diana's shoulder to cut her off. "Don't worry about us," she said. "We'll manage."

Taken aback by Jane's unexpected acquiescence, Elizabeth hesitated a second before she asked, "Which way did he go?"

Diana smirked. "What, the listening and tracking devices you put in our gear aren't helping anymore? Did you think we wouldn't find them? We've known about them since Meteora and thought it would be easier to keep track of you if we told you where we were going. I hope it worked okay for you because it made our task easier."

"There's no need to antagonize them, Diana." Jane pointed to the small hill ahead of them, and said, "He's gone that way. But, I'd advise you not to pursue him. It's too dangerous, and you don't know what you're getting into."

"Why should we listen to a squib?" one woman shouted. "I'll never understand what Lady Yvaine sees in you."

Jane shrugged. "I've heard those kind of remarks for years, so they don't bother me anymore. But, ye should heed our warning and don't blame us if anything happens to ye."

Elizabeth, who'd been listening to the exchange, trying to make sense of the girls' combative attitudes, suddenly got an uneasy feeling and asked. "What do you know about what's ahead of us? Is he planning to ambush us or something?"

"Ye don't know yer grandson if you think he's what ye have to worry about," Jane replied. "He's not up here to take a hike around the mountain. He's planning to walk into an active volcano and get rid of the Omphalos. So, if I were ye, I'd turn around before it's too late."

"Enough of this," Sophie screamed. "You're trying to scare us off." Glaring at the other women, she said, "If none of you are willing to go forward, I am." Without saying another word, she headed off in the direction Jane had pointed.

Elizabeth shifted the pack on her back and followed Sophie. But she'd only gone a little ways when a sizzling ball of blue energy zipped past her head and exploded a few feet away. She whirled around and saw the same giant bearded man who'd wrecked Meteora running towards them, leading two other men. One ball of energy hit the ground near Jane, bounced, and blew up Diana's phone. Another hit the woman at the back of the column, sending her crashing to the ground where she lay, never to move again.

Instinct took over as Elizabeth shouted, "Run!" while simultaneously conjuring up a fireball. Stepping into her throw, she hurled it at the trio of men and smiled with grim satisfaction when it caught one of the men in the chest, setting his clothes on fire. Seeing the giant point his staff at her, Elizabeth dove, wincing when she hit the lava rock.

The next minute was chaos as the standing Druids threw fireballs while the giant warlock and his remaining assailant hurled energy spheres back. Elizabeth heard screams all around her, then moans.

With the fighting ended, the warlock ignored the remaining Druids and ran through them, following the same path Alex had taken. It took Elizabeth another minute before she'd gathered her senses and scrambled to where the nearest Druid lay – dead.

Of the women who'd eagerly jumped off the helicopters, she and Sophie were the only ones unharmed. Three of their number were dead, while the rest lay injured.

She'd never been a fan of Jane Roland, but when she saw the lanky girl running to their aid, she thought she'd never seen a more welcome sight. Elizabeth became so distracted helping the wounded that she didn't hear the bellowing sound a few minutes later on the mountain above, nor the roar of fire and ensuing curses.

CHAPTER 40
THE CHERUFE

Alex's stomach churned uncomfortably as he watched the carnage unfold a short distance from him. He started pulling himself out of the hole to go to the aid of the Druids, but stopped when he saw the giant warlock spot him and throw a sizzling ball of energy at him. Alex dropped back into the ground and felt the little looped cross's force field spring up around him – just in time to deflect a sizzling ball of energy that hit the edge of the hole and ricochet onto a nearby boulder, sending chunks of rock flying everywhere. One, somehow passed through the forcefield and gashed his leg, sending him scrambling into the tunnel.

An ear-splitting roar caused him to pause and chance a peek out of the hole. Even though he'd always been impressed with Diana's magical abilities, he knew dragons were much more powerful. He had no idea how much more until he saw Chrys diving at Erra while conjuring up a car-sized sphere of white-hot flames that appeared to erupt out of the dragon's mouth. As the magical fire hurtled towards Earth, Erra held up his staff and shouted something in a strange language, causing a force field to pop up and sending the flames curling harmlessly around him.

"I can't defeat the Atlantian. His staff gives him much greater powers than mine," Chrys said as he pulled up and back-flapped his wings to hover in place. *"I'll try to distract him and buy enough time for you to destroy the object. Now go! Otherwise, everything is for naught."* Chrys conjured up another fireball and hurled it at their attacker, but it was only half the size of the first. Needing

no further urging, Alex hobbled deeper into the mountain, wincing with every step.

At first, the sunlight from the entrance was enough to see where he was going. But as Alex headed further into the mountain, the light dimmed, eventually becoming so dark that he had to reach into his pack for his flashlight – only to remember he'd left it in the car, along with most of his supplies. Feeling the gas mask Diana and Jane had given him, he pulled it out, strapped it around his waist, then grabbed his staff and limped after Sadie, who flew deeper into the mountain, leaving him alone in the gloom.

He'd only gone a short distance when he noticed an eerie yellow-green glow up ahead. When he reached it, he saw the light came from bits of phosphorescent stone embedded in the walls of the tube, enabling him to see several feet ahead.

Alex kept following the tunnel, but it grew increasingly hotter the farther he descended. Sweating profusely, he had to keep pausing to wipe the sweat off, but eventually realized it was futile and pressed on, letting the salty liquid sting his eyes and drench his shirt. But the heat was only one problem as breathing in the sulfurous-smelling air pouring over him became more difficult.

The tunnel headed steadily down, occasionally twisting back and forth, until it emptied into a large chamber with stalactites and stalagmites scattered throughout. Seeing several chambers leading off the room on the other side, he paused, trying to figure out which one to take. He checked the ankh for a clue, but it lay inert against his chest. Not knowing which opening to take, he chose the center one and started across the room. Before he reached halfway, though, a large lake blocked his progress.

Alex turned and skirted the lake's edge, heading towards the left wall. Just before he reached the end of the lake, he heard rushing water. Curious, he approached the lake's outlet and was surprised to see the water flowing into a tunnel with a small stone pathway to one side. When he felt the Omphalos trying to pull him away from the stream, he knew he was on the right track and plunged into the small tunnel.

The path followed the watercourse ever deeper into the Earth. Other rivulets merged, quickly turning the once placid trickle into a rushing torrent that splashed over the rocks and onto the path, forcing Alex to grow more cautious and feel his way down to prevent from falling.

Spray from the cascading stream seemed to subdue the sulfurous fumes and cool Alex, making his passage bearable until, suddenly, the stream plunged into a hole to continue its descent into the bowels of the Earth. Alex immediately felt hotter and smelled more noxious-smelling air swirling around him. Feeling light-headed and unsure whether it was from the fumes, heat, or exhaustion, he put on his gas mask. The instant he put it on, though, he felt suffocated. Worse yet, the mask reduced his visibility making it nearly impossible to see where he was going. Fearing he would trip and hurt himself and be unable to escape the literal hell hole he was in, he turned and started descending sideways to reduce his chance of tripping.

With his clothes drenched and his throat on fire, he yearned for a drink, but he couldn't bring himself to remove his face mask and risk succumbing to poisonous gases. Despite thinking his plan to get rid of the Omphalos in the heart of a volcano was the dumbest and most dangerous thing he'd ever done, he pressed on.

It seemed like he'd been going downwards forever when he finally spotted an orange-red glow far below. Hoping he was nearing the end of his journey, Alex picked up the pace only to run into Sadie, who agitatedly flapped her wings in his face and squawked while sending him images of a giant burning monster. Alex picked up the little dragon, hoping to calm it down, and said, "Relax. It'll be okay. It's hot down here, but I haven't burned up yet and am not about to. Besides, it looks like I'm almost at the end of my journey because that glow has to be from magma."

His words of encouragement didn't calm Sadie as she continued sending him images of the burning monster. Alex tried petting her to quiet her down, but the little Ryūjin dragon wouldn't have it and flew out of his arms, and up the passage he'd just come down. Unsure what had upset her, but desperately wanting to get rid of the Omphalos, he continued his descent.

The air soon became so stifling that sweat poured out of every pore in his body. Needing a break, he paused and briefly lifted his mask to gulp some water. Despite the fumes, the respite from not having to breathe through the mask felt invigorating. But no sooner had he resumed his journey than he hit some loose stones and found himself skiing down a mountain of loose rocks. Despite the pain shooting through his injured leg, he stuck his staff in the rocks and leaned back, using it as a ski pole to keep him upright. Just when he thought he was safe, though, his staff hit a hidden boulder, sending him tumbling head over heels down the slope until he crashed onto a scalding stone floor.

Feeling like he'd bruised every muscle in his body, he saw he was less than twenty feet away from a pool of magma. It took him a few seconds for his head to clear, and realize the heat from the rock underneath him was burning through his clothes. He jumped up, but didn't move, as all he could do was stare at the bubbling molten rock – the most beautiful, but terrifying sight he'd ever beheld.

With waves of heat rolling over him, the temperature was unbearable, made worse by the sticky hot blood mixing with sweat dripping down his arms. He briefly considered bandaging his arms, but he was so close to his goal that he figured a little more blood wouldn't kill him.

He shook his head to clear it, then pulled off his pack. But as he was pulling out the Omphalos, he sensed movement in the magma pool. Looking up he saw a giant Cherufe emerge from the molten rock, looking exactly like the image of the burning monster Sadie had sent him.

As Alex stared at the twenty-foot-tall beast with flames leaping off his lava-like body, a rumbling voice that shook the ground asked, "Who dares enter my domain?

CHAPTER 41

BETWEEN A ROCK AND A HOT PLACE

Not waiting for an answer, the monster swung his arm out, sending a long, thin line of flames shooting towards Alex.

Alex dove, burning his hands and knees when he slammed into the sizzling floor. Luckily the Cherufe's fiery whip-like flames whooshed past him, just inches above his head. With the ankh not coming to his defense, Alex did the only thing he could think of to stave off disaster. He raised his gnarly staff above his head and slammed it onto the ground. The magical hammer hit so hard that it caused the Cherufe to stagger and sent magma sloshing over the sides, nearly reaching Alex.

Surprised by the attack, the Cherufe stood in the pool of bubbling magma, uncertain what to do about the puny human. At last, he said, "Leave, human, before I lose my patience. Your presence disturbs me."

Alex pulled the Omphalos out of his pack and held it up. "I'm sorry, but I have to destroy this thing. And the only way to do it is to throw it into the heart of this volcano."

The Cherufe waded through the magma as a person would walk through shallow water. When he got close to the edge, he bent over and poked a fiery finger at the object, knocking it out of Alex's hands and sending it rolling a few feet away. "Why is it so important you destroy it?" the monster asked. "Is it a sacrifice to your gods?"

Alex backed up a couple of steps to get relief from the Cherufe's intense body heat. "No. This is a magical object that people have fought over for centuries. It brings out the worst in my kind," he replied in a voice heavily muffled by the gas mask.

"Then take it away. I don't want such things polluting my world."

"Please, I've worked too hard to get here," Alex said. "The object isn't what's bad. It's the greed and lust for power it inspires in my species. If I can destroy it, I'll be ridding the world of something no one should have made in the first place."

"Very well then. Throw it in, but only if you promise you'll never return," the fiery monster said before slowly sinking back into the magma.

"I guarantee I'll never come back," he replied to an empty cavern. Mumbling to himself, he added, "There's no way I'd want to inflict this type of torture on myself again." Alex then stepped over to the Omphalos and was about to pick it up when a ball of energy struck only a few feet away.

"Leave it alone, Boy. That object is mine."

Alex's eyes widened when he looked up and saw the bearded giant striding down the lava tube. Unsure whether the ankh would help him, he tried bluffing his way out of the situation. "Back off before I hurt you," he shouted.

Caught off guard by the unlikely challenge, Erra threw back his head and laughed. "You and what army, Boy?"

Stung by the giant's dismissive attitude, he replied in a hurt voice, "Don't underestimate me. I might be a lot smaller than you, but I have, uh … hidden talents."

Despite his obvious advantages of size and magical powers, Pythia's warnings about the boy caused Erra to pause. Needing time to think through the situation, he temporized. "Take that blasted mask off so I can understand your ramblings," he growled.

Seeing the warlock wasn't suffering from the fumes, Alex hesitantly pulled his gas mask off and hung it on his belt, ready to put it back on if he started feeling dizzy. The relief from suffocating inside it was immediate.

"Stay out of my way, Boy, and maybe I'll be generous and let you live."

Alex didn't know how to respond, but doubted the giant would spare him. He looked for a way out of his predicament, but saw nothing that would help him. With the ankh giving him mixed signals, he turned to his staff. Raising it above his head, he was relieved to see it shimmer, then turn into the magical sledgehammer. Calling on all his built-up frustration, he slammed it into the ground as hard as he could. The ground shook so hard that rocks came crashing down, some falling into the magma and causing the hot liquid stone to splash all around.

"What are you doing?" Erra cried out. "Are you trying to get us both killed?"

Inching closer to the Omphalos, Alex retorted, "I thought you said you weren't worried about me."

Pythia's warnings about the boy caused Erra, for the first time, to worry he might lose the encounter. "No you don't," the warlock shouted thrusting out his staff and sending another blast of energy at Alex.

With the ankh not having been much help since he'd entered the lava tube, Alex was relieved when he felt its force field pop up around him, causing Erra's blast to harmlessly bounce away. His relief was short-lived, though, as Erra leapt off the path, landing only a few feet away from the Omphalos. Drained by the heat, Alex didn't react quickly and watched as the Atlantian grabbed the object and started running up the tunnel."

Seeing all his hard work rapidly disappearing, Alex threw his hammer at the retreating figure – but missed. The magical weapon struck the tunnel wall instead, causing the volcano to shudder and send rocks raining down around the giant, knocking the Omphalos out of Erra's hands.

Alex ran towards the bouncing bullet-shaped rock, scooped it up, and was about to throw it in the magma pool when Erra grabbed it from behind and tried wrestling it out of Alex's control. Despite the Atlantian's overwhelming size and strength advantage, Alex held onto it long enough for the ankh to send a powerful electrical shock through his body, knocking the giant off him.

Exhausted from everything he'd been through, it took Alex a few seconds to realize he still had control of the Omphalos. With his last bit of strength, he hurled the stone towards the magma but was shocked when the Atlantian leapt for the object, grabbing the stone with one giant paw just before it splashed into the magma pool.

For several agonizing seconds, the Atlantian teetered near the edge, flailing his free arm in a desperate attempt to avoid falling in. But his lean was too great, and he slowly toppled over.

Alex watched in horror as Erra fell into the bubbling magma, wincing as screams of pain echoed through the chamber. A second later, flames engulfed the warlock. The Omphalos lingered a little longer on the surface, seemingly fighting not to perish. In its last gasp, before it disappeared forever, it flashed brightly, sending a powerful shock wave through the cavern, hitting Alex squarely in the chest and knocking him across the room.

Dazed by the blast, he sat on the sizzling floor, only dimly aware of his surroundings. An ear-splitting shriek shook him out of his funk and caused him to look up – just in time to see the Cherufe emerge from the magma pool. "How dare you sacrifice a human in my home. You promised me you weren't here to do that. Now, you'll pay for your lies."

Knowing arguing with the fiery monster was useless, Alex struggled to his feet and stumbled up the lava tube. He'd only taken a few steps, though, when a roar caused him to look back. To his horror, he saw the Cherufe ripping boulders from the sides of the magma chamber and throw them around in such a fury that the volcano started violently shaking. Thinking it was the end, Alex briefly thought about giving up and ending his misery. But the ankh wouldn't let him and jerked him up the tunnel.

Alex took a few shuffling steps, but was so exhausted that he paused and looked back. The last thing he remembered seeing was the Cherufe's fiery lash coming at him.

***

Enjoyed *The Omphalos*?

If you enjoyed this story and have a moment to spare, I'd appreciate a short review on Goodreads or the site where you bought this book. Your help spreading the word is greatly appreciated, as reviews make a huge difference in helping new readers find the series. Thank you!

Book 6 in the Maqlû – Pandora's Box

After destroying the Omphalos, Alex Scire, and his friend Chrysophylax head for the dragon world of Berellus, to seek help for their quest to find and destroy the remaining Maqlû.

When they return to Earth, though, Alex discovers that he has even more numerous and dangerous foes than ever before. And, to make it worse, the Druids are using Diana as bait to lure him into a trap.

But the biggest challenge, will be trying to find the mythical city of Atlantis.

ALSO BY THE AUTHOR
The Maqlû Series

AUTHOR'S NOTE
Historical accuracy of *The Omphalos*

Whenever I think I have hit the limits of fantasy, I learn something new about the real world we live in that encourages me to keep pushing the boundaries in my books. For instance, recently, scientists from around the world gathered to discuss if they got *The Big Bang Theory* (not the TV show) wrong and determine whether the universe is older and bigger than they thought (they concluded it was at least bigger). Therefore, I thought readers might wonder what is fantasy and what is fact. Below are some of the more interesting facts and history I've incorporated into the book. Enjoy.

Although I have taken literary license to portray their **characters**, many of the ghosts were inspired by real and legendary people.

Agnodice – Is a legendary figure, purported to be the first female physician in ancient Athens (around 4th century BCE).

Ariadne – In Greek mythology, Ariadne was the daughter of King Minos of Crete. There are different variations of Ariadne's myth, but she is known for helping Theseus escape the Minotaur in the labyrinth.

Cherufe is a Chilean mythological monster believed to inhabit the magma pools of Chile's volcanoes.

Erra was the Babylonian god of war, destruction, death, strife, mayhem, and pestilence.

Gilgamesh was a king of Uruk, Mesopotamia, who lived sometime between 2800 and 2500 BCE. The *Epic of Gilgamesh* is considered the first significant piece of literature, carved onto stone tablets long before the Old Testament with some of the same stories (e.g., the Garden of Eden).

Gugalanna, in the Sumerian religion (an ancient Mesopotamian civilization), is the husband of Ereshkigal, the Queen of the Underworld.

Minotaur is a creature in Greek mythology, part man and part bull, located in the infamous labyrinth of **King Minos** in Crete.

The Pythias were also known as the Oracles of Delphi. They were the most prestigious and authoritative oracles in the ancient Greek world from the 7th century BCE through the 4th century CE. Their most famous prophecy was given to Croesus, the king of Lydia. He asked Pythia whether he should make war on the Persians. The Pythia told him that a mighty empire would be destroyed if he should go to war. It turned out to be Croesus' kingdom, not the Persian's (woops).

Socrates (470-399 BCE) was a Greek philosopher credited with founding Western philosophy.

Susan Picotte (1865-1915) was a member of the Omaha Native American Indian tribe. She was the first Indigenous woman to earn a medical degree.

Ute Indians are an American tribe that historically lived in the Rocky Mountains of Colorado and Utah but hunted over a much broader area. They currently have three reservations in southwestern Colorado and northeastern Utah. They are the tribe that roamed closest to where I grew up on the plains of Colorado.

Many of the **locations** in the book are based on places I've visited;

<u>**Berellus**</u> (the Dragon's home planet) is based on the planet Kepler 442-b and is considered to potentially be one of the most habitable planets in the universe. It is slightly more massive than Earth and is just under 1300 light years away (a little less than 8,000 trillion miles).

<u>**Delphi**</u> was an ancient temple complex on Mt. Parnassus dedicated to the Greek god Apollo and home to the Pythia Priestesses. The ancient Greeks considered Delphi to be the center of the world and marked it with a stone monument known as the Omphalos. It's now a UNESCO site.

<u>**Fingal's Cave**</u> is a spectacular sea cave in the <u>**Hebrides**</u> (both a sea and a group of islands that lie off the northwest coast of Scotland) with a geologic structure comprised of hexagonal jointed basalt columns similar to the Giant's Causeway in Northern Island.

<u>**Greece**</u>

- **<u>Acropolis of Athens</u>** sits on a rocky outcrop above the heart of the city and contains the ruins of several ancient buildings, including the Parthenon.
- **<u>Agia Roumeli</u>** is a small town on the southwest corner of Crete at the southern entrance to the **Samaria Gorge**. Tourists usually start at the northern edge of the gorge and hike down through the scenic trail, then take a ferry back to the other side of the island.

- **<u>Ancient Agora of Athens</u>** lies at the foot of the Acropolis and was the central meeting place for the Ancient Athenians.
- **<u>Crete</u>** lies about 100 miles south of mainland Greece and is the largest of the Greek Isles.
- **<u>Delphi</u>** is situated on the southern slope of Mt. Parnassus, several miles above the **Gulf of Itea**. The **<u>Temple of Apollo</u>** (built in the 4th century BCE) is the most famous building in Delphi as it was home to the Pythias.
- **<u>Meteora</u>** is a stunning rock formation with a half dozen Greek Orthodox Monasteries situated on top of several of the sheer conglomerate rock formations in the area.
- **<u>Mount Olympus</u>** is situated in the northeast corner of Greece and is its largest mountain. It was believed to be the mythological home to the ancient Greek and Roman gods.

<u>Italy</u>

- **<u>Mt. Etna</u>**, is situated on the eastern shore of Sicily, and rises over 10,000 feet. It is one of the most active volcanoes in the world. The lava field Alex crosses in the book is based on an actual field created in the early 90's.
  - o **<u>Catania</u>** is a medium-sized city sitting at the southeastern base of Etna.
- **<u>Mt. Vesuvius</u>** is an active volcano on the southwest coast of Italy near **<u>Naples.</u>** It's most famous for its devastating eruption in 79 CE that covered the cities of **<u>Herculaneum</u>** and **<u>Pompei.</u>**

One significant difference between Mt. Vesuvius and Mt. Etna is that Naples lies much closer to Vesuvius' crater, and has over 600,000 people living in the volcano's danger zone.

Stirling is a Scottish city of about 40,000 people situated approximately halfway between Glasgow and Edinburgh.

Some of the **backstories** in the book are based on historical events or local legends, including;

Ankh is the ancient Egyptian hieroglyphic character for life. The Egyptians believed that living was only part of life and that the ankh symbolized our mortal existence and the afterlife. Its first known use was about 5,000 years ago.

Chiton is a loose-fitting gown, or tunic, held in place by pins at the shoulders and a belt around the waist, and worn by both sexes in ancient Greece.

Druids Very little is known about the ancient Druids, but they are believed to have been the educated professional class (religious and judicial leaders) among the Celtic peoples during the Iron Age (roughly 1200 BCE to 1 BCE). Unlike most cultures, female Druids held prominent roles in Celtic society. Unfortunately, the Romans wiped out their culture.

Some of the key terms associated with the Druids in this book are:

- **Bandruí** is an Irish word for Female Druids.
- **Groves** are how Druids organize themselves (similar to how Wiccans organize by covens). Since the ancient Druids were closely linked to

nature, many of their meetings took place in groves of trees.

The Five Elements were believed to be the most fundamental parts of the universe on which everything is based, but they varied according to belief and tradition. Four are common among most traditions (Earth, wind/air, fire, and water). The fifth element varies (e.g., aether, wood, metal, spirit).

Cup of Jamshid in Persian mythology is a divination cup that also contains an elixir of immortality. Many Persian authors have credited the cup with the Persian Empire's successes.

Magic can be anything from extraordinary supernatural powers to illusion, certain religious practices, and advanced technology. In many ancient Mesopotamian societies, magic was used for various purposes, from understanding omens to protecting oneself against spells cast by some witch. The concept of magic started taking on negative connotations in Greece, where it was thought to be used mostly by frauds. But it wasn't until Christian churches began preaching that magic was the work of demons and such that witchcraft became a hazardous occupation.

Magma is liquid/semi-liquid rock *below* ground (lava is *above* ground)

- **Lava tubes** are formed when a hard outer crust of lava cools off, and the lava inside empties out before it cools.
- **Magma/lava temperatures** are not quite as deadly as I thought. You would get a terrible burn if you touched magma, but a person

wouldn't necessarily die if they fell in – as long
as they could climb out quickly enough.

Maslow's Hierarchy of Needs is a theory of what
motivates humans. It assumes basic needs (e.g., food and
shelter) must be met before a person can focus on higher.

Mjölnir is the Norse God **Thor**'s (also known as **Donar**
to the Germans) magical hammer. Thor was associated
with lightning and thunder and was the protector of
humankind and fertility.

Occam's Razor is a philosophical principle developed by
a 14th-century Englishman who stated that the simplest
explanation for a problem is usually the best.

The Omphalos (naval of the world) are sacred stones
(often meteorites) believed to be endowed with life.
Delphi has two different versions of the Omphalos.

Red Crescent Society is similar to the Red Cross, but
operates primarily in Muslim countries.

Runes are letters in runic alphabets. They were used to
write various Germanic and Scandinavian
languages before the adoption of the Latin alphabet.
Later on, Norse mythology attributed runes to divine
origin.

Ryujin is one of the eight dragon kings in Japanese
mythology and the sea god. I have used the term for the
small dragon species in my books.

Scrying is a method of divination that can take many
forms (crystal balls and silver dishes being the most
common. In my books, it's a secure communication
method for the Druids, similar to Skype.

Sharur in Sumerian mythology is Ninurta's
(Mesopotamian god associated with farming, healing,

hunting, law, scribes, and war) mace. It's a powerful weapon that can fly over vast distances and communicate with its wielder.

Tilley Hat is a versatile and durable hat made in Canada. They enjoy a cult-like following among some people.

Time Dilation is the difference in elapsed time, as measured by two clocks, due to a relative velocity between them (special relativity).

Tonsure is the practice of cutting or shaving some or all of the hair on the scalp as a sign of religious devotion or humility. It is most often associated with certain Roman Catholic monastic orders.

Triquetra (also known as the trinity symbol) consists of 3 interwoven rounded triangles and was often used by Druids as a religious symbol.

UNESCO (United Nations Educational, Scientific and Cultural Organization) is an agency of the United Nations that promotes world peace and security through international cooperation in education, arts, sciences, and culture. World Heritage Sites are those sites considered to be of outstanding value to humanity.

Wakan Tanka, in Lakota spirituality, is the term for the sacred or divine. It can be interpreted as the power or sacredness that resides in everything.

Wormholes (also called Einstein-Rosen bridges) are one aspect of the theory of relativity. They theoretically link two different points in space-time via a 'shortcut.' Wormholes change (punch through) the fabric of the space-time continuum.

For more information on the historical places, events, and characters in this book, go to my web page, where I have posted a more complete glossary.

ABOUT THE AUTHOR

JC Holmberg is the author of the Fantasy Adventure series – *The Maqlû*. He and his wife, Mari, live in *The Kentucky Wildlands*. John splits his time between working on his forestland in the mornings, writing in the afternoon, and continuing his travels to research settings for future books.

The picture below is of the author in Athens. In the background is the world-famous Parthenon.

FOLLOW THE AUTHOR

Although *The Maqlû* is a fantasy series that includes ghosts and magic, the books are set in the amazing real world with fascinating historical characters. To learn more about the author, the background of each story, and some fascinating fun facts included in the books, go to,

www.jcholmberg.com